W9-BZE-117

FAT ANGIE

Rebel Girl
Revolution

e.E. Charlton-Trujillo

CANDLEWICK PRESS

This is a work of fiction. Names, characters, places, and incidents are either products of the author's imagination or, if real, are used fictitiously.

Copyright © 2019 by e.E. Charlton-Trujillo

All rights reserved. No part of this book may be reproduced, transmitted, or stored in an information retrieval system in any form or by any means, graphic, electronic, or mechanical, including photocopying, taping, and recording, without prior written permission from the publisher.

First edition 2019

Library of Congress Catalog Card Number pending
ISBN 978-0-7636-9345-9

18 19 20 21 22 23 LSC 10 9 8 7 6 5 4 3 2 1

Printed in Crawfordsville, IN, U.S.A.

This book was typeset in ITC Giovanni.

Candlewick Press
99 Dover Street
Somerville, Massachusetts 02144

visit us at www.candlewick.com

For Zeke, who reminded me Angie could still change lives.
And for Mags, who never stopped believin'.

There was a girl. Her name was Angie. She had fallen out of love. . . .

Well, not exactly.

Cruel Summer

This was the beginning, again. Angie bit the end of her thumbnail, standing with a JanSport kitten-rage backpack given to her by KC Romance evenly secured on her husky shoulders. She had walked 3,239 steps from her home in the cul-de-sac of Oaklawn Ends to William Anders High School, as counted by her father's once-relished red pedometer. One of the few relics left behind when he moved out two years earlier.

Her unexpected walk on the first day of tenth grade, after a sad-beautiful-sad-better rerun of freshman year, had been marred by the canary-yellow, glitter-dipped ribbons that were tied to the four tree trunks in the front of the high school. A sum total of 573 ribbons adorned the mostly quiet community of Dryfalls, Ohio.

Angie did not like the color yellow.

Angie's sister had not liked glitter or yellow.

Angie cringed at the sight of the ribbons in front of her school.

Feeling less the girl with gusto who had earned a coveted spot on the infamous Hornets' Nest varsity basketball squad the year before and more the loser who'd walked away from it, Angie stood, nervously sweating at her hairline, fearing that there would, in fact, be more lows than highs. With her requited love, KC Romance, on the lam since late July, Angie found herself swallowed by the doldrums, longing for the intense girl with a hunger greater than the number of waffles served at Waffle House (800 million and counting).

Lost in a nostalgia often reserved for montages in teen movies, Angie looped KC's parting words before her reluctant relocation to Texas to "reconnect" with her not-so-long-lost father.

"Baby, sometimes, love just ain't enough," KC had said.

With that 1990s throwback song lyric by the legendary Patty Smyth, featuring Don Henley of the Eagles, Angie's hopes of finally starting sophomore year on the right foot went left. Any hopes of a long-distance relationship were dashed, because KC did not believe in long-distance relationships — a unilateral decision that confused Angie. Nevertheless, she had watched, weepy-eyed, as the only person she thought she could ever love vanished through the long, shoulder-to-shoulder security-checkpoint line. KC had waved tearfully with her one-way ticket on Southwest Airlines, flying to Dallas Love Field.

Fast-forward.

Now.

Tuesday, not Monday.

Four weeks, five days, eight hours, and forty-two minutes since leaving said forever-first-and-likely-only love at the airport, according to Angie's Casio calculator watch. Angie, who in KC's absence felt more "fat" Angie than ever before. According to the expensive scale her couldn't-understand mother, Connie, required her to weigh in on since a recent doctor's visit, Angie was, as a matter of fact, heavier. By several pounds, though she could not admit the exact number even to herself.

Angie dipped her head toward the student parking lot with teens leaning on car hoods or in truck beds. Girls flirting—working angles with a slight shift of a hip, a slip of a grin, their confidence vested in their thin waistlines. Nothing to encumber them. Nothing to keep them from being . . . normal.

Self-consciously, Angie pulled at her Jackalope T-shirt, finally deciding to cover her stomach with her arms. Still waiting for Jake Fetch to pull into the parking lot. Jake, who had promised to pick her up but pulled a no-show. Jake, who had promised to walk in with her because she could not fathom doing it alone. Jake, who had become a series of broken promises since returning from a summer-camp job in rural Wisconsin. All the while denying anything was wrong, but something was clearly not right. Because Jake was a good boy from a good home with both parents, who were happily married and owned a dog that liked his name. The dog's name was Ryan. Even if Jake and Angie seemed like the most unlikely of friends because of his acceptance into popular social circles, he had shown up for her when she needed him the most. Until his recent foray into breaking promises, anyway.

The first bell rang. Staring at the throng of students pouring into the high school, Angie knew not a one of them could know the primitive nature of her gentle, pudgy psyche.

Her chin was up. Though it still doubled.

Her heart was beating. Though it was broken.

Her dreams were big. Though she could not really remember them.

She was, in Fat Angie terms, alone. Truly. Deeply. Painfully alone. This was not fun. In no way, whatsoever, any kind of fun — and finally getting to sophomore year, when she should have been a junior, was supposed to be fun . . . ish.

Angie let out an audible sigh as a bizarre Celtic/Tejano music mash-up wedged its wacky way into her gray matter. It was not the soundtrack first days of school were made of. Nonetheless, there it was — in stereo in her mind. Louder and annoyingly louder, and she suddenly felt a most definite urge to pee when someone shoved her from behind. She lost her balance and fell to her knees.

HARD!

"Watch it, dyke!" Gary Klein said.

Necessary Facts About Gary Klein:

1. He was a senior who read at a seventh-grade level.
2. He was very good at the sport of football.
3. He often smelled like raw onions and root beer.
   IBC root beer, to be specific.
4. He disliked Angie. Immensely.

Gary's crew of friends laughed, pointing down at Angie. All but one: Darius A. Clark. The most unlikely person to hang out with someone like Gary Klein. While a football player, he did not fit the moronic ensemble Gary currently surrounded himself with. A collection of boot-wearing multi-sport jocks who were mostly white, mostly monosyllabic, mostly on the path toward a future of sexual harassment.

Darius did not look or act like them. He did not wear boots and had said very little in Angie's elective film history class the previous year. Though she wondered if she would have said very much had the teacher constantly asked her about every fat and/or gay character after watching films the way he had asked Darius about every Black or Mexican American. Surely, that was uncomfortable, to be singled out that way.

"Hey, fat ass," Gary said. "You feel like squealing for us?"

Gary reached for Angie's belly. She scrambled to her feet. Her eyes darted around. There were students watching from nearby, pausing before going into the building. These were not unfamiliar looks for Angie. The whale-down or wacko-fatso look. The look only a girl who'd had a very public nervous breakdown during a high-school pep rally could attract.

"Leave me alone, Gary," Angie said.

Gary's grin — something was different. His meanness had mutated into something distinctly darker since the end of the previous school year. There was a raw hunger in his eyes. His sneer was more informed by hate rather than just ignorance. Gary was no longer the obnoxious jockhead simply posturing for the masses. His dislike for Angie had, in essence, evolved.

"Leave it alone, man," Darius said. "C'mon. I don't want to be late."

Gary did not like being checked by Darius, as could be ascertained from his disapproving reaction, but it tempered his focus on Angie.

"Stay out of my way, fat ass," Gary said to her.

Angie kept her eyes on Gary as he walked away. Her head dropped. Her anxiety ticked higher. Angie's mind flooded with the seemingly real fear that it would truly be a rerun of last year — her second freshman year. Before KC had come on the scene. Angie did not deal well with this level of anxiety — of —

Breathe, she thought.

It was an obvious-not-obvious therapeutic technique suggested by her new woo-woo therapist. *"When you feel your thoughts racing, try and slow them down. Breathe. In through the nose. Out through your mouth. Slowly."*

After several deep breaths, Angie repositioned her lop-sided backpack, a pang pushing along the center of her diaphragm. What she privately referred to as the Hole was aching. It was also on her List of Dislikes. The Hole that had made itself known on July Fourth when she and —

The warning bell rang. She waited. Hoping that Jake's retro Datsun 280Z would whip into the student parking lot.

It did not.

So . . . regardless of her reluctance to enter the build-ing alone, it was now or tardy. And calling attention to her-self in any way whatsoever was the last thing Angie needed on the first day of school. It had to be a different year. No pep-rally suicide attempt. No freak-outs. No anything that would make her more of a pariah than she had been to her classmates — with her couldn't-understand mom. Especially with her couldn't-understand mother.

Deep breath.

Bigger deep breath.

Angie entered the double doors of the school, keeping her arms pressed close to her body. Trying to make herself as small as possible given her girth. Her heart raced. Her eyes looked down. This was her worst nightmare. Having to walk the halls alone. Without KC or Jake. Just her . . . Fat Angie. She could not do another year of being that to all of them. But what would she do should it turn out to be a recycled sequel of her rerun freshman year? Angie did not like sequels. By their very nature, they rarely met the expectations of the consumer.

Failed Sequels:
Jaws 2
Troll 2
Free Willy 2
The Karate Kid Part II
Weekend at Bernie's II
The NeverEnding Story II

Angie was deep into the mental listing of failed sequels when the unthinkable became thinkable. Stop the mixtape! Holy Spicy-Spicy Guacamole from Betty's Muy Mexican Casa!

There *she* walked . . .

She was not new to William Anders High School, but somehow after a summer semester of study abroad, the she-who-walked had been retrofitted, remade in the image of a teenage boy's dateable, kissable, undeniable . . .

"Hey, Angie."

Jamboree Memphis Jordan?

Named after the 1992 RV and city she was conceived in, Jamboree Memphis Jordan parted the mass of students all Red and Sea with her stride. A paisley-print binder at her side. A purse slung over her shoulder. Her otherwise ginger mane reshaped into layers whose sheen, flowing sunset ombre, would not be flattened by the fluorescent lights. The electricity of her movement could not be tamed.

Fat Angie's pulse on the engine that was hormonal drive cranked. Jamboree's voice had sounded like toffee — her lip gloss glistened naughty. Two grade levels apart, and the mystery of Jamboree ghosting Angie three years earlier had solidified a distance that it seemed would never be crossed. A wound that had never healed for Angie. A hurt Angie had learned mostly not to think about, but in a single phrase — "Hey, Angie" — a much thinner, trendier Jamboree had been officially reintroduced into Angie's world. And apparently everyone else's at William Anders High School, because heads were turning!

Jamboree had transformed from book/band/Model UN nerd with an affection for fashion invisibility into the creative revolution that was rock-star stepping, boho meets grunge, down the crowded hallway. Her effortless stride had lathered an otherwise typical morning.

Fat Angie quickly tallied the libidinous looks from guys that followed Jamboree's more slender curves — her strut.

She was tall.

She was vivacious.

She . . .

TRIPPED!

and ate the floor in the worst possible way.

Epic cool entrance evolved into epic fall in front of the junior lockers.

Fat Angie witnessed the immediate awkward that surfaced on guys' faces.

Girls giggled.

Giggling girls made Fat Angie's blood, in cliché, boil.

But then . . . it stopped. It really, truly stopped. No pomp. No gossip circumstance. That NEVER would have happened to Angie. Her folly would have been the fodder for a story that leeched the lunchtime chatter for weeks. Was there a Get Out of Taunting card for girls who lost weight and dressed sexy? Because Jamboree Memphis Jordan had eaten wax and stood to walk another day.

Maybe things would be different at William Anders High School this year.

Maybe Fat Angie could be just Angie, even without KC.

Under
Pressure

It was lunch.

Lunch sucked. Angie added this to her List of Dislikes in the journal that her new woo-woo therapist had encouraged her to keep. Much to the resistance of Angie, who did not like seeing her thoughts written out. Nevertheless, she was making every effort to comply. She was a rule follower, after all. Well, mostly.

Angie picked a spot in the corner of the courtyard that she estimated would have the least amount of foot traffic. The cafeteria crowd had been entirely too intimidating for her to go it alone. And it would be alone because Jake had not been there to meet her. She fired off another text to Jake, who had not texted her back all morning. She did not like this and added it to her List of Dislikes while finishing a MoonPie.

Clipped to her hip was the abandoned Sony Walkman, with AM/FM and audiocassette capabilities that had been a favorite of her father's. Like the pedometer, it was one of the few leftovers from his moving out, divorcing her couldn't-understand mother, and upgrading to a new, less defective family unit.

1 old dad + 1 younger wife + 1 son + 1 daughter = 4 happiness^2

Angie still struggled with the fact that he had taken the family dog, Lester. Lester, who did not like his name, as he would never respond to it. A name that had been her couldn't-understand mother's idea, which was clearly misguided. Of the plethora of potential dog names, Lester was fairly lackluster. That much Angie was certain of.

Angie adjusted the foam headphones. The music of Tori Amos's "Cornflake Girl" crunched and pumped through her ears from one of the three mixtapes KC had made her before leaving.

Angie liked the number three.

Angie missed KC.

Angie unwrapped an Almond Joy and began to eat it.

She checked her phone for the fourth time in the last ten minutes. Jake had still not texted her. He had promised they would eat together on the first day of school. He had promised he would pick her up that morning. He had promised many things that had not come to fruition. Why had he become a promise-not-promise person? It did not fit the predictable pattern of Jake. Even if their friendship had been birthed from a promise he made to her military sister, Jake had said Angie was a great friend — a best friend. As evidenced by their talks while playing basketball in her driveway or sharing the dinner special at Betty's Muy Mexican Casa restaurant. They had stretched out in dual hammocks in his backyard, wishing on all the stars that did not fall. Maximizing their possibility of wish fulfillment.

After Angie's sister's funeral, Jake Fetch was the one who got her. Even though he himself came from a perfect home, with a perfect lawn, and a perfect family that had dinner together every night. And his dog, Ryan, liked his name.

Somewhere in all of Jake's seemingly perfect existence, Jake saw Angie. Not the Fat Angie almost everyone else seemed to see.

Angie flipped a few pages ahead in her therapeutic journal. She continued her thoughts about director/writer Mr. John Hughes. Over the summer, she had seen *The Breakfast Club* in addition to *Sixteen Candles*. Though there were other films in the director/writer's repertoire, she felt these to be the most relevant at this point in her life. Even though she had never been in detention nor had anyone forget her birthday, significant plot lines in each of the films, she believed Mr. John Hughes would have understood her plight. Understood the undeniable pain and heartache she felt as an outsider who was gay-girl gay in small-town Ohio.

A young woman who had been shunned by her community of peers. A girl who had found love in one immensely brilliant, funny, and unbelievably beautiful KC Romance. Only to have her teen-love bliss dashed.

And while Mr. John Hughes didn't write lesbian or gay characters and made some truly questionable directorial choices regarding race and women, Angie held out hope that had he known *her*, he would have understood. Wouldn't he?

Angie quickly tore the page out and wadded it up. She turned up the volume, trying to drown out the noise of everything — Jake; KC; lunch absolutely sucking; the very thin ice she was on with her mother, who, despite her recent foray into Hot Chic Yoga and a brief stint of birdsong meditation, rarely subscribed to the philosophies of the new woo-woo therapist Angie's father had agreed to pay for. With her fallen sister's statue dedication looming — with television producers booking candid interviews with her family — Angie's hope for a better day was truly waning. And the day wasn't even half over.

Angie dropped her head to the side and watched from her secluded-ish corner of the Loser-verse as Jamboree took a seat atop a concrete table. At the center of the group, she reeled everyone in to a story — a joke — something that captivated them. The magical allure of having been gone and returning with the makeover of the millennium.

Jamboree's attention flicked away from the group. She motioned for someone to join them. Angie followed the group's turned heads to . . . Stacy Ann Sloan?

Seriously?

Angie leaned ever so immediately forward when she realized the salvage-punk-dressed girl in maroon Doc Martens was Angie's former tormentor. The queen of sting, the heartless hater, the original mean girl of the William Anders High School junior class — Stacy Ann Sloan. Cloaked in a garb of messy, not her usual preppie, with a bob haircut, this was not a Stacy Ann Angie had ever seen. No power clique of teen girls following her in a V formation. Just her, a messenger bag, and a calzone.

Angie's jaw ceremoniously dropped.

It had been four and one-half months since Stacy Ann Sloan, the she-who-should-not-be-named-but-was-named-for-clarity's-sake had crossed Fat Angie's path. But there she was, laughing and eating pepperoni calzones at the same table with Jamboree Memphis Jordan, a girl she would have all but made fun of a year earlier. KC would have surely attributed all of it to Mercury in retrograde.

Mercury in retrograde (v): An astrological event thought of as a planetary reversal whereby people attribute their misfortune to Mercury in reverse. A time rumored to be marred by technological and life failures.

Not a super fan of the astrological movement, Angie was uncertain if this was the reason for such a surprising, upside-down reality. But there, Stacy Ann joined the lunchtime hootenanny with Jamboree and her friends. And at some point in Angie's obvious staring, Jamboree's attention was caught. But it was not until Stacy Ann turned toward Jamboree's gaze, interrupting the line of shared vision, that Angie snapped back into real time.

Angie's stomach dropped. It could have fallen to the bottom of her left foot. She had been noticed during a miserable and lonely first-day-of-school lunch. She shoved her journal into her backpack and was plotting her escape when Jake jogged up and sat beside her.

"Hey . . ." he said.

His hair was disheveled, his clothes more sweaty and sporty than usual. It was a level of unkempt she rarely saw in his polished-relaxed attire.

"What's up?" he said. "Thought we were meeting in the cafeteria."

Angie turned up the volume on her Walkman, bobbing her head to the somber, girl-aching-with-piano-and-violins "Foolish Games" by Jewel. Clearly, it was not head-bobbing music, but she made the best out of a frustrating situation that was the reality of a mixtape.

"Angie?" Jake said.

More ridiculous bobbing.

Jake pulled the headphone away from her ear.

"Hey," Jake said.

"What?" Angie said, looking-not-looking at him.

"You're mad," Jake said.

She slipped the headphones off, the echo of the music still playing.

"I'm sorry," he said.

"For which part?" Angie asked, still not directly looking at him. "For not picking me up? For not returning my texts?"

"I was out last night," he said. "Late, and I just . . . I'm sorry I didn't pick you up this morning."

"Like you were sorry you didn't meet me for pizza on Thursday last week. Or the movie marathon on Saturday. Or the half a dozen times you've said sorry for stuff, but didn't actually mean it."

"Look, I just had things . . ." said Jake. "Lots of things are happening, okay? Can you just understand?"

Angie nodded. *Things* was where the conversation stopped. Whenever she asked what was going on because she knew something was, in fact, going on with Jake, he would say "things." Since returning from his summer job, he had talked around topics. He avoided eye contact. His sentences were incomplete. All traits that were normal for Angie, but not for Jake. Most of all, he promised what he could not deliver.

"Are we not friends anymore?" asked Angie. "Like is this some kind of . . . friendship breakup?"

"What?" he said, genuinely surprised by her question.

"I told you how Jamboree ghosted me," said Angie. "That's how you're acting. Very — ghosty."

"I'm not Jamboree, okay?" Jake said. "I'm not KC. I'm not your sister or your mom or Wang or everyone else who disappoints you. I'm me. Jake. I just need . . ."

He kicked at the cement sidewalk with the toe of his sneaker. There was a noticeable tear along the right shoe's outer stitch. It became a detail that Angie fixated on in the pause hovering between them. The pause filled with shoe stomping.

"Look, we're friends, Angie," said Jake. "It's just . . . I don't know."

"Uh-huh," she said.

But there was something swelling in the four and one-half inches of physical space between their elbows. Something that Jake was not telling Angie.

"There are things," Jake said.

"You already said that."

"I'm under a lot of pressure," said Jake.

"But you don't talk to me," she said. "About pressure. You — make excuses. You avoid me, like when guys are about to break up with a girl by text. Only I'm not your girlfriend, and you have historically been nothing like my brother. So stop lying to me. It sucks, Jake. It feels like shit."

Angie was startled by her use of profanity. It was not a part of her lexicon the way it was with her slightly older brother, Wang. Who was of the profanity-using, poser-criminal element.

"I just . . ." Jake said.

And before he could say anything else, Jake's attention slipped past Angie. It was brief but long somehow. Angie followed the invisible-visible trail of his look. It fell in the direction of Jamboree's table, only it was not Jamboree who Jake was looking at.

It was Stacy Ann Sloan!

Jake had shared a look of longing — that way guys look at girls when they've done more than think about kissing. It was layered with —

"Seriously?" Angie said.

"What?" he said, but it was dripping in that I-just-got-busted tone. "It's not what you think — I mean, it is, but it isn't."

"Seriously?" Angie repeated.

"Angie —"

"Seriously?"

"See," said Jake, getting up. "I can't talk to you. You just react. You don't *listen* to me — about *me*. There are things, Angie. Things you won't hear."

Angie pushed herself up from the ground.

"I listen to you," Angie said.

"You don't, because if you did, you'd know — you'd see."

"What, that you're into Stacy Ann?"

"No. I mean, yes. I think. Yes."

"Is that why—you've been, um, not around?" Angie asked. "Because you're dating a hater?"

"She's not a hater, Angie," said Jake.

"Seriously?"

"Can you not 'seriously' anymore and just listen?" he said.

"Oh, I'll seriously if I want to. Seriously, seriously, seriously."

Jake shook his head.

"She—hit me, Jake. On more than one occasion. She turned people against me. She's one of the meanest people I know, and you're one of the nicest, and don't give me any of that opposites-attract-and-you-couldn't-control-yourself-in-the-heat-of-passion crap."

"In the heat of what?"

Clearly, Angie should not have quoted a blurb from a made-for-television romance movie.

"Look, I know what she did," Jake said. "But people can—I don't know. Change."

"What?"

"Not everything is what you think or how it looks or something. You're my friend, Angie. Like, we've become best friends, but . . ."

"Best friends don't date someone who hurts the other best friend. It's a rule-not-rule, but still a rule."

Angie had confused herself for a moment in her defining of best friends.

Jake stared at the ground. Jake Fetch. The best of the good guys and Stacy Ann . . . She could not say it even in her head. It was worse than imagining her parents having sex.

Jake had been dishonest.

Jake had been seeing Stacy Ann.

Jake had made Angie's heart hurt and break.

She was

MAD!

Angie did not like, under any circumstance, to be this level of mad. It often made her cry. It made her—

"Things are just messed up right now, okay?" said Jake, his eyes teary. "Really messed up. I don't know how to do it, and . . . I can't do this with you. I just can't right now, Angie. I'm sorry."

And then in a frustrating teen-television, one-hour-drama homage, Jake turned and walked away. Stacy Ann, who had seen the scene unfold, was not far behind.

What the absolute upside-down cake made by Aunt Meghan for Angie's twelfth birthday had just happened?

JAKE FETCH & STACY ANN SLOAN

Did they Saturday-movie marathon together? Did he take her to Betty's Muy Mexican Casa and sit in the third booth from the door? Did they make out in Jake's well-manicured backyard with Ryan watching? Would he do such a vulgar thing in front of the family dog?

Jake had promised Angie that they would be friends forever. Now, it was tainted with the possible exchange of — she could not begin to think about it.

Angie stood there, adrenaline rushing her body to a shake, thrusting her into emotional overload.

Too much too much Jake.

Too much too much too much Stacy Ann.

Too much missing KC and yellow ribbons and then . . . Angie collapsed.

And not gracefully.

The world looked different from the flat of one's back, Angie quickly realized. Especially when fighting to catch one's breath.

Her heart raced.

Her thoughts raced.

She had an urgent need to pee.

"Angie?" said Jamboree, leaning over her.

Jamboree's hair fell forward, brushing against Angie's cheek. It was soft. The softness was derailed by the crowd that had gathered above Angie.

Angie did not like crowds.

She did not like their stares.

She did not like their cell phones in video mode.

"Get someone," Jamboree said to a girl Angie did not know.

Too many eyes on her. She wanted them to stop look-ing at her. The way they had in the gym when she attempted suicide. The way they all looked on in horror. Some even laughed. Their looks meant pictures and video online. She had promised her couldn't-understand mother not to cause anything that could be perceived as a scene. There could be no scenes. But there Angie was in a lunchtime scene with people all around her.

"Angie," said Jamboree. "Just try to breathe."

Jamboree's voice trickled away.

"Angie, breathe . . ."

It was not Jamboree's voice. It was familiar, but far away. It was warm and safe and before KC. It was before the war when Angie and her sister . . .

It was before she was — gone.

How Does It Feel?

The disposable pillowcase crinkled as Angie turned her head in the nurse's office. Angie had fabricated some story about not eating lunch and low blood sugar. All in an effort to normalize the not normal. To play down her increasing struggle with anxiety, depression, and the Hole.

"Feeling better?" asked the school nurse, pulling the curtain back.

Angie did not know her name, as she was the new school nurse, and her name badge was obscured by her sweater. It was a nice sweater. Blue. Angie liked that color. Significantly more than yellow.

Angie propped herself on her elbows, taking a cup of juice from the nameless nurse.

"Are you sure you don't want me to call your mother?" the nurse asked.

That would be the absolute, unequivocally last thing Angie would ever want any adult to do.

"She's in court," said Angie.

"Mothers love their daughters," said the nameless nurse. "I have two."

There had been two in Angie's house, but the one who mattered had died. Leaving the leftovers, which are never as good as the original. Never.

"I really just want to go back to class," Angie said.

That was a hard and fast lie. What she did not want was to have her couldn't-understand mother show up at the school because Angie had been a "problem." Especially on the first day of school. The ice that Angie had skated on with her mother over the summer continued to be, metaphorically speaking, very, very, very thin. So much so that Connie had hinted on more than one occasion at an "opportunity" for Angie to attend a Catholic boarding school in the city, which was seventy-eight miles away. Connie had suggested the discipline might straighten Angie out and perhaps even slim her down. They did, after all, have a nutritionist on staff.

It did not matter that Angie's family was more of the light-a-candle-when-a-camera-was-on-them variety of Catholics and only attended Christmas mass because Connie's boyfriend, Wang's court-appointed therapist, expected it. Connie took Communion even though she really believed there was no God because what kind of God would take her only good daughter and leave her with an adopted, semicriminal son and Fat Angie? A question Connie had posed to her best friend Joan, believing no one could hear her talking on the phone one night.

The nurse's assessment was factual. Mothers do often love their daughters. Mothers who were not Angie's.

"Okay," said the nameless nurse, her eyes checking her watch. "Sixth period starts in about twenty minutes. Let me know if you need anything."

Angie finished the juice and dropped her head back onto the pillow. The pillowcase crinkled again. She did not like the sound. It reminded her of Yellow Ridge. The post-attempted-suicide treatment facility her mother had admitted her to last year. Angie did not like that place. Not at all.

The walls were blue gray.

The windows did not break.

The sheets were washed with an abrasive detergent that made Angie's skin itch. It was a prison without bars. A disturbingly nonsoothing place where people smiled in that way that felt genuinely inauthentic. She'd said whatever was necessary to get out, because Angie, in no uncertain terms, did not do well in confinement of any kind.

It was at the thought of Yellow Ridge that the Hole grew an invisible millimeter inside of her. She rolled to her side, covering her diaphragm with her arms. That was where the Hole lived. In her diaphragm. Though undiagnosed by any medical professional, it had been there since what was supposed to have been the most perfect July Fourth weekend. It was a weekend that Angie had thought about for weeks, knowing her couldn't-understand mother would be in the city of sin, aka Las Vegas, with her boyfriend, and Angie could be with KC without blowback from Connie. Marathon-watching the sole season of *My So-Called Life* while eating Snappy popcorn with green M&M's.

And it all had rolled out just like her fantasy, even surpassing her expectations, as she and KC had stretched out on an inflatable mattress in KC's mother's 1999 Toyota Tacoma truck bed. The smell of mesquite wood burning on the grill. The sound of Terence Trent D'Arby setting the mood from the portable AM/FM radio tuned in to 93.5, playing hits from the '70s, '80s, and '90s.

The moment was ultra-even, as KC would say.

Romantic to infinity and beyond times pi, as Angie would say.

Then KC dropped the bomb before the first burger could be served. She had agreed to a trial run to reconnect with her dad, thus moving away from Dryfalls and the Hit Me With Your Best Shot smoothies from The Backstory.

Angie's fantasy July Fourth unraveled rapidly. Panic — fear — panic-fear, if there were such a thing, occurred for Angie. Everything had been perfect, and then it was not.

KC leaned in and kissed Angie.

Angie kissed KC back.

The kissing was an impassioned distraction that should have tempered the terror racing in Angie. But soon there was a pang — a pressure. Angie pushed KC away. She gasped for air.

She could not breathe.

KC jumped from the truck bed to get her mother, Esther, and Esther's boyfriend with the handlebar 'stache. Esther hovered over Angie, caressing her forehead. "Breathe, baby. Just breathe . . ."

Angie was surely dying, without question. Dying in the back of a 1999 Toyota pickup with rust along the truck bed. Dying on an inflatable mattress with Enya on the radio.

She did not want to die to Enya.

Hyperventilating, Angie passed out only to awaken on a stretcher. Fireworks streaked and burst across the night sky as Angie disappeared into an ambulance with KC and Esther at her side.

Angie was, in fact, not dying. She would be diagnosed with panic disorder.

Panic disorder (n): a psychiatric disorder in which a person goes into a deep state of fear, often without an immediate danger, that can cause physical symptoms such as sweating, shortness of breath, and a racing heartbeat.

Her couldn't-understand mother received a bill of $1,500 for the ambulance ride to the emergency room. Connie was angry over the fact that her insurance provider would not cover the expense. This she made very clear to Angie. It did not help that Angie had been with KC.

Connie did not like KC.

Connie had forbidden Angie to spend time with KC.

Connie was, among a myriad of other harsh descriptors, homophobic.

Over the summer, Connie had hoped to reduce Angie's gay-girl-gay tendencies with a few not-so-subtle gifts:

A Bible with a vacation Bible school leaflet.

Copies of *Teen Beat* and *J-14* that prominently featured
    attractive young men.

Blu-ray discs of movie adaptations of Nicholas Sparks's
    A Walk to Remember and *The Notebook.*

Lying on the noisy pillow in the nurse's office, Angie tightened her arms around her diaphragm. She closed her eyes and tried to breathe her nervousness away. To breathe away the image of Jake and Stacy Ann — of the looming statue-dedication ceremony — of everything she felt about her sister that she could not say because it —

"Angie?"

Angie tipped her head toward the edge of the curtain. Jamboree stood shouldering Angie's hefty backpack.

"Can I, um, come in?" Jamboree asked.

Angie nodded, scooting and propping herself against the powder-blue wall, the back of her head rubbing up against a laminated motivational poster.

Jamboree nestled the backpack beside Angie.

"Thanks," said Angie, awkwardly.

After three years of nothing but a passing glance, it perplexed Angie how much it hurt to be in close proximity to Jamboree. What if more hurting made her freak out again? She did not want to freak out again. She had to fit — to be normal — to do what was expected. And there were so many expectations. Most of which she rarely met. Except the ones that were about her messing up. About being nothing like her sister.

"Is it okay if I . . . sit?" Jamboree said, motioning to a chair.

Angie shrugged, pulling the backpack closer to her.

Jamboree sat approximately four feet from Angie. It felt remarkably close somehow.

"So . . ." Jamboree said. "First days always suck."

"Yeah," Angie said.

Silence.

More weird silence.

They were in a perpetual wait-for-the-other-person-to-say-something-else cycle. It was truly uncomfortable.

"Good summer?" Jamboree asked.

Angie shrugged. "You?"

"Yeah, Belgium was cool," said Jamboree. "Got to see Paris."

"Yeah?"

"Eiffel Tower," Jamboree said, looking up at the popcorn ceiling. "It was . . . big."

"Huh," Angie said. "I guess it's supposed to be. Big."

Jamboree shrugged. "When I got back in August, my parents had dusted off the RV."

Angie nodded.

"They let me drive it now," said Jamboree. "I didn't think my dad would ever turn over the keys."

"That's, um . . . cool," Angie said.

"Yeah . . ."

More weird what-are-we-actually-talking-about silence.

"Are you okay?" Jamboree asked. "I mean, the lunch thing."

"Um, yeah," Angie said. "It was just a weird . . . blood sugar thing."

"Like diabetes?"

"No," Angie said, defensively. "Definitely not."

"I'm sorry," said Jamboree. "I just—I didn't mean anything like . . . I didn't mean anything. Anyway."

Pause.

Very weighted pause.

Jamboree's eyes drifted to Angie's wrists. To the scars

peeking from the edges of her Casio calculator watch and a navy-blue sweatband. Angie self-consciously repositioned her arms.

"It's kind of weird, huh?" Jamboree said.

"What?" Angie asked.

"This. Us. Talking."

Angie's eyes searched for a place to land that was not Jamboree.

"I came by your house," said Jamboree. "After the pep-rally thing happened. After you, came back from . . . that place you were at."

That place. It had many names. The treatment facility. The nuthouse. The crazy farm. Angie's return from Yellow Ridge was the fodder for the William Anders High School gossip mill still. *That place* had given her nicknames such as Crazy Fat Angie and Mad Cow Fat Angie! It had made her feel more alone than before she'd attempted suicide. Consequently, for that reason, and others, Angie did not like *that place.*

"Your mom said you weren't ready for people," Jamboree said.

"But you never talked to me at school," Angie said, still not looking at Jamboree.

"I didn't know what to say."

"What were you going to say when you came by my house?" Angie asked, picking at a thread on her backpack.

"Huh," Jamboree said, taking a moment to consider the question. "I don't know."

Angie nodded. Nodded because people nod when they hide what they feel.

"I just thought . . . after what happened. I wanted to —" said Jamboree.

"What about before that?" asked Angie. "When you disappeared? When you just . . . stopped talking to me?"

Historically, Angie had not been successful at confrontation. But there she was, deep in the muck of confrontation. She kind of liked it. Well, sort of.

"Yeah, I kind of messed that up," said Jamboree. "I had a lot of stuff going on, and I just . . . stuff I didn't know how to talk about. It felt like everything was going so fast, and changing and . . . it was kind of complicated in my mind. You know?"

Stuff — complicated. It was like the code words for not telling the truth. Jake did it. Now Jamboree.

The Hole ached in Angie's diaphragm.

"So, what do you want?" Angie said.

"I don't want anything."

"You don't talk to me for three years, and now twice in the same day. The probability of you not wanting something isn't likely. Statistically speaking."

Even though Angie, according to her mother, was not good at the art of numbers, she felt her estimation was correct.

"Angie, I . . ." said Jamboree. "I thought . . . I don't know what I thought. It's been a really strange summer. Shit, it's been just—coming back from—it's been a really strange time. Everything is just so . . ."

Angie glanced at Jamboree. Watching her think so precisely. As if the image of the universal answer was stretched out across her expression.

"I saw you this morning," Jamboree said, exhaling deeply. "I was so . . . I wanted to talk to you. And I . . . don't you ever just want to have an undo or redo or something?"

Angie did not follow the trajectory of Jamboree's question.

"So, yeah," said Jamboree. "I don't want anything from you."

Angie looked-not-looked at Jamboree. Her thinner cheeks. Her clear skin. All the things the two of them had imagined perched in the loft of Jamboree's parents' classic RV. Their self-proclaimed tree house on wheels. Cutting out pictures from magazines of what they wanted to look like—be like. Hours and hours of collaging dreams of being someone else—anyone else who was not who they were, where they were: two pudgy girls in Dryfalls, Ohio.

Now, Jamboree was nothing like Angie. Inside or out. And Angie felt fatter than ever.

"I saw you play varsity last year," Jamboree said. "You really got good."

"Yeah, it just, um, wasn't my thing."

"You played it like it was your thing," Jamboree said. "The way you used to when . . ."

Jamboree stopped herself. The way a lot of people did when Angie's sister's name came up. The basketball legend. The American war hero. The fallen solider. The—Angie tried to reshuffle the images of her sister in her mind. To put them in some order that didn't make her feel angry, because Angie couldn't be angry at her.

"I played it like it was her thing," said Angie.

"Gotcha," said Jamboree.

Awkward pause.

Extended awkward pause.

"Um . . . were you always, you know, gay?" Jamboree asked.

"What?" Angie asked, surprised by the question.

"When we were friends?"

"I don't know, maybe," said Angie.

"I never thought you were . . . gay. Are you still . . . gay?"

Angie's brow furrowed. She had no problem looking at Jamboree now. Her hurt had been filled by another emotion. An emotion with fire.

"What is this?" asked Angie. "Intel for Stacy Ann or something?"

"What?" said Jamboree. "No. Why would you say that?"

"Why? Maybe because you were sitting at lunch together. You never sit at lunch together."

"You watch where I sit at lunch?" asked Jamboree.

"Not in a creepy stalker-y way, no," said Angie. "But I've seen you, and never with Stacy Ann Sloan. And it's no secret how she treated me. What she *thinks* about me. She kind of made a campaign of it."

"I'm not here because of Stacy Ann," said Jamboree. "I barely even know her. I just wanted to see if you were okay. To try and talk to you. To finally just say —"

"Go away," said Angie.

And when Jamboree did not move, Angie pointed to the edge of the drawn curtain.

"Leave me alone."

In that moment, Angie had in fact been very direct in what she wanted. Though she was not sure if that was what she wanted. She was so mad and so confused and so exhausted by the whole entire school day, and it was not even sixth period.

The nameless nursed popped her head inside the curtain.

"Everything all right in here, ladies?" she asked.

Jamboree nodded, leaving Angie alone.

No Hole
in My Head

The school-bus ride home was marked by the color yellow . . . everywhere. The yellow bus. The yellow Dryfalls HORNETS' NEST T-shirts the freshmen were wearing. The banner saluting her sister over Main Street with its yellow background. Of course, dusted in glitter. Where yellow paused, red, white, and blue continued with American flags displayed prominently in front of businesses and neighborhoods. People's patriotism ticked higher than it had during her sister's highly attended and televised funeral ten months earlier — an event that still haunted Angie. The cameras. The spectacle. The interviews with their inane questions about *How do you feel? What do you feel?* Angie had stammered through the answers the way she did in most public situations: Without the poise and grace of her sister. Without an inkling of anything similar to her sister but a gift for playing basketball. And Angie had, of course, quit that.

Everywhere Angie looked was the color yellow. What her couldn't-understand mother had called a symbol. A symbol of honoring soldiers. A symbol of honoring her deceased sister. A symbol of the unveiling of the statue of her sister that was designed by a company based in New York City who subcontracted the materials from the Middle East. The irony was not lost on Angie as it had been on the Dryfalls Statue Planning Committee and even her couldn't-understand mother.

None of it made sense to Angie. Not the scholarship fund started for young women who "aspired to exceptional greatness" by the Dryfalls Women's Rotary Club. Not the bake sale by the Lions Club for a plaque in her name near the mostly defunct and miserably funded public library. Not the little girls who had started wearing their hair back in the style of her sister except with a camo clip clasped to a yellow ribbon.

The ghost of her sister saturated the neighborhoods and streets of Dryfalls. She was in every one of the 3,239 steps from the front door of their home at Oaklawn Ends to William Anders High School. She was in the sidewalk outside Jamboree's house where she, Angie, and Jamboree had stick-written their initials in wet concrete. She was in the conversations of people who had lived through her absolute, unbelievable reign as:

Homecoming queen

State-honored athlete

School-play lead

Student council president

Society of Christian Scholars president

Model UN Club president

Key Club president

Yearbook assistant editor

And of all the things, she was the pulse of the state-winning William Anders High School girls' varsity basketball team. Leading the Hornets' Nest to three consecutive regional finals and one state win her senior year. Angie's sister had been the shining star and single most important person in the community aside from a football player who made it to the NFL. But his knee blew out in his first professional game and he had disappeared into all but obscurity. But her sister, she was a war hero. She was a legend. She was even to become a made-for-television movie on a historically women-focused network.

No one wanted to let her go. At least the *her* they had created from photographs, newspaper clippings, and videos, pre- and post-capture. The midwestern girl with an unstoppable jump shot and a smile ready for a magazine spread. The soldier who had bravely faced her torturous death. She had been everything Fat Angie was not. There was no escaping any of this bitter and brutal reality.

And in the town's excessive focus on the immortalization of Angie's sister, Angie was in an unexpected dilemma. Her once immense missing for her fallen sister had, unbeknownst to her, been replaced with:

Anger

Anger (n): a strong feeling of annoyance, displeasure, or hostility.

Fat Angie had learned about anger from her previous useless therapist. Using a graphic to illustrate Elisabeth Kübler-Ross's 1969 discovery, he slowly explained the five stages of grief, in order, to her.

Denial

Anger

Bargaining

Depression

Acceptance

Angie was neither slow-witted nor invested in his semi-lecture on human emotion. Consequently, her mind had drifted until he insisted Angie was in the anger stage of grief. Which was infuriating, because Angie was the only person who had believed that her sister would come home from Iraq alive. Whether she escaped from the terrorists who had captured her or was rescued by a secret special ops mission, she was coming home. Home to make Rice Krispies S'more

Rolls and watch kung-fu and Mr. John Hughes movies with Angie and even Wang (if he was not being a jerk).

There was no possible way Angie could have been angry at her sister. She was the only one in all of Dryfalls who saw Angie for who she was and loved her anyway. Before KC and Jake, anyway.

But ten months after her sister's funeral and now with the new woo-woo therapist, Fat Angie found it harder to deny what brewed beneath the surface of her conflicted psyche.

Angie was angry.

Angie was very angry at her deceased sister.

Angie did not like being very angry at her deceased sister because she loved her so much.

Plus, it did not fit the order of the five stages of grief, and this perplexed her, but not enough to ask her new woo-woo therapist. Even if this therapist seemed to be on Angie's side, she was ultimately on her parents'. Which meant there were things Angie just could not say.

The school bus idled outside of Angie's home, tucked in the cul-de-sac of Oaklawn Ends. She wedged her body through the narrow aisle, stepping over a cluster of back-packs spilling over into it.

"Hey, fat ASS! Joey wants you to suck him off!" said Corey, an asinine sophomore sitting in the midsection of the bus.

Corey Baker was a relentless bus-ride tormentor of Angie's. His face was dotted with acne. His hair, shaped with product, saluted the roof of the bus. Wearing some rotation of retro T-shirts featuring the likes of Dolly Parton, Billy Ray Cyrus, and anything Cincinnati Bengals, he was everything outcast, but still higher on the social food chain than Angie.

Being a queer, fat girl who had suffered a public nervous breakdown and struggled with social situations made Angie a snowflake in the teen world of Dryfalls, Ohio. And Corey Baker was one of many who would not let her forget it.

"Screw you," the Joey guy said, slamming Corey against the bus wall.

Angie stepped off the school bus literally surrounded by flapping yellow ribbons. Every tree trunk in the neighborhood was adorned with vomitus yellow — the sight of them nearly choked the very air out of Angie. Because for her, it was all fake, phony, fibbing, lying, made-up, fictional, invented to make people feel better. They all relied on the invented story of her sister to feel something that was not real. And Angie, well, she might have questioned what *was* real, but she knew it was not yellow ribbons sprinkled in glitter tied around trees.

Wang's Jeep sat untouched in the garage. Their couldn't-understand mother had finally understood how to get Wang where it hurt: his Jeep keys. After his recent foray into moderate teen rebellion with his friends, their mother took the keys and mailed them to some undisclosed location. A lunacy that had divided Wang and his couldn't-understand mother more and, oddly, brought him and Angie somewhat closer together. Which was an unusual state of truce in an otherwise rocky relationship between them.

To Angie's deepest regret, her couldn't-understand mother's leased SUV sprawled across the greater part of the driveway. An unusual occurrence, as Connie was rarely home before seven-thirty at night. If she came home at all.

The SUV's bottomless black exterior glistened in the sunlight. Freshly detailed, as it was every three weeks, inside and out. A spritz of Excellence air freshener on the floorboard mats generated a smell reminiscent of a funeral home — to Angie, anyway.

Not a single scuff or ding. Not a single visible imperfection to the car. Angie's couldn't-understand mother preferred all things to be that way.

Angie's stomach gurgled.

Fat Angie stood in the archway of the recently redecorated living room watching her couldn't-understand mother meticulously arrange an urn on the mantel.

"What is that?" Fat Angie asked.

Connie, startled by her daughter, jumped ever so slightly, an indication that she had been deep in her curious process.

"When did you get home?" asked Connie.

"I dunno. Like, now."

Connie adjusted the urn one more time before stepping back to admire it.

"It's something, isn't it?" asked Connie.

"I guess," said Angie. "What is it?"

Connie shifted her head to the left, questioning the placement of the urn. She adjusted it. Centimeters, if one were measuring.

"It's an urn," her couldn't-understand mother said matter-of-factly.

"But why?" asked Fat Angie.

"It's a symbol," Connie said, a hint of irritation in her voice.

"Of what?" asked Fat Angie. "She's in the ground. The parts of her they found, anyway."

"Stop!"

Connie's response startled Fat Angie.

Fat Angie, historically, did not like confrontation.

Fat Angie especially did not like confrontation with her corporate lawyer mother.

Fat Angie found herself in what would be considered a pickle, a jam, an incident of inevitable confrontation. Even though Connie had recently picked up Hot Chic Yoga, there was no amount of Zen vibing between the two of them, because the weight of Angie was often more than Connie could bear. Her size, her weirdness, her inability to . . . fit.

Angie stood there swaddled in the unbearable silence, her stomach growling ever so slightly.

Had Angie not flunked freshman year, attempted a very public suicide at a football pep rally, done a host of things that brought attention to her family in the midst of her sister's capture before her body had been found, Angie would still not be the daughter Connie wanted. Because that daughter had died and was now a symbol on the mantel in an empty urn.

"It's necessary, isn't it?" asked Connie.

Fat Angie did not comprehend the directness of Connie's obscure question. It was not passive-aggressive. They were historically passive-aggressive communicators, a term that her previous therapist had assigned Angie, though she struggled immensely with the assessment.

Passive-aggressive (adj.): When someone does not directly address what is bothering them and is actually pretty bothered.

"I don't understand," Angie said.

"For you to question—to destroy anything that *I* value—to distort it by your standards of strangeness. And don't use what that woo-woo therapist said as an excuse. There are people with *real* challenges, Angie. People who can't walk. People who can't see, Angie. Blind people."

Angie was looking at one, metaphorically speaking, but she kept any reaction that would be perceived as snarky to herself.

"Imagine if you couldn't see," said her couldn't-understand mother.

"It's an urn," said Fat Angie, flatly. "You're supposed to put something in it. It's empty."

The purpose of an urn appeared quite obvious to Fat Angie. Her conclusion did not sit well with her couldn't-understand mother.

"Go to your room," said Connie.

"Why?"

"Because I need to not look at you right now."

Connie's direct, flat, emotionally unemotional comment seared Angie quite directly. And when Angie remained frozen in the immobility of rejection and confusion, Connie took it upon herself to leave the living room. Climbing upstairs and disappearing at the top of the refinished mahogany banister.

Angie looked at the urn, considering the emptiness of Connie's symbol. That was when the Hole expanded and squeezed the edges of her diaphragm.

"She doesn't like me," Fat Angie had told her new woo-woo therapist. *"My mother. She doesn't like me."*

"Why do you think that?" the new woo-woo therapist had asked.

"After my sister's funeral, she was on the phone with her

friend Joan. She said, 'Why did it have to be my good one?'"

"That would be hurtful to hear," said the new woo-woo therapist. *"Do you think that—"*

"Can I have a piece of candy from the jar on your desk?"

Wang strolled into the living room eating Spam macadamia nuts. He popped his earbuds out, the bumping bass of rap echoing through them.

"You don't look sick," said Angie.

"Total Ferris Bueller, man," Wang said. "I needed a mental health day, yo."

"It was the first day of school."

"If there wasn't a three-day weekend coming, I would have contracted West Nile to stay home. For real."

"She told you to ride your bike to school, didn't she?" Angie asked.

He punched his tongue against his cheek. Then leaned into her. "I will crawl on my hands and knees — my butt cheeks — before I do that."

Angie snort-chortled. Wang grinned before laughing. It felt good to laugh with him. To be the closest version to what they used to be when their sister had been around.

"Well, it sucked," Angie said. "School."

Wang pulled his phone out of his sweatpants, swiped, then clicked to a video link.

There was Angie in low resolution. Panting. Sweating. Shaking. The level of humiliation was high. The comments immensely cruel.

Jack2Rip: Pregnant cow birth!

Xfly231: Idk, she's crzy.

Ashley7792: Whale ashore!

But there was Jamboree. Holding on to her. The way she had when Angie broke her leg in second grade. That was the second-grade Jamboree. Minus the fully developed breasts, smooth complexion, and fashion-forward wardrobe.

"Please, please tell me you didn't share this with Mom," said Angie.

Wang put his phone away. "Nah . . . but someone will. Probably Joan's daughter. She's a fucking narc about everything we do."

"Maybe you shouldn't have slept with Mom's best friend's daughter and told 'your boys' about it."

"I didn't tell anybody, fool," said Wang. "It was Richie I'm-a-Dick Camacho. For real, he's like —"

But Wang stopped talking as he tilted his head, staring into the living room, confused by the —

"What the hell is that?" he asked, eyes on the mantel.

"It's an urn," said Angie.

He continued masticating, rather loudly.

"It's empty, right?" he confirmed.

"She says it's a symbol."

"Like the fucking ribbons?" he asked.

Angie nodded.

"Man, shit just keeps getting stranger, yo," Wang said. "Did she show you the video of the spotlight?"

Angie shook her head. "What are you talking about?"

"For real, she had some company come out to the cemetery," Wang said, still masticating. "They, like, retrofit the headstone with this Las Vegas Luxor light–looking thing. Legit. It's right on top and activates at night. Kind of a JFK Eternal Flame. Minus the actual flame."

"No way," said Angie. "That's even too far for Mom."

He nodded. "I'm serious. I talked to Frankie Gonzalez. Says he can see it from his backyard."

It was the single most ridiculous effort yet for Connie to elevate her daughter's death to something as monumental as the John F. Kennedy Eternal Flame. Where would the lunacy stop?

"She came home early to meet with the mayor about tomorrow. They got, like, hundreds of seats in the park. Two big massive tents. Military band. Like . . . man, it's insane, you know?"

Tomorrow.

Wednesday.

The afternoon Angie had dreaded for months!

What should have been the second full day of a seemingly miserable new school year would be a half day because of an even more miserable statue-dedication ceremony — an event that should have been held on a Saturday, but Connie dared not compete with a major concert two hours north in Cleveland and the Dryfalls Buckeye Pie & Art Festival. Angie's mother had stopped at nothing short of spectacle.

"Does she really think that many people will show up?" Angie asked.

"Don't you?"

Angie shrugged. "I just want it to be over. All of it."

Wang nodded, tipping the bag of Spam macadamia nuts toward her. She shook her head.

"She really do that with the headstone?" Angie asked.

"Look, I wouldn't lie to you, Biggie-Size," he said.

She punched him in the arm. "Don't call me that."

"Hey," said Wang, gently massaging his arm. "Watch the beauty that is my *new* tattoo."

Wang proudly lifted his T-shirt sleeve, revealing what was, in fact, an actual, nonwashable tattoo.

"Shut the front door!" she said. "Is that real-real?"

"*Shhhh!* Damn, Mom doesn't know."

He showcased the most ridiculous, the most absolutely unfathomable — it was . . . Angie was not sure actually what it was supposed to be.

"It's Bruce Lee," Wang said, matter-of-fact.

It was a matter of fact that it did not resemble Bruce Lee.

"Are you sure?" Angie asked.

"What do you mean? Yeah, I'm sure. Look at that pose. *Game of Death.*"

"Um . . . okay. I thought his jumpsuit was yellow."

"That's yellow. Sort of," he said. "I need touch-ups."

Again, the tattoo did not resemble Bruce Lee in *The*

Game of Death. Unless Bruce Lee looked like a cross between a hobbit, a few pieces of spaghetti, and a martial artist's pose. Then it definitely was a dead ringer for Hobbit Spaghetti Bruce Lee.

"And some shading," said Wang.

"Okay," Angie said, still inappropriately staring at it.

"Mark's cousin did it. He's apprenticing at Red Wall, over by Smokey's Burgers."

"A tattoo shop did this?" Angie asked, a stroke of absolute surprise in her voice.

"No, I mean . . . I'm not eighteen. So he dropped this in his basement."

"Basement?" Angie said. "That's stupid. You're going to get hepatitis."

"Can't you be cool for, like, a second?" He slid his sleeve down. "Ms. I-Dated-a-Smoking-Hot-Lesbian-with-a-Purple-Heart-Tattoo-on-Her-Neck-Until-She-Dumped-Me-for-a-Better-Life-in-Texas."

Angie's chin doubled. Wang, in his need for the upper hand, had hurt Angie. Immensely.

"Look, I'm sorry, okay," said Wang. "But damn, you're weird."

"Did Mom really JFK Eternal Flame the headstone?"

"Dude, with all the press, what do you think? And don't forget. ABC's coming over tomorrow after the dedication ceremony."

"I thought we weren't doing that one."

"*Tribute to a Fallen Soldier?*" said Wang. "Like she's gonna pass on that."

Wang shook his head, looking at the urn.

Angie disliked the interviews. The cameras made a nervous twitch develop above her right eye. Puddles of sweat would pool on the underside of her knees. She could not focus on the questions. It was not that she was unable to follow their meaning. It was that they actually meant nothing. To her, anyway.

"They interviewed Dad and Sharon already," Wang said. "I heard Mom complaining to Joan about it on the phone."

"He's not coming tomorrow?" said Angie.

"Don't know. He sent me a text. Said he was still getting settled in Lexington. Like, he's been there two months. How long does it take to get settled?"

Knowing her couldn't-show-up father, it would take years. Anything to excuse his not being there for either one of them. At least in the ways they needed.

"Like, what the hell is in Kentucky anyway?" Wang said.

"The World's Largest Baseball Bat and the Kentucky Derby," Angie said. "For starters."

"Uh . . . okay, Google. All I know is I hate Kentucky, but . . . I'm thinking about hollering at him. See if he'd let me come and chill down there for a few."

"How few?" asked Angie.

"I don't know. Few-few."

"You don't know-know or—"

"It's just weird around here, you know?" Wang said. "Urns—statues. Shit, everything's still about *her*, and she's not even here, you know? I'm just done, man."

"Okay, so it's super weird," said Angie. "It's always weird. You just can't . . . leave. I mean, who else is going to put Monistat into my toothpaste?"

He grinned. "That was a good one, right?"

"Disgusting, but smart."

He tipped the bag of Spam macadamia nuts toward her again. Giving it a little shake. "Try it."

She leaned forward. The smell was like dirty socks and salt. She pulled out five pieces and tossed them in her mouth. One would have been too many, because her face soured in exactly three precise chews.

"It's foul, right?" he said, grinning. "Yeah, I love it."

Wang jogged upstairs, disappearing into his bedroom. Soon the sound of *ABBA Gold* swept the walls and strutted down toward Angie. And there she was with the taste of stale Spam macadamia nuts, swaddled in the disco hit song "Dancing Queen" and the emptiness of the urn.

Her day could get no worse.

War

Watching your mother make kiss-face at your brother's court-appointed therapist after a hellish first day of school is both nauseating and deeply unprofessional, Angie wrote in her therapeutic journal as she sat at their new mahogany dining room table. The dining room, like the rest of the house, had been redone. Twice since the spring. One time after her sister's funeral. The shade of color, the style of sofas, the guest bathroom — nothing was ever right in Connie's mind. Not that she had been around enough to truly absorb the wrongness. Her job kept her out of town three out of four weeks of the month. And the kids preferred it that way. Mostly.

John/Rick, Wang's court-appointed therapist, had been the unexpected addition in the subtraction of other things in Connie's life. First, as a secret-not-really-secret boyfriend, and then the completely obvious one after Angie's sister's body was recovered. Soon he became the stationary front that would not move past their lives. "Playing" father rather than the boyfriend, he mostly regurgitated textbook/talk-show therapy at the kids. He smelled like cigarettes smoked in the backyard, cheap breath mints, and gym sweat. His smile and abs were likely his best traits, if that were possible.

Wang did not like John/Rick.

Angie did not like John/Rick.

Connie probably didn't like John/Rick either.

John/Rick grabbed beer number two from the refrigerator, popping the cap and leaving it on the counter. A rookie mistake for a guy who was working on getting a drawer in Connie's dresser after a year-plus of dating. Rule #8 in regard to the kitchen: *Everything you use falls within the one-touch rule. If it's trash, dispose of it.*

"What are you writing?" Connie asked Angie, setting a platter of sushi rolls on the table.

"I don't know," Angie said. "Stuff."

"Do it after dinner," Connie directed. "And no more than four pieces. Have some soup. It's low-fat."

Of course, it was. And so began Round One of the game-not-official-game of what Angie named Passive-Aggressive Dinner Digs (PADD). The rules were simple. Connie said one thing but meant another. Angie pretended she didn't know what her couldn't-understand mother meant.

Angie looked to Wang. Wang, who had wisely opted out

of the family festivities from the onset by jamming earbuds into his ears, quietly nodded along with the music while scrolling the Internet, simultaneously stacking a mound of wasabi on a California roll.

"It will give you heartburn," John/Rick said to Wang.

When Wang did not respond, John/Rick tapped on Wang's plate with his fork—a fork because chopsticks would be a dexterity stretch for the midwesterner.

Popping one earbud out, Wang continued to scroll on his phone. "What?"

Angie grinned. Her favorite part of any "family meal" was watching Wang duel with John/Rick.

"You shouldn't eat that much wasabi," John/Rick advised. "It will make you sick."

Wang picked up his sushi roll with the giant portion of wasabi and launched it into his mouth. Within seconds, tears screamed down his cheeks as he grin-chewed and swallowed.

"Wang," said their mother.

"What?" he said. "Now you're gonna tell *me* how to eat? Whatever."

"Don't disrespect your mother, Wang," John/Rick said.

Angie paused, chopsticks hovering over a Philadelphia roll.

"You're not my dad, John/Rick," Wang said. "You have no authority in this house."

John/Rick's actual name was Jonathan Christopher

Rodriguez, but he had told Wang and Angie that they could call him Rick—a name that perplexed them immensely, so John/Rick felt more fitting.

"He's a guest in our house, Wang," said Connie. "Don't act ignorant."

"I'm not acting," Wang said under his breath.

"Guest?" John/Rick said, catching Connie's faux pas.

"You know what I mean," said Connie.

Angie served herself the allocated four pieces of sushi while Wang topped an even larger amount of wasabi on the next roll. He would burn his esophagus out to spite John/Rick—have fiery poop blaze out of his butt for an hour if necessary. Wang was fearless and, of course, not forward-thinking in his rebellion. Fiery poop was, well, fiery. Still, Angie wished she had a fraction of Wang's push-back, but she didn't even eat mild sauce on burritos, so the outcome did not seem likely.

"Did you try the dress on yet?" Connie asked, pouring a glass of wine.

Angie grimaced. "No," she said.

"You need to try it on," said Connie. "It might not fit."

Round Two of the Passive-Aggressive Dinner Digs. It did not matter if the dress actually fit. Well, it kind of did. It was that Angie did not fit into anything. Into small-waisted clothes. Into social groups. Into Connie's idea of a daughter. Into the suburban heteronormative paradigm. Angie simply did not fit.

"It's a nice dress, Angie," John/Rick said. "My sister picked it out. She's a bigger woman. She understands your needs."

Please, please, please make this stop, Angie thought. Her hand itching for the Ticonderoga #2 pencil wedged in the crease of her notebook. Her stomach growling for twelve, not four, pieces of sushi. Her urge to quite literally scream vibrated in her, but she stretched her lips into a smile and said, "Thanks," to John/Rick.

Wang shoveled the fully loaded sushi piece into his mouth, tears ripping out of his eyes. Chewing and chewing and — he did not look good.

"You okay?" Angie said to Wang.

"Don't look at me," he said, swallowing hard.

"You'll learn someday," John/Rick said. "All this show-ing off won't give your soul any real sanctuary."

What? The kids looked at him blankly.

Connie rambled on about something with the sound equipment they'd ordered for the dedication ceremony. Something about the glaze on the chicken for the meal after. Something and more something while picking up pieces of tempura shrimp rolls from their precisely symmet-rical brethren on the oblong plate and dipping them into soy sauce. Talking in that way that was doused in falseness. The pretend, mind-numbing conversation about the dedica-tion ceremony appeared to have no end. Angie, like Wang, had opted out of the listening portion, partly out of what Angie's new woo-woo therapist referred to as "self-care."

"And then Angie will speak," Connie said, continuing to roll through the litany of her list.

Angie sank a little lower in her chair, staring hopelessly at her tiny plate and tiny serving of sushi rolls.

The very idea of standing in front of anyone and speaking was paralyzing. She literally felt the bottoms of her feet tingle numb with anxiety at just the thought. Her mother, well aware that Angie struggled with public speaking, believed that *one must overcome their fear by doing, not watching.*

Wang got a call on his cell and stood up.

"Hey," said Connie. "We're having dinner."

"It's Dad," Wang said.

The temperature, should it have been measured, dropped twenty-two degrees.

"Tell him to call you after dinner," Connie said.

John/Rick kept his eyes on his plate. This was not a round worth stepping into.

"He's my dad, and I'll talk to him whenever I want."

Wang stormed out of the room. Connie pulled her napkin out of her lap and rested it on the table. One hand on the wineglass, the other pressed against her forehead. John/Rick leaned toward her.

"Want me to go talk to him?" he asked.

Connie put her napkin back in her lap and changed the conversation.

This was family dinner.

Angie stared at the blinking cursor in her text window to KC. KC, who had not texted her in over a week. KC, who had promised that their friendship would be forever. Like Joan Jett and the Blackhearts. Forever suddenly felt a lot shorter.

Angie started, then deleted, a sum total of seven messages, each one sounding more pathetically needy than the next. In her estimation, anyway.

She looked out her *Pretty in Pink* curtains at Jake's house across the street. His deceptively cool Datsun 280Z, with original interiors per his bragging, was parked in the driveway. The glow of the nightstand lamp ignited his bedroom on the second floor. Jake Fetch and his dog, Ryan, were sitting on the bed. The moment would have been cinematic if he had seen Angie, rushed to the window, and shouted, "I'm sorry. I'll never talk to Stacy Ann Sloan again."

Only, that did not happen.

Angie cracked open her dresser drawer, loosening a duct-taped king-sized Heath toffee bar from the roof of the dresser. Noticing her sister's infamous number forty-two Hornets' Nest basketball jersey shoved in the back of the drawer. The jersey Angie had been given when she made varsity basketball last year. The same jersey —

"Hey," Wang said.

Angie jumped, dropping the candy into her drawer.

"What are you doing?" he asked.

"Nothing."

He strutted into the room.

"You suck at lying," he said, plopping onto her bed. "I want half."

"Of what?"

"Of the candy you're acting all fake-innocent about," he said.

Angie grabbed the candy bar and sat beside him.

"Mom's on the warpath," he said. "She's downstairs losing her shit on the caterer."

"You didn't make things any better at dinner," Angie said.

"Neither does she," he said, biting into his half of the candy bar.

"I know," Angie said. "It's just . . . sometimes maybe . . ."

"What?" he said. "Cower? Behave? Eat a shit sandwich? Live in Mom's version of reality?"

Angie shrugged. "I don't know."

"Dude, I am *counting* my days in this house — this town," said Wang. "Aren't you?"

Angie had not thought so specifically about the counting of days. Mostly, she just wanted to get through them, and with the least amount of taunting possible.

"All I know is," Wang said, "I can't wait for this stupid

dedication ceremony to finally be over tomorrow."

"Same," Angie said, biting into the candy bar.

The bottom of her feet tingled. *Don't fixate,* she thought. *Don't panic. Don't fixate or panic, and breathe. In the nose. Out the mouth. Only don't hyperventilate.*

But she was fixating and panicking and thinking about white wooden chairs full of people staring at her standing in an itchy dress with lace that had a small but significant tear in the upper right shoulder. She was—

Wang continued to scroll on his phone. "I think if we tell Dad what's been going on with Mom, he might take us."

Angie fell back on her bed, her legs hanging over the edge. Wang fell back beside her, both of them staring at the glow-in-the-dark stars plastered in purposeful constellations on Angie's ceiling.

"What did he say to you on the phone when he called at dinner?" Angie asked.

"It was Carla, not Dad," said Wang.

"You made that whole thing up at dinner?" Angie asked.

"Uh, yeah," he said.

"I'm not telling you to eat a poop sandwich or anything, but do you have to just make everything up?"

"So, you're siding with Mom?" Wang asked. "John/ Rick?"

"Uh, no," Angie said. "I'm not siding with anyone. I just . . . why do you have to lie all the time?"

"Whatever," Wang said.

The quiet-not-quiet hung in the narrow space between them. Narrow in that Angie had a twin-size bed that was unusually shorter than it should have been.

"You know what the difference is between you and me?" Wang asked.

"Ethnicity, waist size, use of pejorative statements, interest in music that—" Angie said.

"*I* want something," Wang said.

Angie half laughed.

"Seriously. What do *you* want?" he asked. "Huh? To escape/date some girl who ditches you? To be like *her*?"

The *her* was always their sister. Always. Because the saying of her name, it was just too hard.

"Fuck that," Wang said. "I'm not going to be another copy/paste like the rest of this town. Stuck in the smallness of driving circles around the Sonic on Friday nights. Sitting in this house waiting for—"

"I'm not waiting for anything," Angie said. "Just because I don't hang out with wannabe criminals and get 'lit' on the weekends."

Maybe their truce was wavering.

"Look," Wang said. "I'm sorry, okay. But . . . damn, you're—I don't know."

The quiet resumed. For precisely eleven seconds. Then Wang's phone chimed, several times before he turned the sound off.

"You still make wishes?" Wang asked Angie.

"What?"

He pointed to the ceiling.

"They're not real," Angie said.

"So?" he said. "It never mattered before. Remember when you wished for a ten-scoop banana split shaped like a hobbit?"

Angie grinned. The visual was strange and yet appealing.

"Yeah," she said. "You and . . . her made it for me."

"Dude, it was her idea," Wang said. "I was just along for the ride."

They continued to look up. Fake stars. No glow. No . . .

"I miss that," Wang said.

"Me too."

"Ask you something?" Wang said.

Angie tilted her head toward him.

"Why do you think we're so fucked up?" Wang asked.

Angie looked back at her ceiling.

"I don't know," Angie said.

For approximately 11.2 seconds, though Angie did not time it, they sat there with only the silence between them. It was the kind of silence that would normally make Angie uncomfortable, desperately wanting to fill it with anything, but she didn't.

Wang got up off the bed. Angie propped herself on her elbow.

"Where you going?" Angie asked.

"I just need to roam," Wang said. "I'll catch you later."

"Hey," Angie said. "You okay?"

It was not a question Angie asked Wang often because he was rarely vulnerable. It was all smart-ass jokes and poser talk.

He nodded and disappeared out her door.

She fell back on the bed and looked up at the ceiling. There were a thousand plus nine things she could wish for. It just wasn't worth the effort.

Gone Away

The dark cloth concealing the statue of her sister flapped along its edges, teasing a reveal as the bleached ropes restrained it. Reporters filmed B-roll for their local or national news stories, two of them eager to continue the conversation they had started at the house earlier that morning. The United States Air Force Honor Guard stood at attention near the edge of the crowd after the presentation of the American flag and national anthem. From the elevated platform where Angie sat between Wang and her mother, it was the two empty chairs in the front row she had been most fixated on. Marked RESERVED for her father and his fun new wife, Sharon. Angie's dad, who had assured her by text that he intended to come.

The wind picked up. Leaves fluttered down around the thousand-plus people who had gathered. The inescapable yellow ribbons now on jacket lapels and breast pockets punctuated the theme her mother had wanted. Everything down to the plastic cutlery under the red-white-and-blue tent had been dipped in some form of yellow, a color Angie wished to be blinded from.

Sitting with an oversize American flag behind her, and the smell of fried-not-baked chicken from the buffet beneath the tent, Angie wanted to be almost anywhere but sitting there. With the mayor of Dryfalls, an air force colonel who knew less about her sister than expected, a senator speaking for the Ohio governor, and the Wright Brass Air Force Band, the insufferable sea of eyes capsized Angie's nerves. Her right leg bounced up and down. It was too uncomfortable to be still. She—

"Will never be forgotten," said the mayor. "A young woman who fearlessly fought for her country and community, saving the lives of her fellow soldiers and those of civilians they had attempted to assist. For us, she was the young woman with an electric and unstoppable dribble, jump shot, and smile. A hero on and off the court . . ."

As if all that her sister had been could be reduced to something as paltry as the mayor's descriptors. That was not *her* sister. That was the *idea* of her. The mayor finished his overly written speech, shaking hands with the master of ceremonies, Mr. Dover, chamber of commerce president.

Angie's stomach ached and growled. Her mother had restricted her breakfast, suggesting overeating would cause her to be unfocused. A logic that confounded Angie as she watched Wang ingest two Sausage McMuffins with egg, a mocha frappe, and a hash brown.

Mr. Dover introduced Carolina Perez, junior at William Anders High School, first-string varsity squad member, and longtime ally of Stacy Ann Sloan, to read her essay on patriotism and freedom. Carolina, who, with Stacy Ann, had rolled out a series of jokes about Angie's "G.I. Joe" sister, was now speaking about the value of patriotism and working up a tear for dramatic effect.

Angie's attention swiveled back to the statue. The cloth concealing it moved in such a way that it almost seemed to breathe. Slow deep inhale. Then fast thrusting exhale. Had her sister breathed like that? Held hostage — shaking and crying and — the Hole ached in Angie. She covered her diaphragm with her arms, annoyed by the black lace dress her mother had forced her to wear. She was certain it made her look like an oversized doily in mourning, not elegant, as her mother had insisted.

"She was a hero to all of us," Carolina said, "an inspiration that redefined patriotism. Thank you."

Everyone clapped. As Carolina left the podium, she gave Angie the ever-so-slightest glance reminding her that it was all a facade. It was Mean Girl 2.0 as usual.

"You ready?" Wang said, pointing to the program.

There in the fearless black and white of Arial font was

Angie's name. Her name after Carolina's. It was now her turn to —

"Angie?" said Mr. Dover, waiving Angie to the podium.

Sweet Jesus jumping on a pogo stick. It was the single most dreaded moment of the entire event for Angie. Worse than the yellow ribbons and the phony, overwritten speeches. It was her turn to be equally phony.

Angie did not like to speak in front of people.

Angie did not like her mother nudging her to get up.

Angie did feel an immediate and urgent need to pee.

Angie approached the podium, overly aware of the platform squeaking as she walked across it. The bottom of her feet — her lower legs — tingling. She tucked herself behind the podium.

Breathe, she thought.

She stood there, staring at the right edge of the printed speech, her skin itching from the lace of her ridiculously too-tight dress. Her pudgy hands crinkled the edges of the paper of her "personal" narrative about her sister, as written by Connie. Not Angie.

While not good at the art of numbers, per her mother's assessment, numbers were all that Angie could think of. Such as the statistical probability of her sister dying from the flu was about 1 in 70. The odds of her being taken hostage by a foreign terrorist and dying were about 1 in 45,808. And it was surprising-not-surprising, given the current political climate and the increase in public execution on social media. The probability of an American soldier taken seemed heartbreakingly plausible, even if the mayor and her mother had used the word "implausible" in each of their speeches.

She did not feel like Angie there on the platform. She did not feel like the girl who had been loved by KC and even earned that coveted spot on the varsity basketball team last year. She felt like Fat Angie. The blob, the cow, the wacko fatso, the shitbag, the dump truck, the everything ugly and horrible that had been said to her or about her.

Fat Angie pulled at the entirely too-tight lace dress.

"Um," she said.

Fat Angie's breath was shaky.

Her head was light.

She saw Coach Laden in the crowd. Coach Laden, who had been disappointed when Angie left the team but still managed to believe in her. She saw Principal Warner, who, like her father, referred to Angie as a "special girl." She saw some girls from the varsity basketball squad, her aunt Meghan, a guy from her math glass who did not like math, Jake and Stacy Ann. The two of them standing side by very-close side. Angie's heart dismantled.

She looked past Jake at the people she did not know, surprised to see Jamboree standing with her parents. While not accurately timed, the moment of looking between them was at least 3.2 seconds.

This was it. This was the inevitable moment six months in the making. Of eyes on Angie, who was supposed to fawn on the overpriced statue of her war-slaughtered sister. An overpriced statue seeming to breathe not ten feet from her. Was she the only one who had noticed the strangeness of it?

Angie's hands squeezed the edges of the paper harder, her palms sweaty. There was no escaping it.

"My sister . . . um, she was an exceptional member of our community," Fat Angie stammered, reading from the paper. "She had been the girl next door who fought for the American dream, so that we could all rest easy at night. And, um . . ."

This speech is absolute, unbelievable bullshit, Fat Angie thought.

"Her act of heroism spared the lives of her unit and seven other civilians, earning her the Medal of Honor," Angie continued. "While she herself was taken into captivity . . . um."

A baby began to cry in the audience. A shrill and loud cry. The baby would not be soothed. The mother hurriedly stood and stepped to exit the seated area.

"Um . . ." Angie looked back down at her speech. "She continued to be the brave face of every American soldier fighting for our, um . . . honor?"

Fat Angie looked to Wang.

Wang knew that the speech was absolute bullshit, as evidenced by his expression.

Then Fat Angie did what would be remembered as an infraction of the highest magnitude.

"My sister was scared. If you look at the hostage videos, you see it. She was . . . swaddled in fear. I don't even know why she was there. She'll never turn twenty. She'll never go to any of the places she wanted. She'll never laugh again. She had—"

Mr. Dover approached the microphone. "Thank you, Angie, and everyone for sharing your thoughts. Without further ado, let's reveal our town legend with the Wright Brass playing the air force's 'Off We Go.'"

Connie's exchange of looks with Angie was not good. Not by a mile. Not by one billion miles, if there were such a thing.

The directions had been simple: Stick to the script.

The directions were, in essence, bullshit.

The trumpet player emptied his spit valve, and with a nod to the band director, they began their somewhat off-key song.

The tear of Velcro along the sides of the cloth, a few tugs of rope, and down the cloth fell, revealing a bronze monstrosity. In some bizarre homage to Two-Face from the Batman movie franchise, half of the statue featured Angie's sister decked in her infamous number forty-two jersey, basketball tucked at her elbow. The other half presented her as a soldier complete with helmet, tactical gear, and an assault rifle at her side. On what planet of statue design was splitting her sister into two parts a genuine way to honor the whole of her? From Angie's vantage point, she could not see either of them truly being who her sister was.

The band stopped playing. Two more speeches followed. And while her sister had done the brave thing they all mentioned — the saving others, the sacrifice — she had also run away. From growing up and telling her mother no. It was something Angie did not know how to fully reconcile, because in going off to save the world, her sister had left Angie behind.

The William Anders High School Band launched into the school fight song as Angie and Wang followed their mother off the stage. Angie tried to get out of her couldn't-understand mother's sight line, but not quickly enough. Connie pulled Angie close, walking her away from the crowd.

"I asked you to just *read* the speech — to read the speech and honor your sister's memory," said Connie.

"It wasn't me."

"You didn't want to write what *was* you," Connie said.

"I don't understand why you wanted me to say that stuff."

"What can you not understand based on your panic disorder or PTSD or whatever the weekly diagnosis is?" Connie asked.

"That's not fair," Angie said.

"No, what's not fair is what you just did. Up there. In front of all of these people."

And CNN, Angie thought.

Historically, this was the moment in a confrontation conversation with Connie when Angie would begin to shrink in place. To feel unbelievably small and insignificant. So it was of no surprise that she felt exactly that way; it merely sucked that she did.

"Can you ever think of anyone but yourself?" Connie asked. "Is it necessary to make us the joke of this town?"

"Don't you have that in reverse?" Angie said, almost to herself.

Connie's squeeze on her daughter's arm was deliberate. "Sit down, smile, and show some kind of respect for your sister."

Angie knew that it was wrong, but as Connie walked away, she screamed obscenities at her. In her mind, of course.

People had streamed into the tent, lining up for the indulgent buffet. As hungry as Angie had been all morning, she could not face any of them. Coach Laden, whom she had avoided all summer. Jake, holding-not-holding hands with Stacy Ann — the hand hold where the fingers stroke the palm but don't commit to a full-on grasp.

Wang stood with his poser, wannabe-more-badass-than-they-were friends. Jamboree's parents held up the back of the line, indulging in their cell phones as opposed to each other. Jamboree, however, was looking at Angie. It was an awkward and unexpected moment. Angie's eyes darted toward the sea of quickly filling-up tables.

Angie walked the perimeter of tables heading toward her aunt Meghan, her mother's younger, pseudoliberal sister, sitting alone. Angie sat quietly with a seat between her and her aunt. A clear plastic cup of lemonade containing three cubes of ice had created a small but noticeable moat around its base.

Her aunt seemed too immersed in her own internal world to notice the falseness of Angie's forced smile.

"Pinterest lies, Angie," said Aunt Meghan.

"I'm . . . sorry?"

"Pinterest. It lies," her aunt repeated.

Angie was familiar with the online platform Pinterest only to the extent that her mother had obsessively referenced it over the summer when redecorating the house.

"Before I got pregnant, I lived on Pinterest," continued Aunt Meghan. "Creating board after board about baby clothes and baby furniture and baby blogs. *What to Expect When You're Expecting. Look What the Stork Brought In. Nothing Compares to Baby.* Pin after pin of quotes and smiling fathers and cute babyness. It was an endless well of wonder and hope. Women always smiling."

Her aunt took a swallow of her lemonade. The ice cracking together before releasing to the bottom of the cup.

"Thirty-three hours of labor, Angie," said her aunt.

"They don't put that on Pinterest. Thirty-three hours of pushing and breathing and screaming and sweating and squatting and hurting. I'm not even going to tell you the things that happen to your body . . . down there."

It was a matter of unquestionable fact that Angie hoped she would not.

"And when you finally have that baby, no one tells you about the placenta," said Aunt Meghan. "Do you know about the placenta, Angie?"

From Angie's expression, she did not, nor did she have any specific interest in knowing. She hoped to suggest this with her nonverbal cues.

She did not succeed.

"Yeah, I didn't either," said her aunt. "Placenta is like *birthing* another baby. See, you've already gone through thirty-three hours of hellish labor, and then you are back to pushing and sweating and screaming—if you can still scream. And then this thing that looks like . . . angry cabbage . . . comes out of you."

Angie's face wrenched in horror. How could such a truth be? Angry cabbage?

"I can't even *think* about cabbage without having this urge to vomit," her aunt said.

Neither would Angie.

Thankfully, it was not a preferred vegetable.

She preferred Brussels sprouts.

"And you come home, and your husband stays for a few

days," her aunt said. "Then he goes back to work. And there you are, Angie. Alone. All day. Every day, and the baby cries in the middle of the night, and your husband says, 'Can you make the baby stop crying? I have to go to work.' Like your job isn't work? You have to make sure that baby doesn't die. Once they begin to crawl — walk, the entire house is a war zone of sharp edges and unprotected electric sockets. Pinterest lies."

Angie was story-shocked by much of the narrative, especially given the urgency and excitement her aunt previously had about having a child. Given the full sheet cake at her baby shower with the image of her fetus on it — a disgusting memory for Angie, who had vomited her piece of the cake, but her aunt Meghan had loved the cake so dearly. Every last bite.

"But . . ." Angie said. "You liked your cake at the baby shower. With the fetus — the ultrasound picture-thing. You liked it so much."

Her aunt leaned into her. Angie tilted her head forward, expecting a sacred secret of some kind. Perhaps one that was less graphic.

"Never have a baby because you think it's cute, Angie. Not even if it's cute on a cake."

Her aunt gently rubbed Angie's arm. Angie nodded even though she had no interest in having a baby. She would forever see cabbage, though. Very angry cabbage.

"Excuse me," said a man, tapping Angie on the shoulder.

Angie turned toward an air force officer.

"Angie," the officer said.

"Hello," Angie said.

"Staff Sergeant Hernandez," he said, holding out his hand. "Rudy."

She shook his hand.

"May I speak with you? For a moment."

"Um, sure. Okay," Angie said.

It took Angie approximately 4.2 seconds to realize he meant in private. She quickly stood and followed him away from the William Anders High School Band's rendition of Lady Gaga's "Bad Romance." An odd choice for a post-statue-dedication song list, it seemed to Angie.

"I . . . I've heard a lot about you," said Staff Sergeant Hernandez. "Your sister became one of my most trusted . . . friends and, uh."

He stopped walking.

"That's not true," he said. "She was my . . . we were engaged."

Angie's eyes widened.

"En what?" Angie said.

"She didn't—we didn't tell anyone," he said. "She wanted to tell you first. In person. Not on Skype or in an e-mail. She wanted to tell you, but then . . ."

He clenched his jaw, clearing his throat. Trying to find his composure. "She was taken. And then everything else happened."

He looked up at the statue of Angie's sister.

"That's a really ugly statue," he said.

Angie laughed. "It is."

"She would've hated it," he said.

Angie nodded. "Yeah, she would have."

He grinned. "She would have hated a lot of things about all of this. She didn't like attention, you know?"

"No," Angie said. "That's all she had here."

The quiet hung between them for a few moments. The way quiet does when there are so many things to say but no sure way to say them. Angie wanted to ask him how they met. Where did they go on their first date? Did her sister still love Pink, Joan Jett, and Prince the way she had in high school? Because if anyone knew about her, it was him.

But Angie just stood there with the questions ruminating, waiting for him to say something, because he seemed to want to.

"You and your brother meant everything to her," he said. "She talked about you all the time. She said . . . you were a sun even though you felt like a shadow. That you didn't get how special you were. I used to feel that way too. Until I met her. It's like she just . . . reflected back all the good things I couldn't see in myself."

He went somewhere else for a moment. Somewhere that hurt him specifically . . . so precisely. Angie knew that hurt.

"She missed watching kung fu movies with you and

your brother," he said. "And eating popcorn with M&M's?"

Angie laughed, a tear escaping. "She'd eat all the M&M's."

"I know," he said, now crying.

"Except the yellow ones," Angie said.

"Because she really hated yellow anything," he said.

They wiped their faces.

"I've wanted to come and talk to you for so long," he said, looking at her wrists. "When I heard about what happened, I just didn't know if it was the right time. I didn't know if I should tell you about her and me and . . . I've truly wrestled with what to do, but . . ."

He reached inside his uniform jacket pocket and emerged with an envelope. He held it out to her. There, on a crinkled and dirt-smudged envelope, was Angie's name and address in her sister's handwriting. Somehow Angie had forgotten how her sister wrote her sevens. Her nines. The shape of the *A* in Angie. How had she already forgotten that?

"The night before she went out — when she ended up being captured — she wrote that. She asked me to mail it, but then things happened, and I . . ."

His eyes fell to her wrists again. This time she self-consciously turned them toward her.

"It's not that it's bad what she wrote," he said. "She read it to me. I just . . . I didn't know if it would hurt you. More. And I came here today hoping I would know. And seeing you up there, I did."

Angie looked down at the letter. The Hole inside her grew. It grew in a new place as if it had metastasized. Could the Hole do that? Spread?

"I'm sorry if . . . I should've mailed it," he said.

"I don't know really what to . . . um, say," Angie said. "Thanks?"

They half smiled at each other.

"You could read it," he said.

Angie exhaled a deep breath. "Yeah, um . . . okay."

Carefully, Angie opened the envelope. Inside there was a letter and a smaller-than-average rectangular postcard. The outside of the letter said:

READ THIS FIRST ☺

So Angie did.

Hey Ang,

Haven't heard from you in a while. Hope you aren't still mad at me. I'm really sorry for what I said. How I said it. It was stupid-dumb.

Anyway, I hope you're kicking ass in high school. Maybe going out for the team because your rebounds are killer. Coach Laden loves a killer rebound almost as much as a killer jump shot.

So keep working on that jump shot. Flick and follow through. Always follow through, Ang.

So . . .

I got a letter from Wang a few days ago. He said things are getting messy between Mom and Dad with the divorce. Said you weren't doing so well with it. That's got nothing to do with you. Mom and Dad's mess. Seriously, you got to hear me on this because it took me enlisting and ending up over here to figure that out. But I'm here now, and I got to make the best of it because I believe being here means something. Even if things are harder than I thought they would be. It's definitely not like playing Call of Duty. You can't just save your game and go do something else. It's real all the time here. Real lives. Real fear. Real people sometimes dying. The dying part is hard.

But sometimes there is real hope. And it's something you can see. Almost multiplying. That's what I hold on to when I feel lost. The hope.

Listen, I'll be back there soon. I can't WAIT to hang out with you and Wang and drink a frothy Slap Me I Dare You latte from The Backstory.

And after we have a Bruce Lee movie marathon, you and I are going on a road trip. Just you and me and the Buckeye state. There's no backing out this time. Okay? Besides I have something really AMAZING to tell you. It's part of the hope thing, and the only way I can tell you first, before anyone else, is if you come with me.

And I want to tell you first, Ang.

So, just to get you ready for our adventure, I've prepared an introductory list of things for us to see/do on the postcard. Don't panic — I'll be there every mile of the journey with you.

Hey, I need to go. I miss you to infinity and beyond times pi. Give Wang a hug for me and look out for him. He's a lot softer than he seems. He loves you more than he'll ever let on. It's a guy thing, I think.

Hope to hear from you soon. Remember follow-through. It's always about the follow-through. And kindness.

Love,
N

Tears streamed down Angie's face. Her throat constricted as she wiped them away with the back of her hand.

"You okay?" Staff Sergeant Hernandez asked her.

She nodded, but she was not okay. She stared at the white-font-and-red-background postcard in her hand that held the phrase: *Why Not?* Angie flipped the postcard over and read the intimidating road trip suggestion list her sister had planned.

1. Roller-skate to Blue Ash's "Abracadabra" at Brookpark Skateland
2. Dance on America's Shortest Street
3. Sing a song with a band in front of an audience
4. Have a picnic at the World's Largest Basket
5. _____ (Angie's choice)

Angie did not roller-skate.

Angie definitely did not dance in front of people.

It was not a List of Do's. It was a List of Impossible. A list that would never happen because her sister had never made it back.

Angie looked blankly at Staff Sergeant Hernandez.

"She really wanted to do all of those things with you," he said. "She had lists and lists of things she wanted the two of us to do. Things she wanted to see on her own. But that letter, those things? It had meant everything to her because you did. You meant everything to her, Angie."

And Angie felt the deepest of conflicting feelings. The hurt from her sister never making it home — the anger Angie still felt. How could such a duality exist? Were the five/seven stages of grief a mere hoax? She did not follow the suggested order of operation.

The postcard in Angie's hands outlined a road trip that would have been another disappointment to her sister had she returned, because Angie was afraid of almost everything. This was not a description she would ever use lightly.

Short List of Things She Feared:
Heights
Germs
Tornados
Public restrooms
Eating in front of people
Being lost
People looking at her
Driving a car
Dancing in front of people
Talking to people
Making wrong decisions
Ants
Making too much noise when kissing someone
Not having candy

From his pocket, Staff Sergeant Hernandez pulled a

piece of paper with the Holiday Inn Express logo on top.

"That's my e-mail and cell," he said as Angie read. "And where I'm stationed for the next six months. Let me know if you need anything. And, um . . ."

He reached beneath his collar and unfastened a necklace clasp. Pulling from beneath his shirt Angie's sister's most prized possession. Her pendant from when she made varsity freshman year. Her sister never took it off.

"She'd want you to have this," he said.

The pendant dangled in front of Angie. Almost whispering. He stepped behind her and fastened it around her neck. The weight of everything the pendant had meant to her sister hung heavy.

"I should probably," he said, looking at the crowd, "let you get back."

"Um . . . thanks," Angie said. "I mean, thank you. For the letter."

He grinned and pulled Angie into a hug, the hold time an estimated 4.7 seconds, and she did not entirely mind the hug the way she often minded hugs from people she did not know. Maybe because it was almost like hugging her sister. Almost.

When he stepped back, his eyes were full of hurt.

"Take care, Angie," he said.

Angie watched him weave through a crowd of people near the park's entrance. He crossed the street and disappeared around the corner of the Pizza Gallery. Right then, something shifted inside of her, only she did not know what it was. It was a feeling with no adjective.

Wang waved Angie over to Aunt Meghan's table. As she got closer, she saw he had two plates of food.

One with . . . cabbage!

Tick
Tick
Boom

It was Thursday.

It was lunchtime.

Lunchtime absolutely, unequivocally, without question sucked. Again!

Angie had retreated into the girls' restroom. Third stall from the sinks, her feet drawn as close to the base of the toilet as possible, her Walkman blaring "Open Arms" by Journey, with front man Steve Perry. Her heart breaking because she had made the mistake of going onto KC's Facebook and seeing KC, immersed in immense glee, with a Metallica T-shirt–wearing girl with avocado-green dyed hair and one gazillion ear piercings. Had Angie already been replaced by such a stereotypical rebel wannabe? The wound was unbearable. The Hole throbbed inside her.

Angie tore into her third Hershey's milk chocolate bar, the trifecta of square molds displaying the company's name crushed beneath her desperate chewing. She unwrapped another bar. Then three Andes mints that she'd stolen from her mother's secret stash in the hollowed-out, fake Aqua Net hair spray can, the place where her mother also stored several hundred dollars and a single marijuana joint. A random burglar would never think to look there, her mother had most likely surmised, but Angie and Wang both knew their mother's detestation for aerosol products. It was one of the few redeeming qualities about Connie. At least, from Angie's weighted perspective.

Still salivating for sugar — anything to ease all that felt out of control — Angie found a squished Almond Joy at the bottom of her backpack. She tore through the wrapper, but before indulging in the trusted go-to, she stopped.

Her stomach ached.

Her blood sugar had elevated.

By all accounts, she did not feel well. Not well at all.

There was no joy to be found in the coconut delight with two large almonds glazed in a silky milk chocolate. This was a first in her relationship with Almond Joy. She did not like this feeling. A rush of panic washed over her. She got up from the toilet, spilling pens, buttons, *Survivor* on audiocassette, and an article on beekeeping onto the grimy damp part of the floor.

She leaned up against the wall of the stall, tipping her

head back, eyes closed. Trying to slow down the racing thoughts in her head. Thoughts of KC and Avocado-Green-Dyed-Hair Girl with her gazillion ear piercings. Thoughts of that stupid, horrific, unmovable statue now eating up a significant part of Dryfalls Park. Thoughts of failing her couldn't-understand mother again and again and again —

A group of giggling girls poured into the restroom, their normalcy choking the very abnormal parts of Angie, which were many.

Angie scooped up her soaked contents and stuffed them in her backpack, rushing out of the stall.

As Angie stepped outside the girls' restroom, she furiously squeezed hand sanitizer into her palm, quickly rubbing one hand over the other. As her new woo-woo therapist recently mentioned, Angie had too many metaphorical tabs open in her mind. The swirl of the last few days, weeks, and years made it impossible to close any of them.

And it was for that reason, as she plowed ahead mindlessly out of the far side of the school building, that she did not see Gary Klein place himself directly in front of her.

Gary held out his leg and tripped her. Fat Angie ungracefully plunged to the cement walkway, cutting open her palm.

It was Thursday.

It was 12:37 in the afternoon.

It was not supposed to be this hard on a Thursday at 12:37 p.m. during the first week of school.

Blood surfaced near the scars of her failed suicide attempt. She did not like to look at her scars. She needed to add this realization to her List of Dislikes.

Angie's face wrenched in pain.

Gary's beefier stature towered above her.

"Dyke down," he said, laughing, pointing at her.

At close range, Angie became fully aware of the increase in Gary's neck mass — his shoulder width. Everything larger and harder and meaner. How could she have not noticed this on the first day of school? How could she have actually *kissed* Gary Klein all those years ago? Why did he need to continue his hate for her simply because she had not liked kissing him? And why did her life suddenly feel like some fat, poorly scripted version of the 1984 classic *The Karate Kid*?

The Karate Kid (runtime 126 min): A film about New Jersey teen Daniel LaRusso, who relocates to Los Angeles and meets cheerleader with a soul Ali-with-an-I, whose bully ex-boyfriend, Johnny, uses his karate to torment Daniel. Until a wise handyman, Mr. Miyagi, teaches Daniel karate by doing a bunch of chores, so he can fight Johnny in the All-Valley Karate Tournament.

Fat Angie, Wang, and their sister had been avid viewers of the *Karate Kid* franchise, Angie never realizing she would be in a somewhat similar scenario someday.

She propped herself up with her uninjured hand and attempted to stand.

"Sit down," Gary said.

The bottom of his boot met her right butt cheek, and she lost her footing, flying forward. Forgetting, of course, Rule #2 in the art of hand-to-hand combat: *Never turn your back to your opponent.*

"Quit it!" she warned.

"Ooooooooo," said two of the guys.

Gary laughed.

"C'mon, man," said Darius. "Just leave it."

"You still sympathizing with faggots and freaks, Darius?" Gary challenged.

Gary ticked his look toward the other two guys. They snickered. Almost in unison.

Darius wanted to be a leader. He wanted to tell Gary and the other guys to f— off. At least, that was the narrative that Angie was writing in her head. Unfortunately, he just shook his head and looked away.

Gary turned his attention back to Angie, his sneer sopping with hate.

"Hey, you feel like squealing for us today, piggy?" asked Gary.

He licked his lips, enjoying the taunt.

"Screw you, Gary," she said.

"Don't you wish, fat ass," he said.

He reached for her stomach, and she slapped him away.

"Better watch out, Gary," said one of the guys.

The other one had his cell phone pointed at Angie. "Show us your mad-cow face, Fat Angie."

In that moment, Fat Angie was angry. Not five-stages-of-grief angry, though recent psychology believed there were actually seven stages. Rather, she was:

Angry at her sister for enlisting.

Angry at Jake Fetch for hooking up with Stacy Ann.

Angry at her couldn't-understand mother's relentless
    focus on weight loss, fake smiling in public, and
    inability to have a genuine emotion.

Angry that KC gave up on their love.

Angry that the Hole continued to grow in spite of her
    therapeutic journaling.

Angry that the whole town was infatuated with an
    "idea" of a girl none of them actually knew.

But at that precise moment, without question, Angie was most angry with Gary Klein and his malign friends — even Darius A. Clark. Because by doing nothing he was still doing something. Darius might not have looked like them or acted like them, but he stood beside them all the same. It was a fact that confused Angie, but it was none theless true.

Gary squatted, pinching Angie's stomach. Angie screamed, and he covered her mouth. Panic shot through her when she could not escape him.

"You know faggots go to hell, right?" Gary said to Angie. "Same for fat-ass dykes."

Gary twisted his grip on her stomach. Her muted scream vibrated in her mouth, filling her throat with a shaking fear. Moron-with-the-Cell-Camera pushed in closer. His moment of cinema verité was at Angie's expense. She had to do something. She had to —

Angie bit Gary's hand, breaking loose long enough to scream. Gary slapped her across the face. The burn was numbing. Blood trailed from her nose.

"Enough, man," said Darius.

"Shut the fuck up, faggot," Gary said.

"I'm a faggot?" Darius challenged. "What's wrong with you?"

Angie scrambled to get up, but Gary hooked onto her ankle and dragged her closer, her jeans scraping along the sidewalk.

"Where you going, little piggy?" Gary asked.

Angie shoved him, but it only made him hungrier. He leaned into her. "Hey, fat ass. Why don't you kill yourself for real this time? I'll even let you borrow my daddy's gun."

Fat Angie's heart raced, her mind speeding through all the mental red lights that would say "Stop. Think."

She was so immensely angry.

She did not like to be immensely angry.

She did not like to be immensely angry because she didn't know how to —

"Breathe," her new woo-woo therapist had said. *"When you feel your mind racing, try and slow it down."*

"It's too fast," Fat Angie had said.

"What is too fast?" the new woo-woo therapist had asked.

The noise in Angie's mind — Chinook helicopters, television news reports, machine guns, Wang crying from his bedroom window, Jake and Stacy Ann, her sister screaming. The panicked montage — Angie fast-forwarded to the third sequel in the *Karate Kid* franchise. Where Daniel was drawn to the dark side of karate:

"If a man can't see, he can't . . ."

Angie thrust her palm into Gary Klein's nose. An audible crack followed by —

"You fucking fat dyke!" screamed Gary.

His pain was palpable as he groaned.

Angie had snapped — seen red. Whatever the phrasing was for what had happened, she had done it. She had struck Gary Klein in his nose and broken it. She stared at her pulsating palm, blood flushed to the surface of her skin.

The brick-shouldered bully dropped to his knees, cradling his nose. Blood seeped through the edges of his meaty fingers.

"You crazy bitch!" said Gary.

The guys tried to help Gary up, but in an effort to save face, he pushed them away. Tears streamed his cheeks. He coughed and spat — bright-red blood speckled the sidewalk. Then his eyes met Angie's with a fury she had never seen in anyone.

Rule #3 in the art of hand-to-hand combat: *Know when to retreat!*

Angie scrambled to her feet and ran. Well, sort of ran. For her current state of out of shape, it was more of a panting, thigh-chafing jog.

She was not too far into the courtyard when Gary tackled her from behind. Angie slammed to the ground, the air knocked out of her.

Gary established his leverage and straddled her. His punches were not pulled. They were hard and intentional. He truly wanted to cause her pain.

She blocked, her sweaty arms aching from his blows. Blood from his nose splashed on her like a Pollock painting. Angie was a fan of artist Jackson Pollock, just not a fan of looking like the early stages of a canvas from his drip period.

"She's a girl, Gary!" someone yelled.

"Oh my God . . ." another person said.

"Get Mr. Warner!" a girl shouted.

Angie's vision blurred with sweat and tears. Gary's arms continued to swing. Her forearms were numb, his fists getting past them, knuckles bearing down on her face.

Jake — Wang — anyone, please, Angie thought.

Then, quite surprisingly, a bunch of guys dog-piled

Gary, knocking him to the ground, corralling him. Stacy Ann hooked Angie under her arms and dragged her away from Gary. Kneeling in front of her, Stacy Ann placed her hands on Angie's bloody face.

"Angie?" asked Stacy Ann. "Are you okay? Angie."

But Angie instinctively scooted away from her one-time tormentor.

"Get the fuck off of me!" Gary shouted. "Get off me!"

When he broke loose, he surveyed the onlookers who formed a mini-wall between him and Angie. He had lost more than favor. He was, officially, despised. Regardless of his exceptional abilities on the football field, there, among his peers, Gary had crossed the line that truly mattered. Even if many of them had made Angie the butt of a joke, none of them seemed to cosign on to Gary beating her up.

"What?" Gary said to them. "That crazy bitch broke my fucking nose."

"Angie?" said Stacy Ann. "Hey."

Disoriented, Angie attempted to stand but collapsed. Stacy Ann helped her get up, but Angie pushed her away.

"I'm trying to help you," Stacy Ann said.

The vice principal and a security officer descended, pushing through the wide circle of kids watching—some still filming on their phones.

Gary, Angie, Stacy Ann, and the guys who had attempted to stop the fight were escorted away from the courtyard. Jake tore through the crowd.

"Angie?" Jake said. "Angie, what happened?"

Angie said nothing to Jake.

"Angie . . ." Jake said.

What could she say to Jake? That she had just broken Gary Klein's nose? Was it a justifiable action, given Gary's very real threat—her fear? She wanted to say something to Jake. Something about how much she had missed him and how their friendship made her feel like she could belong. But she just continued to walk clumsily forward, her backpack strap saddled askew off her shoulder.

Angie saw Jamboree standing atop a concrete bench in the courtyard. She saw the sea of faces staring at her. It should have thrown her into panic, but she was just too . . . numb?

Had she somehow turned to the nefarious, dark side of life? When had this happened? How had this happened? Would it require a new wardrobe? An *en vogue* hairstyle?

How had her life gone from hard but sometimes funny and quirky to absolute, unsolicited teen hell? It did not fit the trajectory of how she had imagined her sophomore year, even though she should have been a junior.

From over his shoulder, Gary glared at Angie. Their conflict was far from over. And as unnerving a reality as that was, there was something more ominous than his fury that she feared.

What would her couldn't-understand mother say?

It's the End of the World as We Know It

Connie did not look directly at her daughter. She did, however, sit in close enough proximity that the heat of her silent rage radiated profusely.

For the record, this sucked even more than lunch had.

Principal Warner continued to speak in a monotone succession. None of it boded well for Angie, who slouched in a painful, silent seethe. Painful in that the chair's arms pressed at the sides of her wide hips. Painful in that she hurt in so many other places, because real fighting was not like movie fighting. Especially when facing real hate. It hurt. Immensely.

"Angie, do you understand what I'm saying to you?" Principal Warner asked slowly.

Angie was not slow. Her mind was a buffet full of words, phrases, and ideas that did not need him or anyone else to speak slowly, even if she struggled to articulate things sometimes. It did not make —

"Answer him," Connie said.

"Yes," Angie said. "I understand."

Principal Warner waited. Doing that thing authority figures do with dramatic pauses intended to emphasize the level of trouble someone is in. Angie did not need a dramatic pause. The anger radiating off her mother would more than suffice.

"Connie, as you know, per signing paperwork during orientation," he said, "we have a zero-fighting policy here at William Anders. Now, I know that Angie has had some special circumstances —"

The word *special* had been at the top of Angie's List of Dislikes. It made her skin crawl. It rolled her adrenaline into full-on fight mode. It was code for "low-functioning," "emotionally challenged," "out of control," "freak," and a host of other derogatory descriptors. Angie did not want to have special anything anymore. She disliked that word almost more than any other thing on her list. Almost.

"Now, I haven't spoken to Gary's parents as of yet," said Principal Warner. "But I have to be honest with you both. This incident could result in possible assault charges for Angie."

"What?" said Connie, a strident tone in her voice.

Assault charges? Against Angie? She had defended herself. She had finally stood up to the man. Well, so to speak.

"That's not fair," Angie said. "None of this is fair. Gary knocked me down. He started all of this. He —"

"Be quiet," Connie said.

"This wasn't my fault. I swear."

Sadly, Connie did not believe her very sincere daughter.

"This is not an assault charge, Principal Warner," Connie said. "I assure you that I plan to handle this at home."

"It's my job to let you know what the situation is and can be," said Principal Warner. "At the very least, Angie will be suspended for a week, and depending on the superintendent, possibly expelled. We take incidents of this nature very seriously and —"

"This is bullshit," Angie said, not caring that she had cursed.

"Watch it," her mother warned.

"I didn't do this," said Angie. "Gary *started* this. He *pushed* me — he knocked me down."

"I've spoken with Gary's friends, and that's not how they tell it," said Principal Warner. "And given your history —"

Her history of being the only girl to have had a very public nervous breakdown during a football pep rally after slitting her wrists in the locker room bathroom, thus winning the invisible but coveted award of nutcase supreme. Of being everything outcast, everything her sister was not. Of now being accused of a crime she had not committed.

Well, not entirely. The semantics felt irrelevant to Angie. What was relevant was who would believe Angie over Gary and his friends? The verdict was already in on Principal Warner and her mother.

"You signed the paperwork, Angie," said Principal Warner. "No fighting on this campus."

"I also signed the zero-bullying policy, Mr. Warner," Angie said. "But that didn't stop the bullying. That didn't stop the pushing and the name calling or the fat roll squeezing. That didn't stop—"

"Enough," warned Connie.

It was not enough. It was not enough, and Angie boiled with frustration. Suspension? Expulsion? Assault? How were these not words related to her flirting-with-juvie-hall brother instead of her? Had the world turned upside down? Would frogs literally rain down from the blue sky?

"Angie, you need to learn to resolve your problems without violence," said Principal Warner. "Do you understand that?"

Angie shook her head. "Right . . ."

"Have a seat outside," he said. "I want to speak with your mother privately."

Angie struggled to get out of the chair, much to the embarrassment of her mother. Angie grabbed her now-dusty and torn backpack and headed out the door. She did not expect to see Stacy Ann Sloan, sitting on a bench outside the principal's office. Sitting with an ice pack over her left cheek. Reluctantly, Angie sat beside Stacy Ann, as it was the only available seat.

"Hey . . ." Stacy Ann said.

Angie continued to stare ahead as Stacy Ann held out the ice pack for Angie.

"For your eye," Stacy Ann said. "The swelling."

In all of the chaos post-fight, Angie had yet to see her face. She pulled her phone out of her pocket. The screen was cracked from the scuffle with Gary. She rolled it into selfie mode, finally seeing the extent of the fight. Her eye was definitely a nod to the final scene in the 1979 film *Rocky*, starring Mr. Sylvester Stallone. Without question, she looked similarly pulverized or, as the phrasing went, "rough."

Angie snapped a photo and attached it to a text to KC before stopping herself. Would KC share the image with her sultry new wannabe rebel squeeze? Surely they were squeeze-ish. The photograph Angie had seen on KC's Facebook had been far too effusive.

Angie deleted the message.

Stacy Ann placed the ice pack on the bench between them. Angie rolled her tongue along the fresh hole inside her bottom lip, scaling her mouth with her tongue, checking for any possible missing teeth.

"We should talk," said Stacy Ann. "About Jake."

"I do not . . . want to talk to *you* about Jake," Angie said, pointedly. "Like, um . . . ever."

Stacy Ann turned toward Angie, who flinched.

"Relax, I'm not going to do anything," Stacy Ann said. "Look, I get why we hated each other—"

"I never hated you. I never did anything to you. You *tortured* me."

Angie's searing stare silenced Stacy Ann, who faced forward again, placing the ice pack back on her cheek.

The school bell chimed. Kids flooded the hallway. Their muted laughter and conversations reverberated against the glass windows. Some kids dipped their heads around Welcome Back posters to catch a glimpse inside the office, a few of them pointing inside before moving on to class.

"I'm sorry," Stacy Ann said. "For what I did. For how I treated you."

"Why?"

"Because . . . it was cruel," Stacy Ann said.

Angie shook her head. "Why are you dating him?"

"You mean, why is someone like Jake dating me? I don't know. I asked him the same thing."

"When did it start?" Angie asked, her eyes on the floor.

"This summer," said Stacy Ann.

"But he was in rural Wisconsin," said Angie.

"Skype? Letters. Texts," Stacy Ann said. "I *really* like him, Angie. A lot. And I'm not asking you to forgive me for how I treated you, but—"

"Thanks," said Angie.

"Look, I'm trying," said Stacy Ann. "I'm really trying."

Angie turned toward her. "You *dragged* me into the locker-room showers last year. Do you remember that? You made it your personal mission to humiliate me every second I was at school — posting memes of me online, turning people against me. So I'm sorry that I don't really care that you're trying, Stacy Ann. Just because you want to screw my only friend."

"That's not —"

"Fuck your try."

Angie stood up and leaned against a wall that did not face Stacy Ann. She had never talked so directly — so unabbreviatedly — to Stacy Ann. A girl she had feared in the hallways and revered on the basketball court only to continue to find her to be a conundrum. A conundrum who wanted to sleep with her only friend. Angie did not understand this level of anger and hunger for confrontation. It made her feel strong, but it also made her feel empty.

Plus, had she really said the f-word in the principal's office to Stacy Ann Sloan?

The door to Mr. Warner's office opened. Connie stepped out, motioning for Angie to follow her. The parting glance from Stacy Ann to Angie did not coincide with any of their previous interactions. It was as if Stacy Ann cared.

This puzzled Angie.

Immensely.

En route to visitors' parking, a parent passed Angie and

her couldn't-understand mother. Connie stretched into that public persona that relayed "I'm fine/we're fine/everything is absolutely fine."

Angie did not dislike that persona. She HATED IT. She did not know if she could put something she hated on her List of Dislikes, but she would consider it.

"Mom —" Angie began.

"Get in the car," her couldn't-understand mother said.

Angie opened the door. A wash of hot air crashed into her. Connie methodically belted herself, put the key in the ignition, and checked her makeup in the rearview mirror. This was her ritual. An apocalypse with dragons and demons bursting through the cracked, molten asphalt could happen, and Connie would still need to complete this ritual. Well, maybe not dragons.

Fat Angie stared out the windshield as Connie slid the gear shift into reverse. The seat belt warning alarm blared. Angie had not belted in. She fumbled with the strap.

Connie jammed the car back into park.

She.

Was.

MAD!

"What were you thinking? Do you — think?" asked Connie.

Connie's grip on the steering wheel tightened. She was trying to regroup, channel her newfound Zen, something—because she took several deep, meditative-like breaths. Angie watched her from the corner of her eye. Not committing to a full-on stare for fear of drawing any more ire.

"I was in court, Angie," said Connie. "Do you understand that I have responsibilities? Not like your father. Out chasing his 'dreams.' Moron. He's not here paying the mortgage. I am responsible. And today. Today was one of my biggest clients."

"They're all your biggest clients," Angie said almost under her breath.

"What?" asked Connie.

"It's what you always say when you're inconvenienced."

"Inconvenienced?"

Angie had put her mother on the express lane to defensiveness. Not a particularly smart strategy, as her mother had yet to detail the level of groundedness Angie would incur.

"Angie, you need to wake up," said her couldn't-understand mother. "This isn't going to just go away. It is a possible assault charge. Do you understand what that means?"

"I did not start the fight. He *pushed* me."

"It's not about what you think happened. It's about possible time in a juvenile correctional facility. I can't believe this isn't a conversation I'm having with your brother."

"I did not start the fight," Angie pleaded. "He—"

"It doesn't matter." Connie's tone was silencing.

Angie wanted to make her largeness as small as possible.

But she was too big. In all the ways that she could never hide.

Connie rested her elbow on the console between them, pressing her fingers against her right temple.

"I called your therapist on the way here," said Connie. "She's out of town until Monday, so I shared something with her that I've been considering."

Connie reached into the glove box. From beneath the proof of insurance emerged a full-color brochure that had a water stain in the top left corner. For clarity, there had never been a brochure or pamphlet from her mother that Angie had deemed helpful. Not the Weight Watchers pamphlet. Not the *I'm Okay, You're Okay* pamphlet. Not even the seemingly harmless pamphlet on getting your period. But this particular pamphlet was —

"Whispering Oak?" Fat Angie asked.

The name sounded like a retirement community, but it was not. Deep in the heartland, aka Iowa, Whispering Oak was a remote, faith-based rehabilitation facility for last-chance/at-risk youth, offering behavior modification treatment for challenging teens. "Initiates" spoke only when given permission. Meals, motivations, classes, and counseling were structured around daily prayer. It offered special focus on teens experiencing a "sexual identity crisis" with the use of conversion therapy.

"Deprogramming?" Angie read, almost like a whisper.

Whispering Oak was, in short, Yellow Ridge 2.0, and Angie was mortified.

She did not like confinement.

She did not like confinement at all.

She most definitely did not like the word *deprogramming*.

"Are you serious?" asked Angie.

"Are you? Because I am at an absolute loss. First, with your suicidal ideations and Tom Petty fixation."

"I was not fixated on —"

"Then your sexuality, and the running all over town after your sister's funeral, acting out, and now fighting again. You can't continue to behave this way. Are you listening to me?"

"I hear you," said Angie. "I hear Principal Warner. I hear Stacy Ann Sloan and Jake and Dad, even when he doesn't call. I hear all of you, but you don't hear me. Why can't you hear me?"

"I am deafened by hearing you, Angie."

Connie put the car into reverse.

That was it. Angie's fate was pretty much sealed.

Her cell phone vibrated in her pocket. She knew better than to check it.

Soon she and her couldn't-understand mother drove past the statue memorializing her sister. Then the street corner where KC had told Angie she loved her for the first time. Every place was riddled with sadness. With heartbreak. With nothing funny, and Angie could have used something—anything—funny right then. Even if it were Wang's lame, self-gratifying humor.

How had everything gotten so hard—so dark? Like season six of *Buffy the Vampire Slayer*. Surely, Mr. John Hughes would have written a better ending to Angie's day. He would never have let Gary punch a girl. He would have found some clever way around the unbelievably graphic nature of the day's violence. However, Mr. John Hughes died of a myocardial infarction, also known as a heart attack, in August of 2009, so he would not be scripting anything for Angie's life.

Rather, Angie was stuck. Stuck in her paltry, quite miserable existence with the likelihood of an extended trip to horrifying Whispering Oak in her very near future. This was not her life. Was it?

Make the World Go Away

"Don't even think about walking out that front door," Angie's couldn't-understand mother said, securing her carry-on luggage into her SUV.

The irony was that Angie had, in fact, just walked out the front door with Wang to watch their mother leave. A two-day business trip to Chicago.

Wang loudly masticated his favorite barbecue potato chips, Grippo's, while watching his mother go through her check-off-list routine.

"I expect you to keep an eye on your sister," Connie said to Wang.

"Right," he said, under his breath.

Wang was still pissed at the slew of rapid-fire questions flung at him from his mother approximately one hour earlier about why he had not been there to keep Angie from "getting into trouble" at school. Connie was attempting to usher Wang into the status of big-brother/protector. A laughable role given that he did not even acknowledge Angie as his sister at school. Much less take on the role of protector. Even if he was a year older.

"Heard John/Prick trying to tame Mom's shrew," Wang said, still loudly chewing.

"What?" Angie asked.

"You didn't hear him use some of that low-rent, therapeutic bullshit on Mom?" Wang said. "Moron. Mom's newfound Zen is one hundred and ninety-nine percent prepackaged, Buddha-on-a-key-chain bullshit. You think Buddha wants to be on a fucking key chain?"

"I'm serious, Angie," said her couldn't-understand mother, shutting the SUV hatch.

John/Rick took the keys from Connie and dropped the SUV's driver's seat back as far as it would go. It failed to fully accommodate his height, as it got stuck unusually close to the steering wheel.

"You messed with the driver's seat gear again, didn't you?" Angie asked Wang.

Wang continued to masticate, as previously mentioned, loudly.

"Angie," barked Connie.

"Yes," Angie snapped.

"Do not leave this house," Connie warned. "Not to

Jake's. Not anywhere. I'll be back Saturday night. I expect your room to be clean."

Wang dug around in the bag, searching for the most seasoned chip he could find. Moments later, the SUV reversed. The nose of the car scraped the dip in the driveway before blowing out of the cul-de-sac. They were, of course, late to the airport.

Angie watched Wang chewing, his thoughts quite possibly in a rare but deep pensive solitude.

"Dude, you're screwed," he said, cackling. "I haven't seen Mom *that* pissed since she found out I was selling downloaded porn."

Angie shook her head and went into the house.

"Like . . . what were you thinking?" he asked, shutting the front door behind him. "Breaking Gary Klein's nose? Not that there aren't a dozen kids who want to, but damn. The guy's a landfill, but man, is he steroid-hard. How did you do it?"

"*The Karate Kid Part III*," Angie said, sheepishly.

Wang covered his mouth. "Awww, snap! When Daniel's in the club, right?"

Wang improvised the film's core karate moves of wax-on-wax-off, paint-the-fence, sand-the-floor, and the signature crane stance.

"It's not funny," said Angie.

"It's kinda funny," Wang said. "I mean, the movie kinda sucked."

It was a sequel, after all.

"Seriously, I would've never picked you to channel all that was the dark side of karate and break that prick's nose. Damn."

"He knocked me down and — covered my mouth and . . ."

Wang stopped in mid-chip bite.

"Did he try to . . . did he *try*?" Wang asked.

"No," Angie said, dismissing the notion of rape. "But he was . . . he was hurting me. Really hurting me and I . . . panicked. And I was so . . ."

Mad.

Angie had been mad.

Mad in a way she did not fully understand, and that scared her.

Wang threw the bag of chips on the entry table and scooped up the fifty-dollar bill their mother had left for them, sliding it into his baggy jeans pocket without a moment of pause.

Angie stared at the urn looming atop the mantel in the living room. Its eerie hollowness, with pretentious engraving, staring back at her.

"Did you know you can get a Green Bay Packers urn?" Wang said, rooting around the back of his mouth with his index finger.

"What?"

"Yeah, I looked it up," he said. "There's, like, an urn for

everything. Superman, Monopoly boards. Like, these big-ass golf balls — and KISS."

"The band?" Angie said.

"Right?" Wang said, grinning. "Imagine Gene Simmons with his mondo tongue sticking out on our mantel."

Angie laughed. Wang laughed. It was nice to laugh together. Even if it was about something as morbid as urns.

"Of all of the cool urns Mom could have picked. I mean, it's not like she's in there, but she would have hated that one."

"Yeah," Angie said. "It's cold."

"Huh?" he asked.

"The urn," she said. "It feels cold."

Wang looked at Angie's bruised and battered face.

"Everything . . . it's just so . . ." Angie tried to find her fractured words. "Hard. You know?"

Angie exhaled, her body wanting to collapse under the weight of the last few days — weeks — years. She was tired of trying. She was tired of therapeutic journals and loneliness. She was —

Wang nudged her with his shoulder and motioned her to follow him into the kitchen. First thing he did was blast hip-hop music from the iPod docked on their mom's overpriced speaker system. John/Rick's iPod, complete with cracked screen and playlists that did not actually, well, suck.

Angie leaned against a counter as Wang dug around in the freezer. Shuffling Lean Cuisine meals to the side, he pulled a bag of chopped mangoes from the back. He chucked the bag at Angie, who fumbled but caught it before it hit the floor.

"Wrap it in a dish towel and put it on your eye," he said.

He reached into the refrigerator, retrieving a small box of leftover pizza and one of John/Rick's energy drinks.

"Three-day weekend, yo," Wang said, sliding up on the counter. "Party over at Henneway's tonight. Rancid Reign at The Backstory. Saturday down at the lake. Me and my boys are gonna get lit."

Angie rolled-not-rolled her eyes at Wang's itinerary of debauchery.

"What about you?" he asked, biting into a slice of pizza.

"Were we not standing out on the same porch?" said Angie, repositioning the frozen mangoes on her face. "I'm grounded."

"Dude, she's not here," he said. "And I'm not gonna tell her if you don't."

"I've got nowhere to go, anyway," Angie said, a defined sadness in her voice.

"Hang with Jake," Wang said.

"That's . . . *not* going to happen. Maybe ever."

Wang threw his pizza crust into the box and wiped his hands on his jeans.

"Because of Stacy Ann?" he said, taking a swig of the energy drink.

"What do you know about Stacy Ann?"

"Dude, at some point," he said, belching, "you gotta

accept that I know pretty much everything that's supposed to be on the down low. Plus, everyone kinda knows."

Angie tossed the frozen mango bag on the counter. She was not part of the "know" percentage of William Anders High School. How could she not see — know — that Jake and Stacy Ann . . . ?

"Look, Jake's your real friend, you know," Wang said. "Like, he doesn't care what anyone thinks. He actually likes you."

"I don't want to talk about Jake."

Wang finished off the energy drink, rolling out a text on his phone, cracking up when one fired back at him.

There was a time Angie could have talked to Wang about a lot of things. Before their sister left. Before she went missing. And in the nostalgia of that memory and the fact that she had no one else to talk to, Angie asked, "What am I going to do?"

He shrugged. "Join a cult?"

Angie shook her head. "Yeah, okay. Thanks."

"Just . . . I don't know. Apologize, or lay low or something. Play the 'my sister's dead' pity card."

"You're gross," Angie said.

"Look, I've been in trouble a lot," said Wang. "You'll get a week at home to watch your flashback TV shows. Then it will be over."

Angie knew it would not just "be over." She slid the Whispering Oak pamphlet out of her back pocket and handed it to Wang. He dusted off his hands and read it.

"Mom wants to send you here?" Wang asked.

Angie nodded regretfully.

"Wow . . . they actually used the word *deprogram*," Wang said, continuing to read the pamphlet. "Initiates? Shit! This place is scary, yo."

"Yeah," Angie said.

"What is she thinking?"

"She's thinking I'm gay and that I screw up because of it?"

"Yeah, but it's like Mom just sandwiches stuff together all stupid. Like you're 'unstable' because you're gay. You're gay because you want attention. You're overweight because you're gay and want attention. She always wants to blame everything on something else that doesn't make sense. It's just . . . it's never what it just *is*. You know? Like, I don't even know why I'm here. Why did she want me? Was it, like, some flash Angelina Jolie adoption phase? Did she just need to fill a gap in the holiday card? Like for real, I just . . . I don't even know."

And for the first time, Angie saw a glimmer of something deeper in Wang. A hurt — a loneliness that she had felt, but could not articulate.

"But this shit?" he said, holding up the pamphlet. "This is bullshit, Angie."

"She says the therapist gets to make the final decision," said Angie.

"So, tell her what she wants to hear," Wang said. "I do it with John/Rick."

"I can't just lie," Angie said.

Lying was contrary to the therapeutic process, as it had been explained to Angie. Lying would not enable her to develop healthy coping strategies. Lying would prevent her from getting past the loss of her sister and her family and —

"You wanna go to this place?" Wang said, fanning the flyer at her. "Initiates are for *The Hunger Games,* not therapy, Ang. You wanna be all *Hunger Games* in . . . Iowa?"

Angie did not like the trajectory of his question.

Iowa was significantly colder than Dryfalls. Plus, the facility was near a large cornfield. After seeing Stephen King's *Children of the Corn* at age ten, Angie had kept away from all things corn oriented. Even corn salsa.

This was a fact.

Angie did not like corn. Much in the way she now did not like the image of angry cabbage. Both equally terrifying.

Wang's phone chimed, and he hopped off the countertop.

"Dude, tell her whatever you have to to get out of it," Wang said. "Otherwise, Mom will ship you off. And seriously, I'd lie, run away, or do whatever before I ended up in a place like that."

Wang fired a text message back.

"I gotta roll," he said, handing the pamphlet to Angie.

He started out of the kitchen, then stopped in the

doorway. Something softer seemed to sweep over him when he turned back toward her.

"Don't just sit here freaking out, okay?" said Wang. "For real. Just go talk to Jake. He'd definitely give you better advice than me. He's kind of that guy, you know?"

Angie nodded.

Wang strutted out of the kitchen, grabbing his oversize hoodie before disappearing out the front door.

Angie was alone.

Alone in her pristine house with all the picture frames perfectly hung. Without dust in any corner of the kitchen. It was perfection. It was everything that Angie was not — could not be. And it was at the notion of all things put into their places — places where she didn't fit — that Angie felt the rise of nervousness, of agitation swelling in her.

She rushed upstairs to her bedroom, passing her brother's room, the bathroom they shared, and the sixteen-by-twenty-four framed military photo of her sister.

Angie shut her bedroom door behind her, locking it.

She pushed play on her audiocassette alarm clock radio beside her bed. Sinéad O'Connor's infinitely heartbreaking "Nothing Compares 2 U" ached through the speakers, each lyric more gut-wrenching than the last.

Angie stretched out on her bed, fixating on her dismal future. On the realities of a place like Whispering Oak. Some quasimilitant, pray-the-gay-girl-gay-away hell on Earth. She rolled onto her side, facing the dusty imprint of where her desktop computer had been. Her couldn't-understand mother had taken it away, along with Angie's cell phone and her iPod Classic. Leaving her with a flip phone that only dialed 911.

Angie sat up on the edge of her bed. She lay back down. Up, down. No position was comfortable. Nothing was comfortable. Agitated, she shot up on the edge of the bed again. She reached beneath her nightstand and fished out a Butterfinger candy bar. With precision, she split the crinkling, yellow-orange wrapper. She chewed and chewed, but it could not wall off the overwhelming noise in her head.

Nothing was comfortable. Nowhere was safe.

This made her more nervous.

She did not like to be nervous.

She tried to do as instructed by her new woo-woo therapist. She tried to "just breathe," but it was not working. Nothing was working.

The reality was that Angie felt trapped. Trapped in the sad vocals of "Nothing Compares 2 U." Trapped in the stupid yellow ribbons and the expectations to be like anyone's sane, rational, slim, cute, funny, smart, boy-crazed, teen-magazine-reading, member-of-the-cheerleading-squad, Nicholas Sparks–fan or similar daughter.

Angie began to kick the floor. She kicked it harder and harder and harder, creating a rhythm counter to the somber music. There were just too many metaphorical tabs opened in her mind. She couldn't find a way to close any of them.

Monday she would be evaluated. The new woo-woo therapist would not believe Angie. She would side with Angie's mother — though they seemed to think little of each other. Angie had been suspended, possibly expelled. The therapist would definitely see Angie as the problem. Angie could not go back to shatterproof glass and sheets washed in harsh detergents.

Angie kicked the floor harder and harder, her voice literally screaming from inside her as she looked down at the scars on her wrists. The scars stretching beyond the confines of her watch and sweatband. And in that moment, Tom Petty's "Free Fallin'" echoed in the panicked recesses of her mind the way it had that day of the pep rally. That day in the girls' locker room, thinking she couldn't live without her sister.

"Please, please, please, just stop," Angie whispered.

Her mind flooded with online video comments, with text messages and taunts from school.

Why don't you just kill yourself?

Die, bitch!

She can't hang herself because the rope will break.

Whale crossing!

Then she heard her mother's voice over all of the noise in her head.

"Why did it have to be my good one . . ."

Angie flew into a blind rage. She knocked everything off her dresser. She overturned it. She flung framed photos against the wall, glass shattering. She threw mix CDs from her sister, gifts from KC. Nothing was safe from the fury of Fat Angie. Not her desk. Not her worn-out sneakers. Not the motivational posters on her wall from fourth grade. She clawed and ripped photos and newspaper clippings featuring her sister from the full-length mirror they were plastered to, leaving Angie with only the reflection of herself. Her sweaty, puffy-eyed, and bruised-faced self. Chocolate coating the corners of her mouth.

She was left with . . . Fat Angie.

"I HATE YOU!" she shouted.

And then . . . Angie cried.

She cried so hard. Her heart full-throttle pounded in her chest while she leaned forward on her knees, sobbing, her throat choking up as the tears pushed along her sore cheeks. This was, she thought, the bottom.

Angie did not like the bottom.

Angie did not like crying.

Angie could really have used a tissue as her snot began to run.

In the moment of ugly cry, Angie noticed something amid the carnage of her bedroom. Beneath scattered paperback books and stuffed animals was her sister's HORNETS' NEST basketball jersey.

Somehow Sinéad O'Connor's sad song had continued to play and began to fade out. In the moment of silence, Angie heard the loudness of herself breathing, the aching of her tears. And unexpectedly, the rebel of rock 'n' roll, Ms. Joan Jett, blared through the speakers with her 1981 smash hit "Bad Reputation."

Ms. Joan Jett had been an icon for Angie. So much so that she kept a photo of the rock queen in her wallet, performing at the infamous Norway concert. And it was then, with Ms. Joan Jett singing, that an unexpected anthem began in Angie, a fire igniting so deep and so immediate in her plump self.

Angie wiped her face with the collar of her T-shirt while clomping through her room, paper and glass crunching beneath her sneakers. Pushing her overturned desk upright, she opened the third drawer from the bottom. Beneath Connie's gifted Nicholas Sparks book–inspired Blu-rays were the postcard and letter from Angie's sister.

With "Bad Reputation" clawing the bedroom walls, filling Angie with ideas of teen rebellion, Angie fixed her puffy eyes on two words:

Why Not?

Why not take the trip her sister wanted to take? Connie would not be back until Saturday night, so why not? Aside from Angie's obvious fears, phobias, and of course, the direct disobeying of her couldn't-understand mother.

Angie stumbled into her closet and pulled out her old backpack. She shoved in some clothes, a ziplock of candy bars, two pencils, one pen, several mixtapes, and her therapeutic journal. She clipped the Walkman to her jeans' waistband.

Angie rushed down the hallway, barging into her mother's bedroom. She unscrewed the bottom to the hollow Aqua Net hair spray can. Three hundred seventy dollars. Two Andes mints and a single marijuana joint. She took the mints and the money. She threw the joint in her mother's toilet and flushed it. It was illegal to possess or use marijuana in the state of Ohio, as her couldn't-understand mother had said to Wang when he was apprehended for using marijuana. Angie was merely helping her mother follow the letter of the law.

Angie jogged down the stairs and made a direct line for . . . her mother's beloved symbol: the urn. She swiped it, a little surprised by the weight, and made for the front door.

She swung the door open and paused.

Big are-you-sure-about-this pause.

Crossing the threshold between doorjamb and welcome mat would be the official breaking of her couldn't-understand mother's "don't leave this house" rule. Until that moment, everything could be returned to its original place. Everything could go back as it was, with the exception of the torn posters. And the broken picture frames. And the flushed marijuana joint. And — she stopped herself from continuing the list of what could not be fixed as Jake and his dog, Ryan, stepped out their front door.

It was now or it was never. It was do or . . .

She stepped out the door, locking it behind her.

She had done it. She had broken the unbreakable don't-step-outside-the-house rule. There was no time to process the weight of the action as Jake crossed the street. Because she was in no mood to talk to Jake.

She was at the edge of her driveway when Jake and Ryan intersected with her.

"What is that?" Jake said, eyeing the urn.

"It's a symbol," Angie said, walking past him.

"A what? Hey."

Jake and Ryan jogged up beside her. The clicking of Ryan's nails acting as a metronome.

"Your face," Jake said. "Jesus, Angie, what really happened?"

"Nothing."

"It doesn't look like nothing."

"It's not your problem," she said.

"It's not my what?"

"It's not your problem to worry about, Jake," said Angie.

He continued to follow her. "I've been calling you, you know. Texting."

"My mom took my phone," she said. "And my computer. And my iPod Classic. My soul is next."

"Stop," said Jake, stepping in front of her. "Just tell me what's going on."

Angie glared at him.

"Really? You're gonna glare at me?" Jake asked.

"I'll glare," she said. "You're not the glaring police."

"This trying-to-shut-me-out thing? This isn't you, Angie."

"Me?" said Angie. "You would have to show up to know me, Jake. You'd have to be honest —"

"I have shown up," he said. "Maybe not always knowing how, but I've been here."

She shook her head. He had been with Stacy Ann for months. FOR MONTHS! Lying to Angie. Poor, dumb little Fat Angie. She was done with his lies. She was done with his secrets and his use of the word *complicated*. She was done.

"You lied to me," Angie said.

"I shouldn't have. It's just . . . It's —"

"Complicated?"

"It wasn't just a hook-up, Angie," Jake said. "I know you think it was that, but it wasn't. It was something else. It was —"

"Breasts? Pom-poms? Waistline?"

"Don't," said Jake.

"Don't *don't* me," Angie said. "Okay? You became friends with me because of what? My sister made you — feel guilty or sorry with some . . . stupid promise or whatever. I don't want guilty-sorry friendships, Jake. So, just go back to your perfectly manicured lawn with your perfectly named dog and your, um . . . perfectly numbered parents. Go do whatever you want with Stacy Ann. Marry her. Have a gazillion babies and shop at Gap Baby."

"Um, it's Baby Gap," Jake said.

"Whatever!" she said. "But there's placenta, Jake. Lots of angry cabbage."

"What?" he said.

"Forget it," she said, storming off.

"Angie . . . Angie, c'mon."

She walked approximately twenty-three steps before turning back to Jake and his adorable, pet-food-commercial-dog, Ryan. They seemed smaller in the darkness. They seemed like strangers, their bodies and faces wrapped in shadows and small pools of light.

They seemed like they belonged in someone else's life. Not hers.

She fitted the foam headphones onto her ears, pushing play on the Walkman. "Ain't No Mountain High Enough" boomed from her cassette titled *Ain't No Mountain High Enough on Repeat Thirteen Times.*

Angie had accepted the challenge of *Why Not?*

She had the urn, her sister's letter and postcard, and the will to finally show Wang she wasn't just another Dryfalls copy/paste sit-and-wait-for-the-world-to-meet-her girl. She was a daredevil. A girl against the grain. A young woman ready for adventure.

Well, it was a goal anyway.

There was only one thing more she needed.

A ride.

Runaways

The weight of Angie's backpack straps dug into her soft shoulders as she stood beneath the neon glow of The Backstory's distinctive sign. In the absence of a mall or even a Starbucks, the indie café/confectionary, nestled in a warehouse-esque setting, was *the* Dryfalls teen haven. And tonight, hometown favorite Rancid Reign was featured on the marquee. The *R* in Rancid drunkenly leaned to the side, collapsing into the *a*. It was not a far-off estimation of the band's recent reputation, as relayed by the lead singer's scorned ex-girlfriend, a woman who had suggested that the band's "extended" European tour was extended only because they could not afford plane tickets home. No one seemed to care what the reason was, because the parking lot was packed.

The vibration of their Nirvana-ish-meets-metal music seeped through the loose edges of the building. Angie reached for the door handle but paused, because the "Ain't No Mountain High Enough" adrenaline high was waning.

Angie did not like crowds.

Angie did not like entering The Backstory alone.

Angie wished she did not struggle with the above-mentioned challenges.

Headlights swung into the parking lot, blinding her before they angled elsewhere.

She knew this was *the* place to find someone in Dryfalls, and there was someone Angie very much needed to find, so she stepped inside.

It was literally a sensory explosion. The band's gritty-grungy music walloped her ears. Beeping arcade games faintly pierced through the sometimes-grueling, off-key guitar riffs. The dance floor overflowed with kids in full head thrash. The tiniest of mosh pits formed near the front of the stage. As terrible as the band sounded to Angie, they had something that drew her into their performance: rebellion.

Rebellion (n): The defiance of authority. Classic rebellions include but are not limited to: the Haitian Revolution, the French Revolution, and the American Revolution. Not to be mistaken for the Beastie Boys' "Fight for Your Right" lyrical revolution.

The lead singer/guitarist (and former Dryfalls Rocket Club president) flailed around the stage, bumping into the bassist, who was booming big chords in her over-modulated amplifier. The drummer popped up and down on his stool, his face scrunched as though giving birth were imminent. The band literally played like there was no tomorrow. Like there was no cloud of town gossip sitting stationary over them. In that moment, Rancid Reign was infinity and beyond times pi in Angie's estimation. Something she could never imagine being.

Angie looked beyond the crowded dance floor to onlookers lining the graffiti mural walls. Her eyes drifted to the shoulder-to-shoulder counter, people clamoring to order signature beverages such as What We Have Here Is Failure to Caffeinate and We'll Always Have Salted Caramel Lattes.

Just beyond the counter and past the iron-railed stair-well, Angie spotted exactly who she was looking for: Jamboree Memphis Jordan.

Angie adjusted the straps of her backpack and wove through people, turning a few heads as she stepped through the crowd and hearing the collapsing echoes of cupped whispers. Of laughter. Eyes noticing the urn.

Angie climbed the stairs. Jamboree's back was to her.

"Jamboree," Angie called out.

Jamboree did not hear Angie. In fact, it was not until a

group of girls standing near Jamboree stopped and stared at Angie that Jamboree turned to notice her.

"Hey," Jamboree shouted over the music.

The girls were not just staring at Angie. They were staring at . . . the urn.

Self-consciously, Angie cradled it with both arms. This was not an attractive or natural position.

"Can I, um . . . talk to you for a second?" Angie shouted.

Jamboree considered the question, throwing Angie's confidence into chaos. Angie had not considered the very real possibility that Jamboree might say no. Angie had, after all, told her to leave her alone. She had been firm, definite, and what some might characterize as rude. What if Jamboree said, "Get out of here, fatso!" or "You're crazy, crazy." What if she hocked a loogie directly onto Angie's face? That would be incredibly disgusting and unhygienic.

"Sure," Jamboree said, noticing the urn.

"It's a symbol," said Angie.

"A what?" Jamboree shouted back.

"A symbol!"

"Okay."

Speak, Angie thought, but the words were tied up in the traffic of her nerves.

"Your eye . . ." said Jamboree.

"Yeah. It um . . . it only hurts if I breathe."

"Don't do that, then," Jamboree said.

Both of them kind of smiled. Then the awkward seeped back in.

Pause.

Extended pause filled with music and laughter that was not their own.

"Are you okay?" asked Jamboree.

"Um . . ." said Angie.

And there it was. The "um." The in-between word that plagued Angie's existence. The inarticulate filler, as Connie referred to it. Angie's couldn't-show-up father was much the same way when put on what was commonly referred to as "the spot."

"I need to ask you for something, um, that—" said Angie.

And before Angie could finish, Courtney Jones crashed into Jamboree, spilling her unauthorized alcoholic beverage onto Jamboree's blouse.

"What the hell?" Jamboree said.

"Aw . . . shit," said Courtney, giggling. "Sorry, Chunks."

Chunks? Courtney was clearly inebriated, drunk, three sheets to the wind as the saying would go. Though Angie did not understand what three sheets and the wind had to do with intoxication. Still, there was nothing "chunks" about Jamboree.

Courtney looked at Fat Angie, realizing for the first time

that she was even standing there. Then she saw the urn and giggle-belched. It was not an attractive sound.

"I'm gonna take a picture of you," Courtney said, fumbling for her phone.

Angie did not like pictures.

Angie did not like Courtney.

Angie did not like that Courtney often hung out with Stacy Ann Sloan.

Courtney pointed her cell at Angie, directing her, "Say 'donut.'"

Before the flash could fully glare, Jamboree grabbed the phone.

"What the fuck, band nerd?" said Courtney.

"What the fuck, alcohol PSA?" said Jamboree. "Maybe *ask* if someone wants their picture taken."

"Give me my phone, *bitch*."

Jamboree took a couple of steps toward the balcony railing, dangling the phone over the edge. Angie's eyes widened. Surely, Jamboree would not drop what was the newest, most expensive smartphone fifteen feet to the concrete floor. While a rarely discussed fact, Angie, Courtney, and Jamboree had been in the same fourth-, fifth-, and sixth-grade classes together. They had shared pencils and pens and Cheetos at lunch.

Now Angie and Jamboree shared how much Courtney did not like either one of them.

After dangling the phone in midair, Jamboree shook

her head and tossed the phone into the cushions of a red velvet sofa.

"It doesn't matter what you look like," Courtney said, sizing up Jamboree. "You're still a fat band nerd inside."

"Well, you're a self-hating anorexic who gets drunk to not have to deal with the fact that her *dad* is sleeping with the school counselor."

Snap! Crackle! POP!

Courtney considered her move. She was traveling alone, not with her usual flock of followers, thus eliminating her bullying-in-numbers ability. So she picked up her phone, threw Jamboree what was referred to as "the look," and walked away. Just like that, the rumble at The Backstory was over.

"Is her dad really doing that?" Angie asked.

Jamboree shrugged. "I guess so. I was just fishing."

Jamboree's phone screen lit up. She glanced at it but put it away.

"Do you want to . . . ?" Jamboree nodded toward a corner near the bathrooms. "It's at least one decibel quieter. Maybe one and a half."

Angie nodded and followed Jamboree. A few people seemed to notice them, but most were glued to their cell phone screens or the band down below.

"So . . ." Jamboree said. "What's up?"

The asking part. The standing on the balcony of The Backstory with Jamboree Memphis Jordan — the remastered and remixed version, in skinny jeans, a bohemian top, and soon to be a member of the coolest of the cools, her induction inevitable despite Courtney Jones.

"I, uh . . ." Angie said. "I kind of need to go somewhere."

"Okay," said Jamboree.

Angie reached into her back pocket and handed Jamboree the letter and postcard. Jamboree's phone lit up again, but she ignored it. She finished reading the letter and flipped over the postcard, then looked at Angie.

"Where did this . . . ?" Jamboree asked, holding up the letter.

"It's kind of . . . she . . ." Angie said. "She wrote it before . . . what happened. I just got it."

"How just?"

"Dedication-ceremony just," Angie said.

"Wow," Jamboree said, looking back at the letter.

"I want to do those things, Jamboree," Angie said. "On the postcard."

"When?"

"Um, now."

"Right now?" Jamboree asked.

Angie nodded.

"Okay," Jamboree said. "Um, I thought you didn't want to talk to me. Not that I'm saying — I just . . ."

"I have to do this now because . . . well, because after today, what happened at school. My mom . . . she's, um, done with my . . . She's just done, I think. With me. She wants to send me away."

"What kind of away?"

"It's a treatment facility place," Angie said. "I don't know when I get to come back to Dryfalls. If I get to."

"It wasn't your fault what happened with Gary," Jamboree said. "Anyone would say that."

"Yeah," Angie said, knowing it was bigger than Gary Klein, "except, um, no one did. It doesn't matter anyway. My mom's . . . I don't . . ."

"Won't you get in more trouble for doing this?" Jamboree asked.

"She's out of town until Saturday night. And I, uh . . . I need to do those things. For my sister."

Jamboree looked at the postcard again. Her phone lit up in her pocket, but she ignored it.

"You know, Ohio is technically not a big state," Angie said. "Not like, um . . . Texas. I mean from Wascom, Texas, to El Paso it's —"

"Eight hundred thirty-one miles," Jamboree said, grinning. "I remember."

One of the many factoids they had memorized together, looking at the maps in Jamboree's parents' RV when they were kids.

"Why not ask Wang?" Jamboree said. "He's into anything that annoys your mom. At least, he said that to me."

"You talk to Wang?" Angie asked, surprised by the reveal.

"Yeah," said Jamboree. "Sometimes. I mean, not a lot but just texting . . . you know. To see how you are. Mostly when I was doing the study abroad thing."

Jamboree talking to Wang? Pause for more from Dryfalls and the Theory of All Things Upside Down.

"My mom took his Jeep keys and allegedly mailed them to an undisclosed location," Angie said.

"What?" Jamboree said, laughing.

Angie kind of laughed. "Yeah."

Jamboree's phone lit up again.

"Just a second," she said, sliding her phone out of her jeans. "It's my friend . . . Holy shit."

"What's wrong?" Angie asked.

"C'mon," Jamboree said, leading Angie down the stairs. "We have to hurry."

Jamboree pushed through the crowd, dragging Angie behind her.

They shot out the front door, running toward the side of the building.

"What's wrong?" Angie said, catching her breath.

Jamboree pointed to a crowd near the Sonic. Gary Klein was in the center. Gary Klein and . . . Darius?

"Hurry," Jamboree said.

"Hurry where?" Angie asked, reluctantly following Jamboree.

Jamboree ran to the side of her parents' RV, which was parked across the street.

"Zeke!" she called up toward the roof.

Zeke leaned over the edge of the RV, a lollipop in her mouth, a camcorder in video mode, filming Jamboree and Angie.

"Dude, where have you been? This shit is like junior Fight Club," said Zeke.

"Get down," Jamboree said. "We have to do something."

"*We?*" said Zeke. "He's a Judas."

"Come on," Jamboree said to Zeke, stepping into the back of the RV.

Patricia Ana Corona-Morales, otherwise known as Zeke, sprang off the back RV ladder, dust rising up as her Converse sneakers hit the ground. She was the element of brooding cool with her dark hair, short along the sides and curly-wild on top. Known for her purposive slam poetry, an anomaly in Dryfalls, and her self-published punk/feminist zine, *Don't Bleach My Skin*, Zeke had stirred the community like few others during her sophomore year. Rumored to be lesbian, bisexual, asexual, transgender, she was a mystery never fully revealed. A stanza unfinished. A sentence without a period. But for all the things that made her stand out, Zeke, unlike Angie, had never had a public nervous breakdown. And that still counted for something on the outcast scale of William Anders High School.

Zeke's attention and camera lens immediately fell to the urn.

"It's a symbol," Angie blurted out. "My mom . . . says it's a symbol."

"Okay," Zeke said, continuing toward the RV side door.

"It's empty," Angie quickly added.

"Would've been cooler if it wasn't," said Zeke.

Jamboree stepped out of the RV, handing Zeke a baseball bat. Arming herself with a glittery-blue can of mace.

"You're not really going to help him?" Zeke asked Jamboree.

"What exactly are we doing?" Angie asked.

"Saving the Judas, apparently," Zeke said, clearly not thrilled.

"He's not a Judas," Jamboree said, heading in the direction of the fight.

None of this added up for Angie, who did not, under any circumstance, want to see Gary Klein ever again. Much less twice in the same day.

Zeke craned her neck to Angie, who was still standing by the RV. "You coming?"

"Um . . ." Angie said.

Was this teen rebellion at its height? Baseball bats and mace? It seemed like a very violent way to simply get a ride.

"Ms. Joan Jett, Ms. Joan Jett," Angie muttered to herself. "What would Ms. Joan Jett do?"

Angie stepped away from the RV, jogging, urn still in

hand, to catch up with Jamboree and Zeke, her heart literally pounding as the three of them approached the crowd of fight gawkers.

"Do we have a plan here, Jam?" Zeke asked. "Seeing how violence leads to more violence and all."

Jamboree considered the question but offered no response.

"Okay," Zeke said. "Just putting it out there."

Soon the three of them were pushing along the edges of the crowd. Angie saw Darius scramble to his feet, his legs wobbly.

"What's wrong with you?" Jamboree said to everyone. "Huh?"

Gary turned toward her, his eyes locking on Angie. Angie, who literally could have peed herself at the darkness of his look.

Gary charged in Angie's direction. She panicked. She truly, unquestionably, panicked. She grabbed the mace out of Jamboree's hand and firmly extended her arm. Pressing and squinting—

She sprayed Gary Klein on the hand and knee and crotch.

But then . . . in the eyes.

"Whoa . . ." Zeke said, camera in record mode.

"You fat bitch!" cried Gary.

He dropped to his knees, wailing, a series of expletives ripping from his mouth, also dripping with mace, it seemed.

Wide-eyed, Jamboree and Zeke stared down at Gary. Clearly, they had not anticipated truly having to use the mace.

"Damn," Zeke said.

Angie's hand nervously pointed the mace nozzle from side to side. As if anticipating an additional attacker.

"Híjole," Zeke said, placing her hand on Angie's wrist. "Holster your glitter weapon, Annie Oakley."

Zeke lowered Angie's arm and took the mace from her.

"C'mon," Jamboree said to Darius.

Jamboree helped Darius up and led him to the RV.

Gary was still writhing in pain. What had Angie done?

"C'mon," Zeke said, pulling Angie away.

Darius grimaced, holding on to his ribs as he fell into the soft-cushioned chair behind the passenger seat.

Angie gulped, looking between Darius in the RV and Gary at the Sonic. Not only had she broken Gary's nose, but she had pepper-sprayed him. Even in self-defense, was this an offense punishable by law? How had she become a semblance of Wang? She did not have Wang's confidence or overworked swagger.

"Angie?" said Jamboree. "Get in."

Angie climbed into the RV, shutting the door behind her. Zeke plopped onto the dinette bench and filmed Darius.

The RV pulled away from the Sonic. Away from the neon glow of The Backstory sign. They drove past the seemingly endless yellow ribbons and the Main Street banner. They drove past Angie's sister's bronze statue. Past the cemetery and the eternal flame blasting through the treetops, beaming brightly into the night sky.

The whole world Fat Angie knew faded into the darkness as they entered the on-ramp to the interstate, the RV merging into the quiet highway with a few eighteen-wheelers.

No one asked where they were going. Which seemed, well, weird, because they were going somewhere. Right?

Are You Gonna Go My Way?

From the dinette bench, Angie stared at the miniature, fuchsia-colored Jesus stuck to the RV dashboard. Lit with a ministring of multicolored lights, his arms glowed in their outstretched position beside a chipped, sun-bleached bobblehead of Rosie the Riveter. A silver disco-ball ornament swung from the rearview mirror, scattering slices of light along the console.

The radio frequency clogged with patches of static and intermittent bursts of George Michael's 1987 classic "Faith." They had driven for the duration of the prior two songs. And in that time, Angie did not know what the intended destination was, because Jamboree plus two were not talking.

"Oy," Zeke said.

Zeke, who had been distracted by a back-and-forth series of texts, flipped her phone facedown on the table and leaned toward Angie. Angie leaned ever so slightly toward Zeke. Anticipating a question, a comment, a declaration. Only . . .

Angie waited.

And waited.

And—

"Love," Zeke said.

"Yeah?"

"Curdled," Zeke continued.

"Okay . . . ?" Angie said.

"Soured."

Angie sensed a dairy theme emerging.

Zeke leaned away from Angie, flipping through pages of a notebook plastered with stickers. She scribbled, nodding to a beat that was likely not George Michael before slamming the notebook shut.

Angie asked, "Soured?"

Zeke rubbed the bottom of her chin and pushed away from the dinette booth. She threw a disgusted glance at Darius before climbing into the passenger seat. A hand-drawn sign was taped to the back of the headrest:

Co-Pilot
Extraordinaire

"So what's the plan?" Zeke asked Jamboree. "I'm just asking because we were supposed to be at Raquel's. Instead we're on the interstate with"—Zeke leaned toward the mileage gauge before reading from a small spiral note-book—"maybe fifty miles of gas and—"

"Seventy-three," Jamboree said.

"Whatever," Zeke said. "Where are we going with an urn, the town legend's outcast sister, and Judas?"

"Screw you, Zeke," Darius said.

"Screw me?" Zeke said, tipping her head in his direction. "Screw you, backstabber."

"Hey," Jamboree said.

"Nuh-uh," said Zeke. "This vato does not deserve a Get Out of Jail Free card. Not after what he did."

"Yeah, I'm the asshole," Darius said.

"When genius speaks," said Zeke.

"Look, I didn't ask for your help," Darius said.

"Man, you can send your didn't-ask-for-help right over to Jamboree and Angie, because you'd still be lying on the ground if it were up to me."

Angie had been plunged into what was a very heated conversation. She did not like being in such conversations.

"I didn't . . . really have a whole lot to do with it," Angie stammered.

"Dude, you maced Judas's BFF," said Zeke, filming the interstate.

Darius ticked his glance to Angie. Neither of them had much interest in the other. Darius had lied, corroborating

Gary's story, as it was referred to in police television series. Darius's cowardice or meanness or whatever had left Angie in jeopardy of expulsion and an assault charge. Who knew what was on the docket of offenses after spraying mace at Gary? Was there such a thing as assault with a glittery-blue, key chain–size canister of mace? It truly was self-defense. Her *self* definitely warranted defending but . . .

"Just drop me off," Darius said.

"We're in the middle of nowhere, Judas," Zeke said.

"Lay off that," Darius said.

"Man, it's like *The Scarlet Letter*," said Zeke. "You're just gonna have to wear it."

"Jamboree, *please* drop me at the next exit," he said, grimacing as he shifted in his seat.

"I'm good to drop you on the side of the road," Zeke said.

"Then just pull over," Darius said.

"You see me behind the wheel, cabrón?" Zeke fired back.

Jamboree slammed the brakes. The RV fishtailed. Angie grabbed the edge of the table. The urn rolled away from her and toward the cab, landing at Zeke's feet.

"What the hell, J?" Zeke said, bracing herself on the dashboard.

Jamboree straightened the wheel out and stopped along the shoulder of the road.

"Okay," Jamboree said.

She thrust the RV into park, slammed the hazard button, unbuckled, and crawled into the back. Sitting across from Angie, Jamboree considered what to say.

"You were a dick to Zeke and me after the party," Jamboree said to Darius. "You know it, and we know it."

"I know that she showed up with Raquel *after* I asked her not to," said Darius. "Got drunk and made everything weird."

"Are you seriously blaming me for what happened?" Zeke asked, stepping into the back of the RV.

"You shouldn't have been there," he said.

"We were your real friends, Judas," Zeke said. "Not those pendejos you call friends, but whatever, race traitor."

"I'm a race traitor?" said Darius. "What about you?"

"I've never betrayed my people cosigning with a homophobic bigot. Which is exactly what Gary is."

"At least he didn't turn his back on the church—his family."

"He's a racist homophobe and—"

"You published screen grabs off my phone in that stupid magazine and YouTube show that you—"

"Journalistic expression."

"You bullied me and Gary and anyone who didn't think like you, Patricia," Darius said.

"Zeke," she corrected. "My name is Zeke."

"Right, because you're gender-neutral-something-dyke-something—"

"¡Pinche cabrón! ¿Te escuchas?"

While Angie's grasp of Spanish was limited to the minor conjugation of verbs and asking where the bathroom was, she sensed some bad words somewhere in what Zeke had said.

"I do hear myself, Patricia," Darius said.

"Zeke. My name is Zeke. And I am not a dyke-something, *Judas*."

Angie leaned into Jamboree. "Is he truly a Judas?"

"It's complicated," Jamboree said.

"Is she a . . ." Angie whisper-whispered. "Dyke?"

"I can hear you," Zeke said, turning to Angie. "You want to know if I'm a dyke, big girl?"

"No. Uh-uh," Angie said. "I mean, maybe. In fairness, I don't actually know the right answer."

"To what?" Zeke asked.

"Enough," Jamboree said.

"You don't leash me, Jamboree," Zeke warned.

"Picking on Angie is not an option, *Zeke*," Jamboree said. "Okay? It's not who we are."

Zeke stewed, quiet-not-exactly-quiet, with her arms crossed over her chest.

"Look," Jamboree said to Zeke and Darius. "Maybe you all need to never talk again. Though I think that would be really stupid."

"So now I'm stupid?" Zeke asked.

"Oh, my God. Quit taking everything so personal."

"Personal? I'm not you, Jam. My parents didn't pay for me to go Belgium for some extended early summer, so I could eat waffles and French fries and —"

"Belgian fries," Angie interrupted.

"What?" Zeke asked.

"They don't call them French fries," Angie continued. "While sometimes disputed, Belgians assert they created the fry. So, they're Belgian fries not, um . . . French. Fries."

Darius half grinned.

"Jamboree and I used to talk about Belgium all the time," Angie said. "When we were, you know, just before and stuff. Anyway, sorry."

Angie cleared her throat. Self-conscious that she had blurted out random factoid #122,199 in a conversation she had wanted very much to stay out of.

"Whatever," Zeke said. "My point is that I've been here in Dryfalls. Putting up with the fallout of his shit from my family. So don't be telling me not to take anything personal, Jamboree. Okay?"

Darius shook his head.

"Yeah okay," Jamboree said. "Sorry."

Weird quietness.

More weird quietness.

"Look, let's just forget it," said Zeke. "Let go to Raquel's."

"I'm not going to Raquel's tonight," Jamboree said. "I'm . . . going with Angie. On a road trip."

Jamboree handed the letter and postcard to Zeke.

"There are some things Angie needs to see," Jamboree continued. "To do."

Darius leaned toward Zeke to read the letter, but she angled it away.

"Dude, can you even sing?" Zeke asked Angie.

"I gurgled mouthwash and made it sound like 'Silent Night' once," Angie said.

Zeke grinned. "Hell, yes!" She exclaimed. "I'm in."

"Darius?" Jamboree said.

"Uh-uh," Zeke said. "I'm in so long as he's out. This is the Estrogen Club."

"Just drop me off at the next truck stop," said Darius. "I'll get somebody to pick me up."

"What are we waiting on?" Zeke said, resuming her seat as Co-Pilot Extraordinaire. "Let's go."

Jamboree smiled at Angie. "We're on an adventure, right?"

The classic phrase from years past had suddenly been dusted off. Was the adventure really happening? Just like the ones they had made up years ago? Was Angie truly embarking across the great state of Ohio with Jamboree Memphis Jordan in an RV with concert posters, Christmas lights, and the smell of old books and Kool-Aid? Did it matter that Jamboree had ghosted her, and Angie never knew why?

"Yeah," Angie said. "We're on an adventure."

Jamboree climbed back into the driver's seat.

"FYI," Jamboree said. "There are rules to the road trip."

"Road trips are antiestablishment," Zeke said, activating a GPS app. "There can be no rules."

"Rule #1: Paper maps only," said Jamboree, reaching in the glove box.

"Paper maps?" Zeke asked.

"It is how road trips are done," Angie said.

"Yeah by the settlers," said Zeke. "But okay. If you wanna be all Luddite."

"It isn't Luddite," Jamboree said. "It's nostalgic. Besides . . . it's how Angie's sister would have wanted it."

Angie grinned. It was a real grin. An honest feeling-seen grin. Which was something Angie had only done with KC, Jake, and . . . well, her sister, of course.

Jamboree turned over the ignition, pumping the gas pedal several times before the engine coughed to life.

"We can look up food places and addresses online," said Jamboree. "But the basic route is all paper maps."

Jamboree held the Ohio map out to Angie. "Brook Park."

"We're going to skate first?" Angie said, a ping of panic in her voice.

"It's the closest," said Jamboree. "I think."

Angie unfolded the map at the dinette table while Jamboree merged NASCAR out-of-the-race-pit style onto the interstate.

"Rule #2," Jamboree said.

"Ay, Dios mío, enough with the constraints," Zeke said. "You are punking my chi."

"No playlists," Jamboree said. "Radio or audiocassette only."

"Not a Luddite, huh?" Zeke said, scanning the radio.

Country, NPR, more country, classic rock, then . . .

"That's perfect," Angie said. "There."

Tracy Chapman's nod to escaping your life, "Fast Car." Was it a sign? Divine intervention from the universe? Not that Angie entirely understood the universe. It was more of a KC concept than an Angie one.

The tempo and downbeat ignited in the song. Something renewed sprang in Angie's would-be plump soul.

She was infused with hope.

She was infused with excitement.

She was infused with —

"I'm turning this depressing shit off," Zeke said.

With the rotation of the tuner dial, guitar riffs and snare drums pounded through the speakers, the music literally vibrating in Angie's chest.

It was not that Angie disliked the energy of the song or even Zeke rocking out air-guitar style, though she felt very strongly that Zeke should rebuckle her seat belt instead of squatting in her seat.

Angie liked the music very much, but there was a sadness she had not expected. She turned her head toward the urn. Even though it wasn't her sister, she just needed to pretend it was. She put it on top of the map and began to plot their course.

Into
the
Wild

Unisex Please Knock!

was taped to the men's restroom door outside the creepy-ish gas station. Written in a frenzied straggle of letters with blue ball-point pen, the ink seemed to run out by the *c* and *k*.

Angie stood there debating whether to knock or simply hold it. She had needed, very much, to go to the bathroom. Angie, however, struggled with the use of public restrooms. More specifically, the use of the men's room. With the women's restroom barricaded by three folding chairs corralled with flagging tape and a Caution Wet Floor sign, the men's was her sole option. Her only hope. Her . . . the point was clear.

However, her idea of the men's restroom had been largely tainted by Wang. Wang, who had proudly recounted how he and his "boys" urinated in gas-station sinks or on toilet seats. It was simply a disgusting act that could not be disremembered by Angie.

The pressure in her pelvis increasing, Angie had almost willed herself to knock on the door when Zeke stepped in front of her, messenger bag slung across her chest, camcorder in record mode and in Angie's face.

Angie did not like cameras.

Angie did not like how much she needed to pee.

Angie did not like how a camera pointed at her made her want to pee even more.

"I'm documenting my entire year," Zeke said. "Everything. School. Hanging out. My asshole brother. My cousins 'cause they are always at our house. Mi abuela, who is the fucking bomb. My dad when he's around. My mom when she's not up my ass."

"Um, okay," Angie said, feeling uncomfortable. "And right now, you're documenting me because . . . ?"

"Because how often does Dryfalls' primo outcast road trip with European Extreme-Makeover Jamboree Memphis Jordan?"

Angie crossed her arms self-consciously over her stomach. "We used to be friends."

"I know," said Zeke. "But now you're not. And here you are."

"I just needed a ride."

"What about your girlfriend?" Zeke asked.

Zeke's interrogation filming was unsettling to Angie.

"I don't have a girlfriend," Angie said. "Um . . . anymore."

"You say 'um' a lot," said Zeke. "Did you know that?"

"Um, I guess," Angie said. "I mean, yeah."

"My mom's a word warden," Zeke said, still filming. "She's like 'Patricia, speak like a proper young woman. How are you ever going to find love with your foul mouth and boy clothes?' Then I roll my eyes, and she threatens to pull them out of my skull. How is that proper?"

"Yeah," Angie said, blinking at the image of eyeball removal.

"So, what's your story?" Zeke asked.

"Story?" Angie said. "Um, nothing really . . . story-wise."

Zeke dropped the camera to her side. "You've been on the cover of *Time*, *People*, and on, like, *Good Morning America*. Twice. Girl, you've got a story."

Angie shrugged. "It's not really my story. It's my sister's."

Zeke went back to filming.

"Aren't they kind of the same?" Zeke asked Angie.

Angie did not know Zeke.

Angie did not like the direct questions.

Angie still, very much, needed to pee.

"It's messed up, you know," Zeke said, pausing the recording. "What happened to her. Like, I used to think maybe I could join the army but . . . I couldn't do what she did."

"Die?" Angie said.

"Be that selfless," Zeke said. "For country and all."

Selfish, Angie thought.

Zeke pulled out a bag of Reese's Pieces from her jacket pocket and tipped it toward Angie.

"I'm good," Angie said.

"It's the supreme mix of chocolate and peanut butter."

"They don't actually have chocolate in them."

"They're Reese's."

"Yeah, it's, um . . . a vicious marketing ploy," Angie said. "Reese's were basically failing as a candy until Steven Spielberg's movie *E.T.* The success of the film, um, propelled Reese's into a sort of cultural stardom, but they don't have any chocolate in them."

"No shit," Zeke said.

"Um . . . no shit," Angie said

Zeke flipped over the bag, reading and filming the ingredient list.

"Hey," Jamboree said, walking toward the convenience store. "Y'all want something?"

"Mountain Dew and M&M's," Zeke said, turning toward Angie. "They have chocolate, right?"

Angie nodded.

"How about water and beef jerky, so you don't explode your bag all over the RV again?" Jamboree said.

Zeke rolled her eyes. "How about you don't mother me?"

Jamboree disappeared inside.

"Bag?" Angie asked.

Zeke lifted her T-shirt, revealing an oval wrapped in checkerboard duct tape on her right side.

"Ostomy bag 2.0," Zeke said. "Hot-pink-and-white design by Jamboree. I'm more of a black-and-red."

"Um . . . what is it?"

"So you know how the poop comes out the shoot?" Zeke said, dropping her T-shirt back down. "Mine doesn't. For now, anyway. Because my bowel was super messed up, and I was going to the bathroom like twenty times a day. No joke. I really was. So I would miss a bunch of school. Take a bunch of different meds. Miss more school. Then I had this emergency surgery, and I woke up with my small intestine sticking out."

"Wow," Angie said.

"Right? It's freaky. And basically I wanted to die. Like *really* die because who wants to poop out their side, right?"

Angie was not sure if it was a rhetorical question, so she nodded in agreement.

"My dad just made it worse. I'd walk around in an undershirt, and he'd be like, '*Patricia, don't wear that. People will see it.*' I'm like, fuck you for making me hate my body. And my brother with his zealot shit about how God was punishing me for being queer. And I didn't even know if I was queer, but I was like, 'Dude, ulcerative colitis happens to straight, God-loving people, too.' So one day, after some stupid, stupid shit, I'm staring at this thing . . . this stoma on my side and hating myself. And then . . . I just named it. I was like, screw it. I'm being friends with this thing. It's cute, in a reddish-pink, part-of-your-small-intestine-sticking-out way."

"What do you call it?" Angie asked.

"Clair Voyant," Zeke said. "It's my stoma's roller girl name."

Angie grinned. "That's really cool. Like, that you can . . . not be ashamed."

"Why should we be?" Zeke said.

It was a question Angie had not truly considered so specifically before.

Zeke motioned toward the men's restroom.

"Anyone in there?" Zeke asked. "I need to do a dump. Of the bag."

"Um, I don't know," said Angie.

"Don't worry," Zeke said, camcorder recording. "I pledge as tribute."

Zeke grinned and pressed the door open with her shoulder, not knocking when the sign had explicitly said to knock.

Angie tugged at her excessively snug jeans that were

crushing her crotch. Her couldn't-understand mother contended that Angie would lose weight when she could no longer fasten her jeans, a rather heartless and torturous method toward weight loss that had failed to be effective, because Angie had not been able to fasten her jeans for some time.

Zeke tipped her head outside the restroom door.

"It's dude free," Zeke said. "C'mon?"

"Um. No, I'm um . . . good."

"You don't have to go?" Zeke asked.

"Nope."

Lie.

Excessively bad lie.

The thought of sharing a public restroom on the side of a creepy-ish gas station with Zeke was daunting for Angie. As taught to Angie by her couldn't-understand mother at the age of four: *Potty time is private time.*

There would be nothing private about this moment. Perhaps she could hold it. Perhaps — no. She needed to go.

"I'm mean, it's scary as hell, but it's empty," Zeke said.

Angie sighed and walked in, immediately slapped with the smell of . . .

"Wow," Angie said, sticking her nose inside the neck of her T-shirt.

It was more of a *what* than a *wow,* in all honesty.

Water had overflowed from one of the toilets. It clapped against the bottom of Angie's shoes as she walked. The urinals were filthy with cigarette butts and a couple of crushed beer cans.

The door to the first stall hung off its hinge ever so slightly. Another handwritten sign taped to it read in all capital letters:

DO NOT FLUSH
FEMININE FEMALE PRODUCTS

Angie reread the sign three times, finally concluding there was a significant error in the description.

"What do you do with the butch tampon then?" Zeke asked.

Angie blinked at her two times. She did not follow the trajectory of Zeke's humor.

"As opposed to feminine female one?" Zeke said. "Butch tampon."

Angie still did not follow the trajectory of Zeke's humor.

"Is that a pun?" Angie asked.

Zeke half laughed. "Girl, you're funny." She shook her head, walking past Angie to inspect the other stalls. Camcorder recording, she tipped one open with the toe of her sneaker.

"Oh . . . man!" Zeke said, her face wrenched in disgust. "Wow!"

Flies fluttered above the definitely not-flushed toilet. A maxi pad hung over the lip of the seat, as if it were making a desperate attempt to climb out of the bowl.

The remaining two stalls were only slightly better.

"Just hover," Zeke said, entering the stall closest to the wall. Grimacing at the condition of the remaining stall, Angie reluctantly entered. Covering her face with the neck of her shirt, she flushed the toilet with the bottom of her shoe, saying good-bye to what must have been a very unfortunate experience for someone.

Angie unfastened her jeans and squatted in the hover position as suggested by Zeke.

"What the hell do guys do in here anyway?" Zeke asked.

Quite possibly pee on the seats and sinks, as Angie had feared. In that state of still hovering above the toilet, something went incredibly wrong for Angie. She had what could be best described as performance anxiety. Zeke was in the stall next to her.

There was no protocol for this level of hovering-over-a-germ-infested-toilet anxiety.

"Shit," Zeke said. "Hey, Ang."

"Yeah," Angie said.

"I started my period."

This was an exclamation Angie rarely heard.

"Can you go buy me some tampons?" Zeke asked. "I'll pay you back."

"What about your bag?"

"Completely different plumbing, dude," Zeke said.

Angie hovered in place. Debating the issue while imagining the germs surely permeating her exposed skin.

"C'mon, Ang," Zeke said. "These are my favorite underwear."

"Okay," Angie said, zipping up her jeans.

The neck of her shirt slipped from her face. She writhed in the painful stench, gagging.

Jamboree had her cell pressed to her ear when Angie stepped out of the restroom. She seemed to be in the throes of a serious conversation.

Angie entered the convenience store, the bell above the door ringing. A spiky-haired clerk grinned and nodded at her.

"How you doing?" he said.

"Um, good," she said, walking around a stack of boxes.

"Inventory," he said.

Angie stumbled, but recovered with awkward half steps.

She quickly walked the aisles from chips to licorice to mileage notebooks and work gloves. There was even a dilapidated clothing rack with deer and big-truck T-shirts. She noticed the clerk watching her. Smiling but watching.

"You seem familiar," he said.

Angie fake smiled. She practiced this action in the mirror because smiling was mostly an effort to her.

"I'm not from here," she said.

"Most people aren't," he said, still smiling. "We're the only all-night stop for thirty miles."

Angie continued down aisle after short aisle, but no

tampons. Was it a physical impossibility? There were multiple options for hand sanitizer, pork rinds, and condoms. Finally, she approached the counter, noticing the clerk's crooked nametag: The Ethan.

"It was my brother's when he worked here," he said. "He told me it was a, uh . . . conversation starter."

"Um . . ." she said. "Okay."

The Ethan looked like dozens of guys who sheepishly walked the halls of William Anders High School. The Ethan was the guy girls walked by because their muscles were not thick enough. Because their voices still squeaked when they stood up to give a presentation in class. Because they were some combination of:

Too nervous

Too short

Too skinny

Too fat

Too desperate

Too sensitive

Too nice

Too chatty

Too quiet

Too awkward

Too _____ (fill in the blank to infinity times pi)

In *On the Origin of Species*, written by Mr. Charles Darwin, guys like The Ethan fared poorly in the ecosystem of high-school dating. Without the likes of Mr. John Hughes writing their lives, it was difficult to catch what some often refer to as "a break."

"Couldn't find what you were looking for?" The Ethan asked.

Just say it, Angie thought. *Just say . . .*

"Tampons?" Angie said. "Um . . . asking for a friend."

"Uh-huh." He grinned, reaching beneath the counter. "You'd never believe how many boxes of these get stolen. Boss makes us keep them behind the counter."

He slid a box of tampons between them.

"Personally, I'd go for the Advil PM or even the organic gummy bears," The Ethan said. "The clear ones are the best."

"Sure," Angie said.

He keyed in the price on the cash register.

Uncomfortable. Uncomfortable. The moment felt it would never end.

"I've got two sisters," The Ethan said. "There's nothing embarrassing about asking for feminine female products. Bag?"

Feminine female products! Angie had caught The Ethan red-handed, metaphorically speaking. He was the one who'd fathered the grammatically incorrect men's restroom sign. Anyone with two sisters plus one mother would have to know that was inaccurate phrasing. And according to Zeke, it omitted the butch tampon. Though Angie was not entirely sure this was an actual product.

"Bag?" he asked again.

"No, I'm, um, good," Angie said.

He grinned. "Have a better night."

Angie walked briskly back to the men's restroom, noting that Jamboree was still on her phone in what continued to be a serious conversation.

Angie paused outside the men's room. Deep, deep breath. Hold it . . . Angie stepped back and saw Zeke lathering up her hands.

"Ang, can you believe they have soap?" Zeke said. "Three squares of toilet paper and half a gallon of soap."

Angie held out the box of tampons, covering her nose with the neck of her T-shirt once again.

"Thanks," Zeke said. "Keep 'em. I found a pad at the bottom of my bag. Besides, tampons suck, right?"

The sound of the hand dryer blow-blared.

Angie left Zeke in the restroom, setting the box of tampons on one of the chairs barricading the women's room door. She stood there, in the middle of nowhere, watching Jamboree writing in a small pocket spiral. Thinking—

"Jamboree!" Zeke shouted, stepping out of the men's room.

Angie had not expected Zeke to shout so close to her ear.

Jamboree looked up from the spiral.

"You really need to see this restroom!" Zeke shouted again.

"I'll pass," said Jamboree.

Angie followed behind Zeke to the RV.

"Hey," Jamboree said, her attention on Angie.

"Hey," Angie said, her eyes ticking to Darius.

Zeke looked around the gas station parking lot. "Where's your ride, Judas?"

Darius clenched his jaw.

"I mean, no need for a long good-bye," she said, a spark of enjoyment in her eyes.

Angie made note of said Zeke-enjoyment spark. Should she have a similar spark?

"Unless those putos aren't coming to get you," Zeke said. "Boom!"

Zeke filmed Darius. "Darius Clark, cast out from the kingdom of fake righteousness. Stuck at one of the freakiest gas stations in the state, probably. With his dyke cousin and her band of wayward friends to throw him a lifeline."

Angie whispered to Jamboree, "They're cousins?"

"I can hear you," Zeke said to Angie. "Distant cousins."

"Very distant," Darius continued.

"What will he do now, with his ego as bruised as his face?" Zeke said.

"Enough," Jamboree said.

"Feels like shit, doesn't it?" Zeke asked, pushing the camera in his face. "To be rejected? To be —"

Darius shoved the camera out of his face.

"Whoa," Jamboree said, stepping between them.

Zeke seemed to savor that she had gotten all the way under Darius's skin.

"Whatever. Let's go," Zeke said, walking toward the RV.

Jamboree looked to Angie, took a deep breath, and said, "Darius is coming."

Zeke backed around to the group.

"No," she said to Jamboree. "No way. He deserves to be stuck out here."

Angie raised her hand. Hesitantly, of course.

"Dude, you don't have to raise your hand," Zeke said to Angie. "This is the Estrogen Club . . . plus one temporary. So screw the patriarchy. We speak when we want."

"Then let her speak," said Jamboree, turning to Angie. "And I don't know what the Estrogen Club is. This is a new thing."

"Um . . ." Angie said. "I kind of need to second Zeke, reluctantly. I mean, this trip is about my sister and . . . I don't want a Judas-maybe-not-Judas to —"

"He's a Judas," Zeke said, pointing at Darius.

"I'm sick of — I messed up, okay?" Darius said. "But I'm done shouldering all the responsibility."

"Shouldering?" said Zeke. "Like, who are you? You sound like — I don't even care what you sound like because I don't care about you, primo."

"Because you don't care about anyone but *Patricia*."

"Zeke."

The bickering volleyed back and forth. Jamboree put her hands on her head. There seemed to be no good end.

"How am I supposed to get home?" Darius asked Zeke. "Huh?"

"Just a while ago, you didn't care if we dropped you in the middle of the interstate. So I —"

Angie raised her hand slowly. Zeke paused.

"Sorry about the hand-raising thing, but," Angie said, "you don't like Darius."

"I think this cabrón is an asshole," Zeke said.

"Darius doesn't seem to like you," Angie said. "And I don't like him either, but . . . leaving him here is wrong. So. What if he comes with us until we can drop him at a bus station."

Jamboree eyed her watch. "It will have to be after roller-skating, because they close at eleven. If we make it."

Zeke considered her options.

"Okay," Zeke said. "This is your thing, Ang, so okay. You're lucky, Judas. Because you know what? She may be weird and gay and all the things your church and your friends hate, but she's a decent person. Willing to help your weak ass. Even knowing you'd never do the same."

Darius shook his head, seemingly frustrated with being Zeke's punching bag as she walked toward the RV side door. Jamboree and Angie weren't far behind her. Darius remained in place for approximately 5.7 seconds, possibly reconsidering his decision. Then he stepped into the back of the RV, resuming his seat from before.

Angie slid into the dinette booth while Zeke filmed a piece of paper taped to the wall.

Rules of the Road Trip
(as Outlined by Jamboree Memphis Jordan)

1. Paper maps only.
2. Don't drive the RV over 54 miles per hour or the engine will something-mechanical-something-bad, so just don't.
3. The world is our oyster, but don't eat them. I got food poisoning from them once and it sucked immensely.
4. Spontaneous song and dance is encouraged in motion or in park.
5. No fighting. Seriously.
6. FM or cassette music only.
7. Troy Wilson is a dick.

Number seven confused Angie as she had no frame of reference for a Troy Wilson. Nonetheless, she would make note of it in her therapeutic journal for later consideration.

As the engine coughed to life, the Smiths filled the air. They were setting out to do — to see . . .

"Dude," Zeke said, flipping the camcorder screen toward Angie.

It was the men's room.

"This is gonna be golden for my documentary," Zeke said. "Urban Herzog, right?"

"My germs have germs," Angie said.

"Yeah, but I never would have made it to Cleveland. Bathroom's broke on the RV."

Angie still had not peed.

Repeat. Angie still had not peed!

"WAIT!" Angie shouted.

Jamboree slammed on the brakes. Angie jumped out the side of the RV and ran toward the gas station.

Night Like This

An hour away from the most disgusting restroom in gas-station history, the dull white glow of the retro Brookpark Skateland sign, complete with Pepsi insignia, welcomed Angie plus three into an otherwise darkened few blocks. The parking lot packed with minivans, SUVs, and a couple of throwback pickup trucks left little room for the eighteen-foot RV to squeeze into. So they pulled up along the curb across the street.

"This is it," Jamboree said, looking out the window with Angie.

This was absolutely, unequivocally it, and Angie kind of wanted to vomit.

"Excited?" Jamboree asked Angie.

"That's, um, not exactly the feeling," Angie said.

"It's going to be great," Jamboree said.

Angie's lower left leg tingled. It tingled because she had broken it in second grade skating to the 1980s smash hit "Physical," by Olivia Newton-John. Angie had, as a primary lyric suggested, heard her body talk that hot day on the crowded rink. A swarm of skaters had gasped in unbridled horror at the rotation of her leg. The toe of her roller skate had literally kicked her in the butt. But her sister was there with her. Trying to diminish her level of freak-out. Her sister and Jamboree.

Angie tightened her grip around the urn as they all piled out of the RV.

"Hey, Ang, why did your sister want to come here?" Zeke asked, filming. "Not to diminish your adventure, but it's like a big box in the middle of nowhere."

"It's one of the oldest skate rinks in Ohio," said Angie. "And it's got the biggest, um, skating floor. My dad used to skate here a lot when he was a kid. It was kind of a big deal to him."

"So, you've been here?" Zeke asked.

"No," Angie said. "Um . . . it was . . . my mom thought it was silly. She said she didn't see the purpose of going in circles. Plus, I broke my leg at the one in the city, and it just kind of ended it."

Zeke turned the camera on Angie.

"How are you feeling right now?" Zeke asked Angie, camera still rolling.

"Why?" Angie said.

"Girl, we're documenting," Zeke said. "You. The urn. A soldier's last wish. It's perfect for your story."

"Ignore her," Jamboree said. "She filmed me scrambling eggs the other day."

"Hey, Judas, get out of my shot," Zeke directed.

Darius stepped to the far side of Angie.

"Angie," Zeke directed, "look longingly at the skate sign."

"Could we not, please, film?" Angie said. "Just for a while, maybe."

"Dude, don't you want the world to know your story?" Zeke asked.

Jamboree rolled her eyes, pulling Angie away from Zeke. "C'mon. They're closing in forty-five minutes."

C+C Music Factory's "Gonna Make You Sweat" pulsed and pumped along the edges of the building.

Zeke swung the glass door open. The muddy mix of music and roller skates plowed into them.

It was LOUD!

Zeke immediately wandered off, filming the retro of all that was Brookpark Skateland.

"This is cool," Jamboree said to Angie. "Better than that place where you broke your leg. DJ and laser lights. Snack bar with . . ."

It was not that Jamboree had stopped talking. It was that there were so many people — little kids, teens, adults.

Loud talking. Loud music. Loud skating. Little kids screaming. A baby crying by the snack bar. It was, by all accounts,
loud-loud.

"You okay?" Jamboree asked Angie.

"I don't know if I can do this," Angie said. "Any of this."

"She thought you could do this, Angie," Jamboree said.

"She also thought I was a walrus when I was born,"
Angie said. "I think we have to have some latitude about
what she thought."

Jamboree cracked up. Soon Angie cracked up. They
were in a full-on cracking-up fest. It felt good to laugh with
Jamboree. The way they had before everything got strange
and Jamboree ghosted Angie for reasons still unknown. All
Angie had to do was ask. Right then. Right there. Dispel the
mystery once and for all. Just ask why she—

"It makes sense that you're nervous," said Jamboree.
"You broke your leg the first time you roller-skated. Like
really broke it. I'd be absolutely freaked out."

Jamboree's retelling was not helping things.

Zeke waived Angie and Jamboree over to the skate-
rental counter.

"But just try to remember it's going to be fun," Jamboree
said.

"Okay," Angie said, unconvinced.

Skate rentals were $3.50 per pair. Locker rentals were
fifty cents each. Angie covered the cost, which was $14.50.
It seemed an exorbitant amount to Angie, only because her

and Zeke's scuffed skates smelled like parmesan cheese and Odor-Eaters. Zeke's face wrenched at the discovery.

"Hey, you gotta give me another pair, man," Zeke said. "These smell like dog shit."

Angie had not considered that as an odor option. She smelled hers again. No, hers were definitely parmesan cheese and Odor-Eaters. Without question.

The rental guy slapped a pair of skates on the counter, his eyes cutting to the urn.

"It's a symbol," Angie said.

Because that made a lot of sense, really.

"These are the wrong size," Zeke said to the rental guy.

"It's those or dog shit," he said.

"Whatever," Zeke said, walking off with Angie. "Patriarchy."

Angie was quite certain that the patriarchy was not the reason Zeke's skates were half a size too small. It was likely her use of profanity, which seemed ill timed.

"Can I ask you something?" Angie said.

"Only if you want the truth," Zeke said.

"Troy Wilson?"

Zeke sighed and stopped short of Jamboree and Darius, who were lacing up their skates.

"You know that guy in movies that the girl picks and you're thinking how could she be so stupid? I would never pick that guy."

Angie nodded.

"That's Troy. Only it isn't some movie where the girl gets smart to how loser he is, so it's worse."

"Wow . . ."

"Jamboree met him at band camp last summer," Zeke said. "He's this brooding, mysterious, look-at-me-don't-look-at-me percussionist who can play nearly every instrument."

"That's a lot," Angie said.

"It's sickening, really, because girls go crazy for that. I'm a filmmaker. I make things. Lots of things. You think girls go for that?"

"Do you want girls to go for that?" Angie asked.

"I don't know, but that's not the point."

"Okay, sorry," Angie said.

"Don't apologize," Zeke said. "You're Angie."

"Yeah . . . ?"

"Girl, you have a story," said Zeke. "Women who have a story don't apologize. Mi abuela, she has sooooo many stories. Híjole. Stories of men, stories of women — of activism. She was a badass. She still is. And she told me one day when I was apologizing for who I was, 'You don't apologize when you have a story.' And you have a story, Ang."

Angie was not 100 percent certain of Zeke's declaration. She decided it was best to be an active listener and note it later in her therapeutic journal.

Zeke looked at Jamboree.

"But Troy, that vato . . . he's slick," Zeke said. "And he's cheated on her at least twice that she knows of. Like, how can you manage that and still have any kind of power over someone?"

"Sure, yeah, of course," Angie said.

Knowing that if KC sent a message via courier pigeon asking for Angie's wounded heart, she would give it to her in an instant. Maybe that made her weak. No, she was definitely weak. Maybe.

"But she said he was a, um, you know . . ." Angie said.

"A dick?" Zeke half-laughed. "She *always* says that when he does something that hurts her. Then he sends something in the mail, shows up in Dryfalls. Apologizes. Writes her a song. Whatever. And she falls for his false love all over again. Which is stupid, right?"

"Sure, I guess. I mean, yeah."

Angie could not square how Jamboree could be susceptible to a Romeo-not-Romeo con. It did not fit the logic of what she had imagined about Jamboree.

"The thing is," said Zeke, "it's not even who she is. It's who she thinks she's gotta be."

"Who is she?" Angie asked. "I mean, who is she supposed to be?"

Zeke grinned. "That's not for me to say."

Zeke had been more than generous to share everything up until that point. Why would she hold back now?

"Let's lace up," Zeke said.

Angie and Zeke sat on the bench with Darius and Jamboree between them.

"I'm going to lock up my stuff," Jamboree said. "You want me to take yours?"

Zeke and Angie handed their shoes to Jamboree, whose eyes ticked toward the urn.

"Oh, yeah," Angie said, handing the urn to her.

Angie stared down at her feet. The well-worn orange wheels felt familiar to Angie in a this-is-how-I-broke-my-leg-in-two-places, how-stupid-am-I-to-try-this-again way. Zeke sprang up on her skates like a pro.

"Damn, these are small," Zeke said, rolling back and forth on the skates.

"Maybe you should've kept the others," Angie said.

"Dude, they smelled like dog shit," Zeke said, skating toward the rink.

Angie looked sideways at Darius, who was scrolling through a text. She had expected him to stay in the RV. She had expected him to —

"What?" Darius asked.

"Nothing." Angie shrugged.

Darius put his phone down, rubbing the top of his head.

"Over fifty years," Darius said.

"What?" Angie said.

"This place," he said. "It's been here for over fifty years. I looked it up. I like to look things up. The history of stuff."

"Okay," Angie said.

Even if Angie was interested in the roller rink factoid, Darius was still the turncoat who had all but sealed her fate. He was still the guy who said—

"It wasn't my fault what happened," Darius said. "Today. At school."

"So, it was mine?" Angie said.

"No, I just . . . look, I don't hate gay people. I know what Patricia thinks, but I don't. I don't really get it, but I don't hate people for it. And I don't believe in hurting someone the way Gary did."

"I might get expelled," Angie said. "I'm probably going to have to go to court. And all you can say is that it isn't your fault? You lied for him. You think he's really your friend?"

"I don't know," Darius said, rolling his skates back and forth along the floor. "I don't know . . . what I know right now." He got up off the bench, his hand on his side as he skated toward the rink.

Angie heaved a heavy sigh. Her stomach grumbled. She could not hear it over the music but felt it all the same.

The distance from the bench to the snack bar was approximately eleven feet. Eleven feet between Angie and the salvation of a foot-long hot dog, a large popcorn, and a Diet Pepsi.

It just was not going to happen.

"Song's coming up soon," Zeke shouted, waving Angie onto the floor while skating backward.

Of course, filming.

The song. The skating. A postcard from her dead sister. These were the things that would, of course, be a part of Angie's life. A life that was officially off and running — well, sort of. She wanted very much to be the Angie her sister had imagined. The Angie she was when she was with her sister. But without her and with an empty urn, Angie was not that sister.

She was Fat Angie.

Fat Angie in roller skates.

Jamboree skated up to Angie. "You ready?"

Angie looked down at her feet. They seemed so small on eight collective wheels. Small even in a women's size 11.5.

Jamboree leaned in and whispered into Angie's ear, "You can do this."

Jamboree's warm breath spread into a seemingly infinite linger along Angie's ear. The feeling surprised Angie. Immensely. Was Angie not lovesick for KC any longer? Was she leaping the line of attraction to girls who were clearly not gay-girl gay? Surely that would lead to a life of heartache as well.

Jamboree's smile was warm and inviting and soft and — how had Angie not noticed it with such —

"C'mon," Jamboree said, holding out her hands.

"I got it," Angie said.

Angie, without question, did not have it.

Angie slid-stood-staggered to her feet, her knees straight

then bent. Her body unnaturally shifted into dramatic and strange poses. Angie step-rolled for exactly four and one-half steps. Then she lost her balance, rolling forward and grabbing a pipe rail to steady herself.

There was nothing natural about her pose. Nothing!

Jamboree placed her hand along Angie's lower back. "You're doing good."

"You're not good at lying," said Angie.

"Is this the face of someone who would lie to you?" Jamboree asked.

Angie grinned.

Jamboree grinned.

Grin Fest had officially-unofficially returned.

Angie took a deep breath and loosened her grip from the bar. One hand hovering just inches above it. Her unsteady stance gradually scoot-rolled forward. Clopping her wheels, she lost her balance and slapped her palms onto the support wall at the entry to the rink floor.

Angie struggled to reposition herself as Zeke skated up, camera recording, Angie's fear clearly palpable. Her face was wrenched. Her legs shook. This was not an attractive look for her.

Balance + Angie = ?

"It's literally like riding your bike," said Zeke.

"I don't have a bike," Angie said.

"I can see where this is a problem, then," Zeke said.

Jamboree hit Zeke in the arm.

"Ouch," Zeke said.

"Angie," said Jamboree.

"Yeah," she said, a distinct frustration in her voice.

"You're the only freshman aside from your sister to *ever* make the Dryfalls varsity basketball team," said Jamboree.

"I'm also the only one who ever quit," said Angie.

"Your sister knew you could do this," said Jamboree. "I *know* you can."

"DJ said he'd play the song next," said Zeke, eyes on the camera's LCD. "Apparently, it's like a house favorite or something."

"Abracadabra" by Blue Ash was a 1973 power-pop hit that had been a favorite of Angie's couldn't-show-up father as well as her sister. A song that found itself in regular rotation on vinyl in their house before her couldn't-understand mother lost her luster for fun.

Jamboree held her hands out for Angie.

The last time Angie had held Jamboree's hand she had broken her leg. The odds were not in Angie's favor, but she took Jamboree's hands all the same. The squish of Angie's sweaty palms against Jamboree's nonsweaty palms was deeply embarrassing. Angie ambled along in a series of half rolls. It was a slow process, but she was, in fact, moving. Zeke whipped in front of them, skating backward with the camcorder.

Angie panicked and flailed.

Jamboree and a couple behind them caught Angie just before she hit the floor.

"This is stupid," Angie said, rocking back and forth on the skates.

"Look how far you've come," said Jamboree. "Look."

Angie had somehow made it halfway around the rink.

"Brookpark skaters," announced the DJ. "We're throwing it back to Ohio's Blue Ash. Get ready for the magic of 'Abracadabra'!"

"It's one song," said Jamboree. "You got this."

Angie took a deep breath. She most definitely did not feel she had this, but she let go of Jamboree's hand.

"I can hold on," Jamboree said.

But Angie was determined to try it alone.

"Looking good, Ang," Zeke said, filming.

"Stop filming," Angie said.

"You'll want this," Zeke said. "Trust me."

Angie did not like that Zeke continued to film.

Angie did not like how unstable she felt moving forward.

Angie lost her footing and fell onto her knees.

"Dude," Zeke said, offering her hand. "Give me your hand."

"Just don't," Angie said. "Okay? And stop filming me."

"Okay," Zeke said, backing away. "Sorry."

Angie crawled to the wall and sat there with everyone skating by her. Jamboree skated up and sat beside her.

"This is all so stupid," Angie said. "I couldn't have done this if she were here. I'm nothing . . . that she thought I was."

"I think she just wanted you to have fun, Angie," Jamboree said.

"Does it look like I'm having fun?" Angie asked.

"No," said Jamboree.

"She could do anything—be anything," said Angie. "And what did she do? Huh? Run away. Join the stupid air force just to not have to face my mom. She shouldn't have been there. She shouldn't have ever been there, you know?"

Jamboree nodded.

"And that day, when she left," Angie said. "We were in the airport, and we'd had this big fight, because . . . just because. And she says 'Give me a hug' and I wouldn't. I was so mad at her."

Angie wiped tears from her eyes.

Jamboree took Angie's hand. "Hey."

Angie shook her head.

"Hey," Jamboree said, again.

"Forget it," Angie said. "This was stupid."

"You're just trying too hard," said Jamboree. "So what if you fall down? Who cares?"

Angie half laughed, angry at Jamboree's complete lack of understanding.

"You fell on the first day of school, right?" said Angie.

Jamboree nodded.

"And no one seemed to even care," Angie said. "I just

have to bend over, and I'm a joke for the rest of the year. I just have to breathe — exist — to be laughed at."

"People are hateful," Jamboree said. "I get that."

"But see, that never happened to you," said Angie. "Not even when you weren't a size perfect."

"You don't know anything about what's happened to me, Angie," said Jamboree.

Angie nodded, unlacing her skates. "Yeah, I don't. Because you disappeared."

"I wanted to explain it," said Jamboree. "I tried to explain to you in the nurse's office. You didn't want to hear it."

Angie yanked one skate off and fought to get to her feet.

"This was a mistake," Angie said. "All of it."

"It's all right here, right now," Jamboree said. "Why do you have to be so scared to try?"

"Because I'm Fat Angie," she said, hobbling off the rink.

Give Me
the Meltdown

Angie sat against the wall outside the skate rink. The muffled big bass from inside pounded against her sweaty-cold back. She had sat there for five and one-half minutes after storming off the rink floor and returning her putrid-smelling skates. Sat with her dingy white sock feet drawn as close to her body as possible, regretting she had ever left Dryfalls.

She was, in essence, deep within the throes of a pity party for one.

Angie closed her eyes, imagining herself writing in her therapeutic journal. Noting the following words: *worthless, stupid, ugly, slob, lazy, messy, fat.* It was the last word she lingered on the longest, seeing the letters expand and swell in her mind. Exploding beyond the faint blue lines on the make-believe white pages. Bubbling—ballooning beyond—

A blast of music startled Angie as Darius stood with the skate-rink door open. She glanced at him before picking at a hole in the knee of her jeans. It was her obvious-not-obvious attempt at pretending he was not standing there.

But he was, in fact, still standing there. Standing there with her shoes and the urn.

Some people came out behind him. Too distracted by one another to really notice Angie or Darius.

Quiet.

More strange quiet.

"Hey," Darius said.

More strange quiet resumed.

Darius shifted parts of gravel under his shoe. The crackling rubbing of rocks amplified, sounded like . . .

An airplane barreled above them. Darius and Angie looked up as the round sound of jet engines swallowed the tension between them for a moment. For a moment, they were both looking up. Past the undercarriage of the plane pulling away and up toward the stars. Real stars. Unlike the ones in her bedroom. These had the sparkle, pop, and hum-glow, even if many of them were muted by light pollution.

Darius stepped toward Angie, holding her shoes and the urn out to her.

"Thanks," she said, avoiding eye contact.

"So . . ." Darius said. "They're inside trying to figure out what to do."

"There's nothing to figure out," Angie said, tying her sneaker. "This whole thing was stupid."

Darius softly nudged the toe of his sneaker against the ground again.

"I thought you wanted to do this," he said.

"What do you care about what I want?" said Angie.

Darius nodded.

He turned on his heels and started to go back inside, but stopped.

"What?" Angie said.

"Your sister," Darius said. "Her game was stealth. On point. Her speed. She wasn't just good for a girl. She was just *good*. Every college — she could have gone anywhere. She had that thing, you know? That thing people talk about, but they don't have a word for it."

Angie, like the rest of Dryfalls and the nearby outlying counties, knew that *thing*. That X factor. But deep down inside, her sister did not want to be the *thing* that their couldn't-understand mother, their couldn't-show-up father, or even Coach Laden wanted. She was suffocating — screaming — only no one could hear her. Not even Angie. Not really.

"Gary and me were hanging out in front of the gym after one of her games," Darius said. "She was like a junior, I think. Yeah. She was a junior. Gary wasn't such a —"

Angie looked at Darius. A look that said not to sugarcoat who Gary was.

"He wasn't as big of a jerk then," said Darius. "But that night, your sister pulled out this softer part of him. She was special that way."

"Yeah," Angie said, feeling an unexpected rise of resentment.

Angie had been called "special." Mostly by her father and then by several teachers after her attempted suicide. Their version of "special" was not her sister's version. It was the mark of all of Angie's faults and failings. The direct opposite and overtly disappointing.

A group of guys spilled out from inside the skate rink, laughing, a few of them shoving each other like a cheesy clothing commercial set at the beach. They were just having . . . fun. However foreign and scripted it looked to Angie, it was their reality. A fun reality.

Why was that so hard for Angie? Was she really that broken? That angry? Was she angry? Sometimes she was angry, but —

"You know, Gary and I have been friends since fifth grade," Darius said. "It was really hard to move to Dryfalls from Cincinnati. I mean, we had some family and that helped, but I struggled . . . to make friends. I had this really bad stutter."

"Really?" Angie asked.

"No joke," Darius said. "I *never* wanted to talk. I was . . . it was embarrassing. So I just didn't. And this one day, I'm eating lunch by myself behind the library, and Tommy

Parker and Ben Raker see me sitting there. They started calling me names. Racist shit. Can't even tell you how mad I was, but I was scared too. Because I was alone, you know?"

Darius started running the toe of his shoe over the ground again.

"So when I tried to walk away, they jumped me," said Darius. "And they were beating my ass hard when Gary comes around the corner. I'm thinking he's just gonna get in with what they're doing. But he pile-drives Ben all WWE style."

Angie grinned for a moment.

"I thought he was going to break Ben's back," Darius said. "After that, we became friends. Best friends. Gary was different back then. His mom hadn't married Chuck the Hateful Fuck. But once that guy was in . . . like, little by little, Gary seemed less like Gary and more like Chuck. What he did to you — today? I knew it was wrong, but —"

"But you still lied," Angie said.

Darius nodded. "He looked at me like that guy who stood up to Ben Raker in fifth grade. That guy who was my friend when nobody was my friend. The guy who would lose his spot on the team if I said something different. Football is his only chance to go to college."

Darius laced his fingers on his head.

"I just thought you'd get suspended maybe and that it would be over," Darius said.

"It's over all right," Angie said, grabbing the urn and standing up. "I don't care anymore."

Angie walked toward the RV.

"That's what the fight was about," Darius said.

Angie stopped walking.

"He was bragging tonight," Darius said. "Bragging to everybody how 'crazy Fat Angie' was going to go to jail. That they'd press charges against you. And I knew it wasn't your fault and I told him to tell the truth. To do what was right."

Angie did not know whether to believe Darius or not.

"He said he wouldn't," Darius said. "So when I pushed it, that's when things got . . . stupid."

"Why don't you just tell the truth?" said Angie. "Tell Principal Warner what happened."

"I can't."

"Why?" Angie asked.

"I just can't, Angie," Darius said.

Jamboree and Zeke came out of the skate rink, a stream of people trailing out behind them. It was 11:10 p.m. by Angie's Casio calculator watch. It was closing time.

"Hey," Jamboree said. "What's . . . going on?"

"Nothing," Angie said. "Let's just go home."

"Yeah, uh, no," Jamboree said.

"What?" Zeke said, a spiked surprise in her voice.

"Your sister wanted to do this with you," said Jamboree. "And everything I know about her, she'd still want you to do it. To do — to see all the things that she wanted to see with you."

"Okay, so, um, my perfect sister is dead," said Angie. "She doesn't *want* anything."

"She wasn't perfect, Angie," said Jamboree.

Angie shook her head. "That's the only way people remember her, talk about her. Darius, my mom, the nightly news. She's frozen in red-white-and-star-spangled-blue time. The hero, the athlete . . . the good one."

They all stood in the parking lot of Brookpark Skateland, people piling into cars, the world moving around them. The quiet that settled among them seemed an inevitable precursor to the end of the RV adventure.

"Angie's sister was a klepto," Jamboree announced to everyone.

Zeke and Darius looked at Angie for confirmation.

"She'd steal Twix bars and hair ties and Andes mints," Jamboree said. "We saw her steal a copy of *Slaughterhouse-Five* from the Book Stacks once. I don't think she even liked Vonnegut. Did she?"

Angie half smiled. "No. She did it to piss off my mom."

"Dude, your sister was a book thief?" Zeke said, turning the camera on.

Jamboree pushed the camera down.

"Her sister outbelched Wang on Christmas Eve when we were eleven," said Jamboree. "We made a trophy for her out of a Mountain Dew bottle."

"She never threw it out," Angie said.

"And she had this really gross habit of picking scabs," said Jamboree.

"It was a compulsion," said Angie.

"It was a gross compulsion," Jamboree said.

Zeke half laughed.

"But her sister had the biggest heart," said Jamboree. "I didn't really get it then. Because when you're around something so much, it just seems normal. It's when it's gone that you feel it. The difference. The loss of it. The hole."

Angie's eyes began to tear up.

Angie did not want to cry.

"Angie, your sister wasn't perfect," said Jamboree. "She was the most imperfect exceptional person I've ever known. Except for you."

Angie did not follow the trajectory of Jamboree's seeming half compliment.

"I'm nothing like my sister," said Angie.

"I watched you play that game against the Titans last year," said Jamboree.

Zeke raised a finger. "Saw it too, dude. Before I had to go to the bathroom. Twice. Might've been three times that day. Pre Clair Voyant."

Jamboree waited to see if Zeke was through talking.

"I'm done," Zeke said.

"I barely even played," Angie said.

"But when you did, you didn't play it like it was *her* thing," said Jamboree. "You played it the way you used to when it was just us. You, me, Wang. Your dad and his corny jokes and factoids . . . her. You played that game like it was *your* thing. Like you were having fun again. Like you were alive."

Angie wiped tears off her face. She did not relish her public display of immense sadness. It felt vulnerable and awkward and weak.

Jamboree shrugged at Angie.

Zeke and even Darius waited for Angie to say something.

This was it, again. The now or never. The do or die. The go gaily forward or turn back. These were the kinds of decisions that often riddled Angie with a deep uncertainty. But something shifted inside of her, the way it had in her bedroom.

Why Not? repeated in her mind over and over.

What was there to lose by trying? To be honest, there were many things to lose by trying. Enough, in fact, to fill the front and back of several sheets of college-ruled paper. Still, she returned to *Why Not?*

Angie held the urn close to her.

"Okay," Angie said.

"Okay . . . ?" Jamboree asked.

"Yeah, I'll try," said Angie.

"Rebellion on!" Zeke shouted, startling Angie with her enthusiasm. "So, let's ditch Judas at the bus station and go get something to eat."

Everyone walked toward the RV. Well, everyone but Darius. Angie noticed this and stopped.

"I can't leave," Darius said.

Zeke stopped short of the RV.

"Judas, no one wants you here," said Zeke. "I mean, Jamboree feels sorry for you, but that ain't the same as wanting you."

"There are no buses to Dryfalls," Darius said. "The closest stop is New Philadelphia."

An unexpected wrench in the plan of Darius's departure. One Angie had not anticipated, given that New Philadelphia was approximately 53 miles northeast of Dryfalls.

"Bullshit," Zeke said.

"Look it up if you don't believe me," said Darius.

"I don't believe you, Judas, but you know what? I don't care," said Zeke.

"Zeke, come on," Jamboree said.

"No," Zeke said, walking toward Darius. "Stay here. Hitch a ride. Call your dad."

"And say what?" Darius asked. "That I'm in Cleveland?"

"You think I give a shit if you get in trouble?" Zeke asked. "How many shits did you have to give about me? Huh? When your fucking friends humiliated me. You defended those pendejos. ¿Que no?"

"So, you what? Steal screen grabs off my phone?" said Darius. "Print them in your 'literary' trash paper? Those were people's private thoughts."

"See, you're still doing it," said Zeke. "You're defending them —"

"I'm not defending—"

"Your friends shared a picture of me covered in my own shit. All over everywhere. And what did you say, huh? I'm your family, primo. Even if you can't understand what I am or who I am. I was your real friend before Gary—before all of them assholes. You treated me like dirt."

"Gary didn't do it," Darius said.

"He took the photo," Zeke said. "Jamboree saw him."

Darius ticked his look to Jamboree. A moment later, she nodded.

"Someone else posted it," Darius said.

"Bullshit," Zeke snapped.

"*This* is bullshit," Darius said. "You blaming me is bullshit. You passing out at *my* birthday party and your bag leaking because you can't keep it together is bullshit. I can't control who does what, okay? But I said I was sorry for what they did because it was messed up."

"Yeah, but you never stood up to them," said Zeke.

Zeke's anger softened in a way Angie would not have expected. A picture may say a thousand humiliating words sometimes, but being alone in that humiliation says more. Angie got the alone part. From every time Wang had acted like he didn't know her at school. From Jamboree disappearing three years earlier.

Darius laced his fingers behind his head, grimacing from the pain in his side.

And for the first time in the Zeke-versus-Darius spat/

fight/dispute/showdown — however it could best be categorized — there was silence.

Big gaping where-do-we-go-from-here silence.

Then, to everyone's surprise, even Angie's . . .

"Some female dragonflies pretend to be dead to avoid mating with male dragonflies," Angie blurted out.

What had Angie just said? From what part of the mind-bizarre had she remembered such an unnecessary and irrelevant factoid?

"Really?" said Jamboree.

Angie nodded.

"I wish I were a dragonfly," said Jamboree. "That would make my life easier."

Jamboree started laughing. Zeke cracked up. Even Darius laughed.

Angie, in her characteristically nervous state, had managed to blurt out a truly helpful tension breaker.

Zeke turned on her camera. "Ang, you gotta say that again."

Zeke directed Jamboree to join in with a full re-creation of the scene. And there, in the parking lot of Brookpark Skateland, Angie had defused what had seemed impossible to defuse. Though the laughter and silliness dwindled as Zeke turned the camera off, returning all of them to their previous state of now-what?

"So . . ." Jamboree said.

Angie nodded. "Yeah."

"Y'all should get going," Darius said. "I'll . . . figure it out."

Angie dropped her head. What to do — to say? She was coming up with the too-many-tabs-open-in-her-mind meta-phor. She did not like this metaphor. She would need to add it to her List of Dislikes.

Zeke exhaled deep and long and then pivoted on the gravel toward the RV.

"Like, let's just all go," Zeke said, walking toward the RV. "But I'm driving *and* I get to pick the music."

Jamboree followed behind her, hooking her arm around Zeke's neck. All while leaving Angie and Darius looking-not-looking at each other.

"You cool with that?" he asked. "Me . . . coming?"

Angie shrugged. "Um, I'm . . . cool about not leaving you here."

"That's fair," Darius said.

Zeke laid into the horn, hanging out of the driver's win-dow. "C'mon."

Angie and Darius walked side by side to the RV. Though they couldn't be further apart on all of the things that really mattered. At least, to Angie.

We Can't Stop

"Wake up!" Jamboree said, crawling into the back of the RV.

Both Angie and Darius had dozed off, Angie managing to drool on parts of central Ohio from sleeping on the map. Not an attractive reality to wake up to, and she quickly wiped it away with the tail of her T-shirt. Rubbing her eyes, she tilted the face of her watch toward her. It was officially Friday. 12:42 in the a.m., but Friday nonetheless.

Jamboree twisted the cap off a Mountain Dew.

"Stop," Darius said, midyawn. "Look, I'm cool with a lot of things, but you on caffeine? No way."

"Dude, bring me my Mountain Dew," Zeke said from the driver's seat.

Jamboree filled an empty plastic bottle with water and handed it to Zeke.

"Girl, you are seriously punking my chi," Zeke said to Jamboree. "Give me that soda."

"You drink a soda, and you'll inflate your bag. Again. How quickly we forget the humiliation of bile on your favorite T-shirt."

Angie cracked up.

The disco ball was spinning. The Christmas lights twinkled. And *Hits From the 80s,* on audiocassette, set an upbeat mood for Angie to wake up to as they barreled down the interstate. The low-beam headlights peeled through a murky fog that had descended somewhere between Cleveland and wherever they were en route to — the World's Largest Basket.

Jamboree picked up an M&M from the map that charted their adventure and ate it. Different colors for different legs of the journey. A new color had emerged while Angie had been asleep.

"What's in Cincinnati?" Angie asked Jamboree.

"A friend of Zeke's has a band playing there tomorrow night," Jamboree said, eating another M&M. "They're out of Toledo, I think."

"What kind of band?" Angie asked.

"Loud," Jamboree said. "Really loud."

Angie was unsure if "really loud" fell into a specific genre of music. Regardless, she did not like thinking about singing with any band. Loud or not.

"It's a super small crowd, Ang," said Zeke. "Lash, she's

the bassist, said maybe ten people will show, but it's still an audience."

Angie was unsure if Lash was her given name or stage name. She suspected the latter, but the world was full of originality, she had recently decided.

"I thought Lash quit the band because of V," Jamboree said.

"Lash came back this summer when TFH fell apart," Zeke said.

"TFH?" Angie asked.

"The Flaming Heretics," said Jamboree. "I liked them. Very political. Kind of Salem Witch Trial–meets–Joan of Arc themed. Lots of Renaissance-fair armor and low-end pyro, with a giant uterus backdrop onstage."

"Huh," Angie said, picking an M&M off the map and eating it.

"Rehearsal is at six tomorrow night," said Zeke.

Rehearsal? With a real band with actual instruments? Angie's stomach began to sour.

In the transition from one song to the next, Jamboree shouted, "Oh my God, yes! Turn it up. Turn it up!"

"You're killing me with this music, Jam," Zeke said, turning the music up.

"My host family loves this song," Jamboree said. "We danced to it when I first got to Belgium. Kip curry and 'Mickey'!"

Jamboree reached for Angie's and Darius's hands.

"I'm cool," Darius said, watching a video on his phone.

But Jamboree was persistent. She pulled them both out of their respective seats, Darius's hand clutching his side, the soreness of the fight with Gary seeming to have fully settled in.

"Sorry," Jamboree said to Darius.

"I'm good," Darius said. "Just . . . yeah."

And so it began. What was dubbed the official RV Dance Party started. It didn't seem to matter that the music had more treble than bass. It did not matter that the music was from their parents' generation. It did not matter that the song was excessively repetitive in its lyrics.

What mattered was that the three of them were dancing together. Not fighting. Not outwardly hating. Just awkwardly dancing in the RV. Well, Angie was awkwardly dancing. More like swaying without rhythm.

Dancing was not Angie's strong suit. Not by one mile. Not by 1,999,000 miles. Approximately. It was something she did in the privacy of her room with the lights off and the glow-in-the-dark stars, well, glowing. It was something she had not even done with KC. And KC had very much wanted to.

Unlike Angie, Jamboree swung her hips and raised her arms above her head. Her infectious smile willed a lot of what was shy and inhibited out of Darius. Angie, however, was more of a holdout, as she stood there stiffly swaying.

Jamboree leaned into Angie, hip-bumping her. Angie lost her balance for a moment.

"I'm sorry," Jamboree said.

"It's . . . okay," Angie said.

"We used to dance in here all the time," Jamboree said to Darius.

"I was seven," Angie said.

"But you did a mean robot at seven," Jamboree said.

Darius half grinned toward Angie. And not in that you're-a-loser way. It was . . . sweet. Before Angie could process half a dozen thoughts about Darius and his grin, Jamboree committed the dance crime of all time. She busted out all the *ugly* moves of the robot.

The robot (n): A form of dance first created by mimes in the 1920s, meant to imitate a robot. Later popularized by the Jackson 5's performance of their 1973 hit "Dancing Machine" on television's *Soul Train.*

Darius followed, leaving Angie odd girl out, but truly grinning ear to ear.

"You guys are nerds," Zeke said, the camera over her shoulder as she was driving.

"Zeke," Jamboree said. "Eyes on the road."

"Híjole, Driver's Ed," said Zeke. "I'm a professional. I can film and not look at the same time."

"Come on," Jamboree said.

"Whatever," Zeke said, putting the camera away.

"Just let your hips do the work," Jamboree said to Angie. "That's it. Sort of. How does it feel?"

"Like I'm dropping a Hula-Hoop. A lot."

"You don't have to get it right," Jamboree said. "Just have fun."

Zeke turned the music down.

"Dance Party, do I get off of here soon?" Zeke said.

Jamboree grinned at Angie as she slid into the booth at the table, map splayed out before her, Angie and Darius still dancing for a moment before it got incredibly awkward. Angie took a seat across from Jamboree. Darius climbed up into the loft.

"Should still be a ways. What's the last exit sign you passed?" Jamboree asked, reading the map.

"Dude, I don't know," Zeke said. "Just saw there's a truck stop in fifteen miles with a Denny's attached."

"We're picnicking at the Basket," Jamboree said.

"Jam, I'm starving," Zeke said.

"We can grab White Castle outside Columbus," said Darius. "There's one right before we exit toward Newark."

"Double Cheese Sliders and Onion Chips . . ." recalled Zeke.

Angie leaned over the map the way she had done with Jamboree so many times when they had been friends. Only now they were actually going somewhere. They were Thelma and Louise, Sid and Nancy, Harold and Maude. Actually, they were none of those classic cinematic characters. What was relevant was that they were doing what they had always talked about doing.

"I missed this," Jamboree said to Angie.

"What?" Angie asked.

"Dance party in the RV. Picking places we wanted to go with lines of M&M's."

"It was never real before," Angie said.

"I always wanted it to be," said Jamboree.

Jamboree's cheeks flushed. Why were her cheeks so red?

"Lame, huh?"

"Um, no," Angie said. "Surprising, but not lame."

The look between them lingered. Angie could not understand it. What was that feeling? That kind of look?

"Jam, trade me," Zeke said. "I'm bored."

"I'll drive," Darius said, hanging over the side of the loft.

"Never mind," Zeke said.

"So, you're not bored if I wanna drive?" Darius asked.

"I've seen you drive, D," Zeke said. "Your foot is stupid light, and I'm hungry for something besides Sour Cream and Onion Pringles."

Zeke had not referred to Darius as Judas. Angie made note of it in her therapeutic journal.

"What is that?" Jamboree asked.

"It's, um . . . my new woo-woo therapist asked me to

keep a journal. It's supposed to help me process stuff . . . or something."

Jamboree nodded.

"Does it help?" Jamboree asked carefully. "The therapy?"

Angie considered the question. She had not thought about it so specifically.

"I don't know," Angie said. "Maybe? Not the first one, though. It's like I'd say, 'The sky is blue,' and he'd say, 'It's an apple; do you want to eat it?' But this one, she's okay, I guess. I still think she'll side with my mom on Monday."

Jamboree did not follow.

"My mom said the therapist gets to make the call," said Angie. "If I have to go to, um, the Whispering Oak Treatment Facility or not."

"Can't you talk to your dad?" Jamboree asked. "He was always pretty laid-back."

"Yeah, he's not really around," Angie said, fiddling with the edge of her journal. "At, um, all. You know? He's the stereotypical married-to-a-younger-single-mom-who-had-been-his-secretary. Shake, stir: Insta-Family."

"I saw them at the funeral," said Jamboree.

"You were at the funeral?" Angie asked.

"Of course," Jamboree said. "I loved her too. I couldn't believe it. When she went missing. I really thought she'd come back, you know?"

"Yeah."

Quiet.

More awkward quiet.

"I'm sorry," Jamboree said.

Angie shrugged.

"That I wasn't there," Jamboree continued. "That I wasn't your friend."

There was that look again, only it was different. It was wrought with heartbreak and a fill-in-the-blank that Angie could not fill. What was it?

Awkward quiet resumed.

"Hey, Ang," Zeke said. "You ever play Fact or Fiction?"

Darius leaned over from the loft, attempting to signal Angie how to respond.

"No?" Angie said.

Darius dropped back into the loft bed, shaking his head.

"Oooo. An F-or-F virgin in the RV," Zeke said. "Jam, take my camera."

"It's a dumb game," Darius said under his breath.

"What's F or F?" Angie asked.

Jamboree grabbed Zeke's camcorder. "One person says something. You have to decide if it is a fact or fiction. It's truth or dare without the dares."

"Troy loves Fact or Fiction," Zeke said.

"Do not name he-who-shall-not-be-named," said Jamboree.

"You put him on the list, girl," Zeke said.

"I said he was a dick," said Jamboree.

"Maybe you should have written: 'Blank is a dick who shall not be named.'"

Jamboree turned on Zeke's camcorder, reading from the LCD screen. "What does 'format card' mean?"

"Dude, don't do that," said Zeke.

"I'm messing with you," Jamboree said.

"That's messed up," Zeke said. "Never joke about deleting a filmmaker's footage."

Angie grinned. Jamboree grinned. Soon they had fallen headfirst into a grinfest.

"Ang, you in?" Zeke asked.

"Um, sure," Angie said.

A rare acceptance to a game of chance. While not the gambling type, like her couldn't-understand mother she had watched Wang perfect his lying technique. She could smell an untruth like a skunk in the trunk. Well, so to speak.

"You go, Zeke," Jamboree said. "It's your game."

"Okay. Pig Skull," Zeke announced. "If I were a superhero that would be my name. Enter: Pig Skull. My name is Pig Skull. This is my story. Fact or fiction?"

"Fiction!" Jamboree said.

"Fiction," Darius said, scrolling on his phone.

"Ang?" Zeke asked.

"Um . . . fact?" Angie said.

"Final answer?" Zeke asked.

Was Angie wrong? There were only two possibilities:

fact or fiction. Jamboree and Darius's response would most likely be the correct answer, as they knew Zeke better, but . . .

"Final answer," Angie said.

Zeke drumrolled her palms against the steering wheel. The RV pulled to the right ever so slightly.

"Hands on the wheel," Jamboree said.

"Dude, relax," Zeke said. "You're diminishing my fun capacity."

"You are diminishing our life expectancy," Jamboree said.

"Such a mom," Zeke said.

"What's the answer already?" Jamboree asked.

"Fact, of course," Zeke said.

Darius sat up in the loft. "What the hell kind of superhero is Pig Skull?"

Zeke took a swig of water. "The kind you wouldn't mess with."

"No, no, I get it," Jamboree said. "It's her avenging the-piglets-of-slaughters-past. The PETA undercover video. Remember, where she got traumatized for something like a month?"

"Still traumatized," Zeke said. "Pig Skull. I am the spirit of bacon gone rogue."

Angie laughed.

"Go, Darius," Jamboree said.

"I hate this game," he said.

"You hate that I always win," said Zeke.

"Fact or fiction," Darius said. "I'm enlisting after high school."

"Fiction," Zeke chimed in.

"Complete fiction," Jamboree said.

Darius tipped over the edge of the loft, waiting for Angie's response.

"Um," she said. "Fiction."

"Fact," Darius said, going back to his phone.

"No way!" Jamboree said. "You're antiwar."

Darius scrolled on his phone, offering little more than a distracted shrug.

"Wow," Jamboree said.

Angie could not imagine Darius enlisting in the armed forces. Was it merely a disguised answer to win the game?

"Okay, fact or fiction," Jamboree said. "I have a mole on my inner thigh, and I named it."

"How big is the mole?" Darius said, leaning up on his elbow.

Jamboree pulled a bag of Doritos out of a pantry.

"I don't know . . . a centimeter?" Jamboree said.

"Fiction," Darius said, lying back down. "You'd know the size if it was real."

"I'm not playing because I know the answer," Zeke said.

"Fiction," Angie said.

"Fact!" shouted Jamboree.

"Ewwww," said Darius. "You named your mole?"

"Don't even think of mole-shaming her," Zeke said to Darius.

"Moles used to freak me out, and after Zeke named her stoma, I named my mole. Freak-out gone."

"Revolution!" Zeke shouted. "Things aren't so scary if you name them."

"Body-part-naming revolution," Darius said. "The patriarchy is quivering."

"Your turn, Angie," Jamboree said, biting into a chip.

So much of Angie's life was fact that should be fiction. It was truly difficult to choose just one thing.

"Okay. Uh . . . when I was in fifth grade, I . . ." Angie said. "I made out with Gary Klein under the high school bleachers waiting for my dad to pick me up."

"Fiction," Zeke said.

"Yeah, I'm going to go fiction," said Jamboree, tipping the bag of chips toward Angie.

"He would have told me, so fiction," Darius said.

"Fact," Angie said.

"No way," said Jamboree. "You never told me that."

"It was so weird," Angie said. "He bit my tongue. By accident, I think."

"Girl, I am literally gagging," said Zeke. "Hey, D. Guess your boy doesn't tell you everything, huh?"

Darius's look on Angie was long. Long enough to make her squirm nervously in her seat even though she had told the truth.

"Okay," Jamboree said. "Fact or fiction . . ."

The game continued for miles along the foggy stretch of interstate. While mysteries were revealed, Angie began to let herself be herself.

Well, mostly.

I Still
Shut My Eyes

They had been off the interstate and driving on mostly deserted state roads for approximately forty-one and one-half minutes, the RV sopping with the smell of the mouth-watering White Castle burgers, Loaded Fries, and Onion Chips, Zeke making a play for the last even before they steered out of the White Castle parking lot.

As the RV headlights slit through the darkness, an unmistakable glow surged through the lifting fog.

"Angie," Jamboree said, from the driver's seat, "I think I see it."

Angie knelt near the console between Jamboree and Zeke, gazing out the bug-splattered windshield. About a mile ahead, the unmistakable sight came into vivid view.

It was the World's Largest Basket.

A seven-story picnic basket wrapped in a warm golden-white hue of light: a Guinness record-holder right in Newark, Ohio.

Angie's lips parted; a breath of a sound emerged. Her grin expanded the closer they drove, a warmth coating the cold and aching edges around the Hole. A feeling worth noting in her journal later.

Zeke rolled down the passenger-side window, sticking her hand and camera out and filming their approach as they exited the highway.

Darius leaned in behind Angie to catch a glimpse.

"Wow," he said, his wonderment sincere.

Jamboree maneuvered the RV into a turnout and parked. Angie grabbed the urn from the bench and followed Darius out the side door. The two of them stood there, gazing up. And sure, it was not the Eiffel Tower, the Empire State Building, or even the Atomium. But those had been faraway places for Angie. Something she had only seen with the click of a mouse and a scroll. This was a tangible and towering anomaly of design magnitude. It was her sister to every last letter of *unusual*.

"It's an exact replica," Darius said, standing beside Angie, cradling the food and drinks, "of the company's premier basket. That's what it said on the Internet. Can you imagine getting to come to work here every day? Seven stories up. One hundred and eighty thousand square feet. There's nothing else like it."

"Your pocket protector's showing, D," said Zeke, digging through her messenger bag.

"Whatever," he said.

Jamboree stepped out of the RV, carrying several sleeping bags.

"Hey," she said to Angie. "It's cool, huh?"

"Yeah."

"Jam, we're picnicking, not camping," Zeke said, still digging in her messenger bag.

"The grass is wet," Jamboree said.

This was here — it was really happening. Angie could barely believe it.

"I don't know about y'all, but I'm hungry," Darius said.

The damp grass squeaked beneath Angie's sneakers as she walked toward the basket. A breeze wandered through the trees, their leaves clamoring, almost clapping. It was . . .

Zeke threw a lit smoke bomb in front of Angie.

"What are you doing?" Angie asked, backing away from it.

Zeke lit another and threw it. Clouds of blue swirled in front of Angie as Zeke jogged in front of her.

"Okay, now walk through the smoke and look up," Zeke directed. "Like you're awestruck or something."

Angie was inept in the art of performance on demand, as was evidenced by her lumbering through the manufactured smoke and looking into the camera instead of up at the basket.

"Okay," Zeke said. "Go back. Try it again."

"Isn't a documentary supposed to be real?" Angie asked.

"Girl, I'm adding dramatic tension with the smoke," Zeke said. "It's a visual metaphor. For the war. For you stepping through the haze of your journey and shit. Just trust me."

Angie attempted to follow Zeke's questionable direction again. And again, she looked into the camera.

"Cut," Zeke said. "It's reading false. We'll try again later. I'm starving anyway."

Jamboree and Darius had unzipped the sleeping bags and spread them out on the ground. Zeke collapsed onto her knees and pulled out a Double Cheese Slider.

Angie sipped her watered-down Diet Sprite, staring up at the basket. That warmness inside of her had not dissipated. Rather, it had expanded. Was the Hole gone? Could it be that easy? A giant picnic basket and a bag of White Castle sliders?

"You happy?" Jamboree asked Angie, picking the pickles off her burger.

Angie considered the question, not even glancing at her watch to time her response.

"I'm exponentially happy," Angie said.

"That's big happy," Jamboree said.

"Yeah . . . it is," she said. "It's like, I don't know how to describe it. It's a feeling. It's . . ."

Jamboree wiped her hands on a napkin, her attention fully on Angie.

"I can imagine her, standing there. Her head tilted back, you know? Looking up. Wanting to take at least ten selfies."

Jamboree smiled, taking a bite of her burger.

"And she'd walk to that pond over there, on the side of the building, and make a wish."

"I totally forgot she did that," Jamboree said. "The wish thing. When, she, um . . . when she saw a reflection. It was like a point system."

"One wish for a star," Angie said, head tilted back. "Two wishes for the moon. Three wishes for the sun."

"What kind of wish do you think she'd make tonight?"

Angie noticed that Darius was listening to them between bites of his burger.

"Um . . ." Angie said, shrugging. "I don't know. She never said what they were, but that they usually came true. She'd say, 'I still shut my eyes because I want to see everything I'm wishing for. I don't want to rush a detail.' It sounds weird if I say it out loud."

"That's cool," Darius said. "For real. I don't remember the last time I really wished for anything."

"Maybe you could wish for a backbone," Zeke said, under-but-not-under her breath.

"What?" Darius said.

"Okay," Zeke said, turning her camera on. "Things you hate. Who wants to go?"

Her passive-aggressive dig at Darius still stung the mood.

"Come on," Zeke said.

"Okay, I got one," Jamboree said. "Coconut."

"Really?" Angie said. "What about Almond Joy?"

Jamboree shook her head, sipping her drink.

"Oh, and tampons," Jamboree said.

Angie snort-laughed.

"I hear you, Jam," said Zeke. "The plug rarely plays on this girl's turntable."

"Same," said Angie. "Minus the turntable analogy. Not that I don't like vinyl, because I do. Um, anyway."

Darius shook his head. "I hate it when girls talk about personal-hygiene products. Especially when people are eating."

"Whatever!" Zeke said to Darius. "I hate it when my dad clips his toenails in the living room. And leaves them on the floor."

A disgusted *ewwww* came from everyone.

"I'm never walking barefoot in your living room again," Jamboree said.

"Ang, what do you hate?" Zeke asked.

The question introduced a challenge to Angie, as there were many things she disliked — as evidenced by her List of Dislikes, concealed in her therapeutic journal. Among those, it could be argued that there were many that she hated but felt too guilty to express. Because it made her feel like her couldn't-understand mother, a woman who truly seemed to hate more things than she could ever like.

"I hate . . ." Angie said, "awkward silences. And . . . movies and TV shows where kids have all the answers."

"You never see them do anything real," said Jamboree. "Like laundry."

"Man, I hate laundry," Darius said.

"Or have their mom ice 'em out for a week or longer, pues, because they didn't take out the trash," said Zeke.

"It's because if they did real stuff, nobody would watch," said Angie.

"Because it's not funny," said Darius.

"Because it's *real*," said Zeke. "My mom would rather watch some scripted 'reality' show than really hear about someone like your sister, Ang. When she tied one of those yellow ribbons around the tree in the front yard, I wanted to scream."

"Me too," said Angie. "Not about your mom. Just in general."

"Did you?" asked Jamboree.

The directness of the question struck Angie in an unexpectedly vulnerable place. The answer would have seemed obvious per her couldn't-understand mother's prescriptive rules of normalcy: *Smiles required. Authenticity optional.*

"No," Angie said. "I didn't scream."

"Why not?" Zeke asked.

It was the question that would not stop expanding. This made Angie nervous. The Hole echoed from her diaphragm. It had not gone anywhere.

All eyes and a camera lens were on Angie.

Why had she not simply screamed? She had wanted to. Hadn't she?

Why had she not cried at her sister's funeral? Why had she felt such a distance between herself and the rest of the world—so much so that she had literally run and run and run for days extending into weeks? Some people imagined she had done it to be thinner, to be loved, to act out. But she had run because it was the only way she could not feel guilty.

They all continued to wait for her answer.

"Because, um," Angie said. "You can't make noise. They can't know, you know?"

Angie tugged at the torn thread in the knee of her jeans.

"When my sister went missing, my mom pulled me to the side," Angie said. "Before we talked to the cameras. She said, 'Don't cry. Don't let them know they've hurt us.' Like she thought, I guess, they would just give her back if we weren't crying?"

Angie shook her head at the absurdity of her question. At the absurdity of everything about that moment. Microphones mounted onto a stand—prepared statements and questions and—

"You can't let them hear you," Angie said. "The cameras, the neighbors, the terrorists—the f-ing ribbons. You can't let them hear you dying every second of every minute of every hour of every day. There are 86,400 seconds of screaming-not-screaming in every single day. Crying-not-crying. Feeling-not-feeling. But it's still so loud, you know? How can it be that loud?"

The quiet hung thick and damp. What would have been an internal monologue on any other day had externalized. And on camera, no less. Angie looked at Jamboree, who seemed helpless to know what to say. This made Angie feel weird and different and stupid and strange, fat and —

"I would've screamed," said Darius. "If that had been me. I would've."

Zeke angled the camera in his direction. He ticked an annoyed glance at her.

"This picnic has gotten way too heavy," Zeke said, turning the camera off. "Who's down for rooftop s'mores?"

"I'm in," Darius said, standing up.

"Someone who isn't you, D," Zeke said.

"Yeah, okay," Darius said, heading toward the RV.

Jamboree shook her head.

"What?" Zeke said.

"Why do you have to be like that?" Jamboree asked.

"Because he's still a Judas," Zeke said. "We ain't all cool just because he said he would've screamed."

"He's trying," Jamboree said.

"Look, y'all coming or what?" Zeke said. "It's real Belgian chocolate, Ang. It's got little elephants on the squares. Four fabulous flavors, girl."

Jamboree looked at Angie. There were very few times

Angie had turned down a s'more opportunity. Actually, she could not think of one. But she:

1. Did not like heights
2. Feared she might fall through the roof
3. Wanted to spend time with Jamboree

Even though she did salivate, ever so slightly, at the thought of a burnt marshmallow.

"S'mores make me hiccup," Angie said.

S'mores did not make Angie hiccup. It was, in fact, a terribly produced lie, but she was sticking with it.

"I'm going to hang out," Jamboree said to Zeke.

"All right, whatever," Zeke said, walking away.

"Should I have gone?" Angie asked Jamboree.

"Only if you wanted to," Jamboree said.

Angie thought about it. Then shook her head.

Jamboree stretched out on her back.

"It's perfect out here," Jamboree said. "A whisper of clouds. Skittering breeze across the leaves. I like this."

Angie had not tipped her head up. Rather she was marveling at the shape and sound of Jamboree's voice.

"You know what's weird?" Jamboree said. "When you're lying on your back in Belgium, you're looking at the same sky as right here. I thought it would be different somehow. But it was the same stars and the same clouds."

"Was it as swell as you always thought it would be?" Angie asked.

"More swell," Jamboree said. "Same sky. Different world. Being there meant not having to be the girl named after an RV and an overnight in Memphis after a Pearl Jam concert."

Angie grinned.

"Ever since I got back, my mom's travel itch is at new heights," said Jamboree.

"Which is pretty cool," Angie said.

"It is," Jamboree said. "She wants to do a girls-only trek. Relive that summer she turned eighteen. Drive out to California over Christmas break. See all the same things. Go to some concerts. Make wishes from the roof of the RV, eating grilled cheese sandwiches and creamy tomato soup."

"I can't even think about, um, driving to the grocery store with my mom without feeling . . . sick," Angie said.

Jamboree nodded. "You could borrow my mom."

Angie smiled.

"For a nominal fee," Jamboree said. "I'll take a batch of your lethal Chocolate Chip Around the World Cookies."

"Yeah, I don't really make things like that anymore," Angie said.

"Why not?"

Angie knew why. She knew that fat girls with fat thighs and fat faces did not need to consume something as fattening as Chocolate Chip Around the World Cookies.

"What are you thinking about?" Jamboree asked.

Angie shrugged.

"I was thinking about nothing because I was thinking about everything," said Angie.

"Paradoxical."

Loser, Angie thought about herself.

The quiet resettled between them. It was incredibly nervous making.

"You and KC," Jamboree said. "I just never thought you were, you know. And KC, she's really . . ."

Brief List of KC Romance's Qualities
(in No Particular Order)

Smart

Funny

Charming

Sexy

Creative

Insightful

Super-good kisser

Super-good hand holder

Struggled with depression

Gone . . .

It was the final item on the list that Angie lingered on.

"I was surprised," Jamboree said.

"Because I'm fat, and she's pretty?" Angie asked.

"No," said Jamboree. "Because I didn't know you were . . . you never seemed like you were, you know. But now, you are."

"Yeah, well, maybe not after Whispering Oak."

"You really think she's going to do that?" Jamboree asked.

"I think she's kind of . . . done," Angie said. "With everything that isn't about milking the sympathy for my sister. She—"

"Jam," Zeke called out from the roof of the RV. "This s'more is, like, crazy good."

"Maybe in a sec," Jamboree said.

"You and Zeke are . . . close," Angie said.

"Yeah," said Jamboree. "I mean, as close as anyone can be to Zeke. She kind of keeps everyone in front of the lens and away from her. Life is exposition, right? All the backstory of what happens to us. How we deal with it. That's Zeke. Zeke and Clair Voyant. She tries to be all cool about it, but the bag thing really messed with her for a while. Especially after Gary posted those pictures of her. He's such a dick. Totally denied it too. Said 'someone' took his phone. We knew it was him, but Darius . . . Zeke just can't let go of it. I don't know what it is. But she was so *mad* at him for not taking her side. And I get why she can't let it go, but . . . I think Darius is just scared to be Darius. She doesn't have a lot of room for fear. It kind of makes her think people will just skip out or let her down."

"Yeah," Angie said.

"What you said at the skate rink," Jamboree said, "about

me not getting it? You were wrong, Angie. I don't get your hard the way you do, but I have hard too."

Jamboree propped herself on her palm, hair cascading across her arm, the colors catching sprays of light from the building.

"Junior year," said Jamboree. "It just . . . sucked. I'd lie on my bed, staring at my body in the closet mirror. Looking at all of the wrong parts of me. My nose. My chin. My stomach. Nobody wants stretch marks at sixteen."

Angie was well aware of said fact. Immensely.

"I'd lie there just willing something to change," said Jamboree. "Wanting to be some version of those magazine girls we used to collage."

"Now you do," Angie said. "Look like one of them."

Jamboree shook her head, sitting up.

"It's weird, though," Jamboree said. "I still feel like that girl looking in the mirror sometimes. I don't really know what to do with this version. The attention — the looks. I like it . . . sometimes. Maybe. Not really. The way guys look at me. The text messages. The things they say are just . . . I'm like, what? A year ago, I was a chunky, curvy band nerd. Now, I'm . . . what? It's weird. I'm sorry. Excessive overshare."

"It's okay," Angie said.

"Yeah?"

"Yeah," Angie said.

There was that look again. The one from earlier in the RV. Angie's stomach reassembled the crushed configuration of sliders in her stomach, turning them into butterflies.

A muffled pop rang out behind Angie. She turned toward the RV. Zeke stood on top of the roof, waving and pointing an ember-sparking Roman candle into the air. Each ball launching and ripping through the quiet sky. Tails of golden-white light soaring, bursting into a red ball, and diminishing.

Each launch less like a Roman candle and more . . .

Angie gulped. Her mind flooded with news reports. Bombs — tanks on fire. Helicopters. Her sister's capture video.

The Hole.

The Hole expanding and crushing her diaphragm.

"Angie?" Jamboree said.

"Hell, yeah!" Zeke shouted.

The headline:

Body Found

"Angie, what's wrong?" Jamboree asked.

She couldn't — she —

"I can't breathe. I can't . . ."

"Darius! Zeke!" Jamboree shouted.

Angie tried to stand — to move away from —

Bombs. Bullets. KC at Fourth of July — blood, screaming, her sister —

The coffin. The funeral. She came back — in parts — in pieces. So few pieces some even wondered if it was her. Could it be her? There were so few pieces.

Darius popped out of the side of the RV.

"Help!" Jamboree shouted to them.

Zeke sprang off the RV ladder and ran toward Angie and Jamboree.

"I can't . . ." Angie said, hyperventilating.

"Ang," Zeke said, winded. "Dude, breathe."

"It's a panic attack," Darius said, kneeling beside Angie.

"No shit, genius," Zeke snapped.

"Angie," Darius said. "Look at me. It feels real, right? The fear?"

Angie nodded. Her heart racing. She was sweaty — clammy.

Too much . . .

"Okay, but it isn't real," Darius continued. "Whatever it is, it already happened. It already happened and it's over. It's over now. You're right here."

"Breathe, Angie," Jamboree said.

"Just slow it down," Darius said. "Can I hold your hand?"

She nodded.

"We're here, dude," Zeke tried to assure her, though Zeke appeared somewhat distressed and not 100 percent sure what to do.

"I can't — it's . . ." Angie could not say it.

She could not—

"You can," Darius said. "Stay here. Can you feel my hand?"

She nodded again.

Tears bubbling—rolling out of her eyes.

Jamboree put Angie's hand to her heart.

"We're here," Jamboree said.

"Take a slow breath," Darius said. "Just try and believe you can slow it down. You're here."

Her head felt so light. Like it could just float right off her sweaty, large self.

"That's good," Darius continued. "Just one slower . . . breath."

One shaky deep breath led to a second. Little by little, Angie's panic lessened. It did not stop, but it lessened.

Jamboree eased her back down onto the sleeping bag. Propping her head up with her rolled-up hoodie, her hair cascading over her face.

Angie closed her eyes. Until everything inside of her was . . .

Quiet.

Wide Awake

Angie woke up covered by a soft blue blanket. Jamboree was sleeping beside her, holding her hand, Zeke and Darius bundled up nearby. The urn was at Angie's side. It was 6:42 a.m. per her Casio calculator watch. The sun yawned in big gold and blush pink across the sky. The sounds of cars and semi trucks echoed in the very near distance. And the basket — it was still there, in all its grandeur.

She propped herself up on her elbows, taking the time to see all the details. To notice all the things she might have missed somehow. The Hole ached inside of her, a swell of embarrassment rising. Her freak-out had really happened. In front of all of them. Adventure Angie replaced with Fat Angie in a moment's notice of something as ordinary as Roman candles bursting in the air. Was she really this fragile? This . . . broken? Maybe she did belong in Whispering

Oak. Maybe there was something wrong in all the right parts of her she felt were in there, buried beneath the Hole and the guilt and the relief and the anger and the —

"Hey," Jamboree said, groggy.

"Hey," Angie said quietly.

"You okay?"

Angie nodded even though she was far from okay. Jamboree awkwardly let go of Angie's hand.

"I'm sorry," Angie said.

"What for?" Jamboree asked.

"For being me."

Jamboree tucked her arm under her head. Not saying anything for what felt like near forever to Angie.

"I think you gotta give yourself a break," said Jamboree. "Your sister died. I mean, she just didn't die; it was . . . every-where. Your family kind of disintegrated. And all the stuff at school . . . everything. I couldn't do it."

"Do what?"

"Breathe," Jamboree said. "I could barely breathe when we stopped being friends. I can't imagine everything you have to carry around. And that you still try to . . . that you still try. I was so scared that day. At the pep rally. You on the gym floor. Bleeding. I was scared that I . . ."

"But," Angie said, "you didn't want to be friends anymore."

Quiet.

More uncomfortable quiet.

Then the most unexpected thing happened. Jamboree reached for Angie's cheek.

"I wanted to be more than friends," Jamboree said.

What in the upside-down cheesecake had Jamboree just said to Angie? Angie was cycling through instant replay in her mind because surely she must have misheard Jamboree. But Jamboree's very warm and soft hand was still on Angie's cheek. It was there.

"Shit," Zeke muttered.

Jamboree self-consciously slid her hand away from Angie.

"Jam," Zeke said. "You awake?"

"Yeah?" Jamboree answered, her eyes still locked in on Angie's.

"I sprang a leak," Zeke said.

Angie and Jamboree picked through the rack of mostly camouflage T-shirts at a travel center outside Columbus. Zeke was waiting for them to bring a T-shirt to shower area stall #3.

Neither Angie nor Jamboree had said anything about Jamboree's proclamation of unrequited interest in Angie. All of which was incredibly awkward. And confusing. And awkward and more confusing and — the point was clear. It was weird.

Just yesterday Angie had been in the throes of heartache because KC had moved on with Avocado-Green-Hair

Girl. KC and her in an effusive pose online. Today, Angie's stomach was fluttering with gay-girl-gay curiosity about Jamboree. Wasn't she still in heartbroken love with KC? Could she just move on? With Jamboree . . . is that what Jamboree even wanted? She had said "wanted to be more than friends." The word *wanted* in the past tense. What did she want now?

"This one," Jamboree said, proudly holding up her find.

Centered on a camouflage T-shirt was a bright-pink deer, outlined with silver sequins. A very distinctly not Zeke shirt, as her palette was likely not pink.

Angie chuckled. "It doesn't really seem like her . . . maybe?"

"None of these are," Jamboree said, reading some of the shirt slogans. "'And God Made Truckers.' No, wait. 'Family, Friends, Firearms.' And then there's the wolf-howling-at-the-moon series."

Angie held up a screaming neon yellow shirt with NASCAR IS MY FAST CAR sprawled across the chest.

They both grinned. But the grin turned into something more longing and confused, and that awkward silence settled in between them. It was we-both-know-something-we-don't-know-how-to-talk-about awkward. A soundtrack of pop-country music and spattering, low-end latte machines played in the background.

"I'll just get this one," Jamboree said, heading to the register.

"Jamboree," Angie said.

"Yeah."

And right then, Angie froze. Ice-coating-her-voice-box frozen. All those questions that ached for answers had literally sprinted out of her mind, leaving crumbs of disjointed words in Angie's mind.

In an absolute panic, Angie grabbed a shirt off the rack and held it up.

Someone
in
Ohio
Loves Me

A white outline of the State of Ohio adorned with a cutesy red heart in the center of the state finished off an otherwise unnecessary clothing item for anyone over the age of one. Especially in camouflage.

"Oooo," Jamboree said, walking back toward the rack. "Even better."

"Yeah?"

"Definitely," said Jamboree. "The purpose is to make her squirm."

Angie gulped.

"Oh, well, yeah . . . then it's perfect," Angie said.

That something more squeezed between them again.

Awkward silence.

Really freaking awkward silence.

Angie was screaming in her mind. *Say something! Say anything! Fight the very real fear of being rejected. Just say . . .*

"Thanks," Jamboree said, taking the shirt and walking to the register.

The tally for the morning was:

Fat Angie = 0

Fear = 1

Angie continued to pick through the T-shirt rack, realizing that her current shirt's aroma had traversed the landscape from questionable to straight-up foul. But everything on the rack topped off at XL. Well, almost everything.

There in faded red, with a softer-than-expected fabric, was:

I Wish You Were Pizza

She sighed. It would have to do.

Angie walked to the cash register, picking up a package of vanilla Zingers and a stick of beef jerky. The clerk, Wendi-with-an-I, was nowhere near as chatty as The Ethan had been. She was too distracted by the urn.

"It's empty," Angie said to Wendi-with-an-I.

"Then why do you have it?" she asked Angie.

Angie considered the question for approximately 3.2 seconds.

"Why not?" Angie said.

Angie dug seven dollars and forty-two cents out of her Velcro wallet. A remarkably good deal for a T-shirt plus two additional items, in Angie's estimation. Especially given the softness of the shirt.

The women's restroom at the travel center was a far cry from her experience the night before. The litter-free floors and smell of disinfectant cleansers were a welcome change for a girl who rarely liked change. A woman in mom jeans hoisted her toddler son onto the sink counter, giving the urn and then Angie a polite-not-polite look. Angie continued past her and into a middle stall. She set the urn on the ledge behind the toilet. Digging wet wipes, a borrow from Zeke, out of her backpack, she cleaned behind her neck and the backs of her ears. A quick sniff test of her underarms was all it took for her to grab extra wipes and scrub.

When she came out of the restroom, Zeke was filming shriveled hot dogs rotating on a roller grill.

"Hey," Angie said to Zeke.

Zeke glanced at Angie before doing a double take at Angie's shirt.

"Damn, girl," Zeke said, turning the camera on Angie. "I thought my shirt sucked."

"Don't rub it in," Angie said. "Where's everybody?"

"In the RV," Zeke said, turning the camera off. "I said I'd wait for you. So, like, are you cool?"

"The bathroom was very clean," Angie said.

"I'm not talking about the bathroom, Ang."

"Oh, right," Angie said. "Yeah, I'm . . . cool-ish. Maybe."

"You know," Zeke said, walking toward the travel center

doors, "shit happens. In my case, literally on my favorite shirt and jacket."

Angie grinned as they stepped outside.

"Like, really not that long ago, something like that would've wrecked me for days," Zeke said. "But shit happens. When in doubt, remember mi abuela. Girls who have a story don't ever have to apologize for living it. You just gotta learn from it. Get through. ¿Bueno?"

That was not exactly how Angie remembered the story, but she was going to go with it. Perhaps the narrative shifted depending on circumstance.

"Zeke, you're pretty cool when you're not angry," Angie said, hoping that would not make Zeke angry.

Instead, it simply made her deflect, a term Angie had become keen on through her therapeutic process.

Deflect (v): A tactic by which a person avoids a subject by switching to a different subject. Often to avoid facing stuff that is, well, hard.

"I can't believe I'm wearing this shirt," said Zeke.

"Same," Angie said.

They stepped through the side door of the RV. Darius and Jamboree each midslice of pizza.

"Nice shirt," Darius said to Zeke.

"Don't. Say. Another. Word," Zeke warned, pulling a hoodie out of a cabinet.

"Camo is edgy," Jamboree said.

"Can't hear you," said Zeke.

Jamboree grinned as she slid into the bench seat. She pressed her finger near a green M&M on the map. "So, we've been looking at the map," Jamboree said. "Since Angie doesn't have to be at rehearsal until six o'clock, we have plenty of time to go dance."

Angie cringed inside.

"And maybe stop at a thrift store and get her something to wear," Jamboree said.

"Wear?" Angie said. The panic of shopping for her larger-than-average size with Jamboree was mortifying.

"I don't really need anything," Angie said.

"This is your moment, dude," said Zeke, biting into a slice of pizza. "Jam's right. You want to look the part. Don't worry. I got you on this."

Angie most certainly did not want Zeke or Jamboree to "get her" on the buying of clothes.

"I'll find a thrift store on the route," Darius said, scrolling his phone.

"Like you've ever been in one," Zeke said. "I'll find it."

"Okay, someone find it," Jamboree said, wiping pizza sauce out of the corner of her mouth. "So, I'm thinking if we . . ."

Angie zeroed in on Jamboree's mouth in a way she never had before, specifically noticing the smoothness of her lips. The ripple of a scar on her lower lip, a battle wound from falling against the sharp edge of Connie's stone coffee table. In wounded-lip solidarity, four-year-old Angie had drawn a similar gash on her own lip in red Crayola marker, even though she'd found the wound incredibly gross at the time.

How had a moment of innocence and disgust become so intriguing to Angie right then?

"So, what do you think?" Jamboree asked Angie.

Angie, of course, had spaced out and heard nothing Jamboree had said.

"Um, sure," Angie said.

Jamboree's smile was contagious. Angie now returned a similar one. A soiree of smiles swam between them and almost canceled out the very loud, all-girl punk music Zeke had started to blare.

"We're on an adventure, right?" Jamboree said.

"Yeah," Angie said.

Jamboree resumed her position behind the wheel, leaving Darius and Angie in the back of the RV. He scooped another slice of pizza out of the box, holding it open toward her.

"Want a piece?" he asked.

She nodded, sitting on the bench across from him, the Ohio map and a few less M&M route markers between them.

Turning over the engine, Jamboree switched the music from punk to pop.

"Destination dance party," Zeke shouted.

Darius shook his head and continued to eat while scrolling on his phone.

"Bellefontaine is—" Darius said, catching a runaway strand of cheese. "Interesting. Lots of history. First concrete street in America. Highest point of elevation in Ohio. Which is funny because it's not really that high."

Angie smiled. Was she really eating pizza and nerding out over history with Darius A. Clark?

He leaned back against the wall of the RV, still scrolling through his phone.

"Thanks," Angie said.

"For what?" he said, still looking down.

"For helping me," she said.

Darius turned his head toward her.

He nodded. "I got my first panic attack when I was six. I thought I was gonna die. Literally die, you know?"

Angie nodded.

"I got lucky; my dad was a therapist," Darius said. "He knew what was up. He . . . he was cool. He was cool about a lot of things back then." Darius shook his head. "It's a bad feeling. Panic. Because sometimes, you just can't explain it."

"Does it still happen?" Angie asked.

He nodded. "Sometimes. Not like before, though. It's more like . . . an uneasy feeling? I just try to remind myself that I've been there before. But I'm here now. That I got through."

Angie wanted to say something. She wanted to do anything besides sit there afraid the Hole — the panic — might not ever go away.

"It's cool," he said, leaning on the table. "This. What you're doing. You're living it, you know?"

"What?"

"Life," Darius said.

Was that what she was doing? Angie nodded.

"Anyway," he said, sliding out of the booth. "I'm gonna crash for a few."

Darius climbed up into the loft, wrapping his arms around an oversized pillow, and shut his eyes.

Pizza for breakfast. A ridiculous motto on her chest. Fiesta on six wheels. It was at the thought of all of this that Angie realized Darius was right. She was living it. And she tried not to let the thought of it scare her the other way.

Just
Dance

"It's, um . . ." Angie said, trying to find the right word to describe McKinley Street, otherwise known as the Shortest Street in America.

"Short?" Zeke said, popping a new battery onto her camera.

"Yeah," Angie said.

"Twenty feet," Darius said, yawning. "Approximately."

Angie stared at the seemingly ordinary street with weathered asphalt, at the stubs of grass clawing through the cracks and crevices of the sidewalk. Other than a lonely set of rusty train tracks on one side of the street and a boarded-up brick building on the other, there was nothing particularly noteworthy about it.

It was simply a street.

A very short street.

The Shortest Street in America. Per the street sign designating it as such.

Angie had no idea what had made McKinley Street so special to her sister. Only that it had been.

Jamboree stepped out of the RV, carrying a small boom box and a couple of cassette tapes, relics of her parents' past adventures.

"Hey," Jamboree said to Angie.

"Hey," Angie said, trying not to act like an awkward person in her I WISH YOU WERE PIZZA T-shirt. Of course, this was an impossibility.

"So, this is it," Jamboree said.

"Yeah," Angie said. "Nothing really special."

"What do you mean?" Jamboree said.

Angie looked left. Then right. Was she missing something?

"It's just like any street in Dryfalls," Angie said.

"Remember what I said," Jamboree said. "Same sky but different."

Angie considered Jamboree's attempt to brighten an otherwise lackluster moment.

"She wanted to come here for a reason," Jamboree said.

"Maybe it wasn't that profound," Angie said.

"Maybe it wasn't," said Jamboree. "Maybe it was just a 'why not?'"

"Ang, can you stand there on the other side of the building?" Zeke said, pointing. "And when I say 'action' walk out and look up at the street sign."

"You want me to look at the yield sign?" Angie asked.

"No, the street sign," Zeke said. "Above it. And don't look at the camera. Cool?"

Angie set the urn on the sidewalk.

"No, no," Zeke said. "Take the urn. It's good for camera."

Angie had no idea what that meant, but she complied. Mostly because she would rather do anything but the thing they were there to do.

Angie walked behind the building, hoping this was not another "visual metaphor" that required smoke bombs for dramatic effect. She waited. A couple of cars crawled by, their drivers' attention on whatever Zeke was doing on the other side.

Be normal. Walk normal. Don't look at the camera, Angie thought.

"Action!" Zeke shouted, startling Angie.

Angie stepped from behind the building, her eyes, as directed, looking up. She had done it. She had achieved normality. She had—

"Cut!" Zeke said. "It doesn't feel right."

Zeke turned to Jamboree. "Does it play right for you?"

"I'm not in this," Jamboree said.

Jamboree slid a cassette into the player, an are-you-ready

look on her face directed at a very not-ready Angie.

Embarrass herself even more than she had at the skate rink?

Dance?

Dance in the very real daylight? In public?

"Jam, you're killing me with the old-school tunes," Zeke said, flashing her cell. "I got my playlist ready, girl."

"It was Darius's idea," Jamboree said.

Darius shrugged at Zeke. "Number six. Rules of the road trip. Plus, it just makes sense. Old school. Angie."

Zeke considered it. In fact, she considered it for precisely 4.7 seconds. Longer than she had considered anything else that Darius had shared up until that point in the road trip.

"You're right," Zeke said.

Confused, Darius said, "Did you just say I was right?"

"It makes sense," Zeke said, sliding her phone into her back pocket.

Darius grinned softly while Zeke decided how she wanted to frame her shot. Angie would definitely make note of that in her therapeutic journal. Without question.

Jamboree pushed the PLAY button on the boom box. The scratchy sound of the audiocassette cuing up hummed.

Angie gulped, setting the urn down on the sidewalk.

This was it. This was the inescapable moment of Dance Party 2.0. And just when all hope felt lost, a distinctly familiar piano intro cascaded in. Angie had anticipated a selection from a '90s greatest hits or something angst/alternative.

Maybe even 1980s pop. What Angie was not anticipating was for the glorious Gloria Gaynor's "I Will Survive" to come crackling out of the speakers.

"Awww, snap," Zeke said, filming. "Perfect song, Jam."

Darius turned up the volume as Jamboree walked toward Angie. What was this eyes-locked-on-Angie-walking-toward-her moment? In front of Darius and Zeke and especially Zeke's camera?

Angie gulped again. This was a different kind of gulp. Much more of the butterflies variety.

"She didn't say you had to dance alone on the Shortest Street in America," Jamboree said, standing in front of Angie.

Was Jamboree serious? Was Angie in a hallucinogenic state as the result of sleep deprivation and the consumption of excessive amounts of pizza for breakfast? Did she suffer from some undiagnosed head trauma post–Gary Klein courtyard fight? Did she care? Because the song Angie and Jamboree had danced wildly to in the back of the RV when they were kids was now playing. And Jamboree . . . she beamed at Angie.

Angie took a deep breath and tried not to absolutely dissolve into a puddle as Jamboree took her hand.

"Why not," Jamboree said.

The beat picked up in the music. Snares, hi-hat cymbal, and all that was the fervor of a timeless disco track. Jamboree's shoulders shifted to the beat.

"It's just like in the RV," Jamboree said, dancing in front of Angie.

Angie's feet robotically short-stepped from side to side, their lift from the ground weighted by the fear rushing through them. Jamboree's infectious smile punctured, ever so slightly, through Angie's stiffness. Jamboree's arms glided above her head, her hips refusing to quit hitting the beat in uninhibited rhythm. She was sexy. She was vivacious. She was dancing in front of Angie.

Doubt squeezed Angie's shoulders, tensing around the back of her neck.

Breathe, she thought. *Don't panic.*

Angie closed her eyes. There was her and the music.

Breathe . . . Only it wasn't Angie's voice. It was her sister's.

Then Angie let herself shake her shoulders. Ever so slightly.

"Go, Ang!" shouted Zeke.

Then Angie shook them a bit more. And without warning, she busted into . . . the robot!

"Get it!" Zeke cheered.

When Angie opened her eyes, she saw that Zeke and Darius had now entered the dance party. Zeke was still filming, and Angie did not even care.

Angie's grin widened as her wrist stiffened and snapped, creating a wave from left to right across her shoulders. Then freezing her body, sharply stepping. Tilting her head up and popping into place. This had been the dance of her child-hood. The only dance she still did, in the privacy of her bed-room, of course. But there she was in front of all of them and the cars driving by, framing her hip-to-torso twitch locks, her arms waving.

She was dancing! Well, sort of.

Angie's nerves had not dissipated, but they were not stopping her.

And there, in the light of day in Bellefontaine, Ohio, on the Shortest Street in America, they all danced together, the urn on the sidewalk beside them.

Brand New

The four of them stood outside a thrift store, staring at the display window, their heads cocked to the side. Except for Zeke, who was, of course, filming. What lay in front of them was a strange, unusual, utterly bizarre barbecue scene. A greasy, paint-chipped hibachi grill with fake apples and oranges sat beside a waterless plastic wading pool. The pool itself was filled with a dump truck, a finless plush shark, and an inflatable cactus ring-toss game. Two mannequins, one male and one female, gripped the handle of a vintage baby stroller, the woman in an ornate wedding gown, the man in cargo shorts and a T-shirt with the logo:

Save Your Marriage
Drink Beer

A large-headed alien submerged in fluid sat upright inside the carriage. A life-size, faded plastic Jack Russell was positioned behind them, the tip of its right ear gnawed off.

"That's just strange," Darius said.

"Do you think the alien ate the dog's ear?" Jamboree asked.

"It was the mom," Zeke said matter-of-factly. "Her eyes are shifty."

"She doesn't have eyes," Darius said.

"Duh," Zeke said, shaking her head.

"Definitely on my list of Things I Wouldn't Buy Used," Angie said, having started the list in her therapeutic journal. "All of this."

"Same," said Jamboree.

Zeke stopped filming and said, "That and a toothbrush."

"And a pillow," Darius said.

"Too obvious," Jamboree said.

"And toothbrush wasn't?" he asked her.

Jamboree shrugged.

"Condom," Zeke said, holding the door open for them.

"You can't buy a used condom," Darius said, walking past her.

"If I could," Zeke said to him, "I wouldn't."

They all looked at the mammoth thrift-store floor. Row after narrow row of hanging clothes jammed together. Bins of purses and backpacks. Racks of stilettos and sneakers. Flip-flops and combat boots. Shelves of books, board games, and bags of repackaged diapers. And vinyl. Boxes and boxes of vinyl filled the length of a long table at the front of the store. It was a cornucopia of unwanted wants. Of discards or damaged goods. Of germs and maybe unwashed garments.

Angie did not like germs.

Angie did not like unwashed garments.

Angie's mind flooded with images. With sounds. With—

"Tweezers, mascara, dentures, tongue scrapers, mattress, bras, gum, plunger, hairbrush, flip-flops, thermometer (baking and human), meat grinder, facial machine, ChapStick, litter box, syringe, retainer," Angie said.

Everyone stared at her blankly.

"Things I wouldn't buy used," Angie said.

"Oh," Zeke said. "Okay, let's shop."

"If it's cool with y'all, I'm just gonna," Darius said, looking up from his phone, "wander."

"Sure," Jamboree said. "Everything okay?"

"Yeah," Darius said.

Only something was clearly not okay, and Angie knew it. She also knew that, whatever it was, she would be the last person Darius would tell.

"Okay," Zeke said, distracted by filming a porcelain pug coffee mug. "Before we get all rebel-girl makeover, let's cover the basics."

There were basics involved in shopping for a performance that maybe ten people would attend? Because while Angie had conquered her dance-in-public phobia, she had not overcome her very real and present fear of shopping with Jamboree and Zeke, each of them well below a 2XL.

"I've got an idea," Jamboree said to Zeke. "If it's okay, maybe Angie and I look for the shirt and maybe some jeans, and you find the shoes and any other rock-star accessories."

Zeke, in very non-Zeke behavior, agreed. No argument. No eye roll. Not even a puff of hostile breath.

"Cool," Zeke said. "We got you on this, Ang."

Zeke wandered off toward the shoes, leaving Angie and Jamboree. A very Fat Angie and a very incredibly:

Short List of Jamboree's Exceptional Attributes (as Imagined by Angie)

Smart

Funny

Nerdy

Sexy

Well-traveled

Polite

Good driver

Adventurous

Gay-girl gay?

Thin

Sure, Jamboree had once sat at the big girls' table, but now she was primed for any table in the cafeteria. Metaphorically speaking, of course. And Angie, well, she still had stretch marks.

"I hope that was okay," Jamboree said. "It was always

weird for me to shop with someone who was a lot thinner."

"Yeah," Angie said.

They perused a few racks of clothes, many of them in order by color versus size, making the task more arduous than expected.

A couple of naked Barbie dolls had been cast among the clutch purses on one of the racks. Jamboree picked one up.

"Remember when Elisa Matthews told us that Barbie was not anatomically correct because she didn't have pubic hair?" Jamboree said.

Angie had purposely displaced this memory. It rushed back to her in a warm wash of red-cheeked embarrassment.

"And we cut off parts of our hair," Jamboree said. "And glued it onto her—"

"My mom was so mad," said Angie. "It was a Collector Edition Barbie or something."

"Didn't you glue hair on Barbie's butt?" Jamboree asked.

Angie cracked up. "It seemed logical."

"We did a lot of weird stuff," Jamboree said. "Fun, but weird."

"Yeah . . ." Angie said. "If you're good at something, just be it, right?"

Jamboree nodded.

Angie flipped through a few more hangers of shirts and paused. It was a beacon in the darkness of shirt shopping, and in her size.

Angie held the shirt up to herself and said, "This."

"Yes," Jamboree said.

Angie punched her arms through the holes of the black mesh football jersey. The phrase GIRL GANG was splayed across her chest in gold felt letters, the normally itchy material guarded by her soft T-shirt.

"Perfect," Jamboree said.

Angie pulled the shirt over her head, fitting it back on the hanger.

"Can I ask you something?" Jamboree said.

Angie nodded.

"Did it hurt?" Jamboree said, looking at Angie's wrist.

"Um . . ." Angie said. "Kind of. I mean, yeah. I didn't want to . . . do it. I just. I didn't want to feel . . . the world without her. It just was too hard."

Jamboree nodded.

"Wang called me," Jamboree said.

Angie's face wrenched, confused.

"Right after we left," said Jamboree. "He said your room was pretty trashed. That, uh, he was afraid . . . he was afraid maybe you were going to do something."

Angie dropped her head, her chin doubling.

Angie disliked that her chin doubled.

Angie disliked that Wang had called Jamboree.

Angie did not know how to feel.

"Hey," Jamboree said.

"Yeah," Angie said.

"I told him that even if you thought about it," Jamboree said, "it wasn't going to happen. Is it?"

Angie considered the question. The answer that kept people from locking up the sharp objects or reaching for 911 was a no-hesitation no. She knew this, and yet for some reason, she was hesitating. Why was she hesitating? She just said she had not wanted to die that day at the pep rally a year earlier. But she had decimated her room. She had looked at her wrists less than twenty-four hours earlier and felt the echo of that want to escape. To —

"Angie?" Jamboree said. "You okay?"

"I did think about it," Angie sheepishly admitted. "I was in my room and everything got so narrow. So thin. Everything but me, and I looked at my wrists. And I . . . I could feel it. Like, that rush that says I can make it all go away. But . . ."

A woman pushed past them.

"But I . . ." Angie continued, "I got so mad. So mad for even thinking about it. So mad at . . . my mom and my dad and my — so I kind of EF5-tornado redesigned my room. It was pretty dumb."

Jamboree nodded.

"Just so you know," Jamboree said, "without sounding like Mrs. Garben's health-class antisuicide PSA, if you kill yourself, you pretty much destroy everyone who ever loved you."

Quiet.

Painful, heart-aching quiet.

Jamboree pulled Angie into a hug. Angie was not good at the art of hugging. Her body tensed. Her arms never knew exactly where to go. But there they were, hugging in the ladies' shirts section, with a guy in a trucker hat squeezing past them.

Jamboree leaned away from Angie, wiping away streaking mascara.

"Sorry," she said.

"No," Angie said. "It's okay. Really."

"Okay, so, jeans," Jamboree said, returning to the rack of clothes.

Angie reached for Jamboree's hand. A bold and forward-momentum kind of move for Angie. So much so that Angie was unsure what exactly to do. Adventure Angie was once again replaced with Fat Angie.

"Um . . ." Angie said. "Maybe we should ask Zeke about the shirt. Just to be sure."

"Yeah," Jamboree said. "Just to be sure."

Jamboree let go of Angie's hand. Angie stood there replaying a dozen appropriate and seemingly meaningful replies that somehow were all but written with invisible ink when she had wanted to say just one of them — to say *any* of them to Jamboree, who had all but bared her mysterious soul to Angie. Well, a sliver of it, anyway.

A Good Idea
at the Time

Steam spewed along the edges of the RV hood as Zeke steered them to the shoulder of the road. Cars whipped by them on the interstate as Jamboree hopped out of the passenger side.

"Pop it," Jamboree said to Zeke.

"I did," Zeke snapped.

There had already been words when the engine had first overheated. When the sound and steam had first erupted.

"Pop it again," Jamboree said.

The reason for said words was that Zeke had been in full-throttle jam-out to her thrift-store audiocassette of Bikini Kill when she had broken Rule #2 of the road-trip: *Don't drive the RV over 54 miles per hour or the engine will something-mechanical-something-bad, so just don't.*

Angie stepped out of the RV with Darius. Jamboree now quietly fumed while feeling for the hood's latch.

"I have to call my mom," Jamboree said.

"And say what?" Darius asked.

The trailing roar of cars bellowed past them, the gaps of quiet quickly filled by more cars. Jamboree looked at Angie. If Jamboree called her mom, Angie's life would be, without question, over. Because Angie's mom would then know she had not only left the house but that she was hundreds of miles away on a very unsanctioned road trip.

"I don't know," said Jamboree, unlatching the hood.

A gust of steam billowed out as she opened it.

"Be careful," Darius said, reaching for the hood.

Angie and Jamboree secured the levers to keep the hood propped open, steam swirling around the engine.

Zeke hopped out of the RV, camera rolling, aimed at the engine.

"What are you doing?" Jamboree asked Zeke.

"I'm documenting," Zeke said.

Jamboree emitted more heat than the engine at that moment. This was clearly not a good time for Zeke to film.

"Jamboree, it's just overheated probably," Zeke said. "That's what D said."

"I said *maybe* it was overheated," Darius corrected.

"I said don't floor it," Jamboree said.

"I'd done it before and nothing happened," Zeke said.

"What?" Jamboree said.

"Ay," Zeke said, turning her camera off. "We have to get places, right? We can't get there driving all slow."

"This isn't about getting anywhere," said Jamboree. "Everything with you just has to be so . . . extreme. The filming, the music, the hatred for the patriarchy. I mean, I get the last one but . . ."

"Look, I'm sorry," Zeke said. "Just get D to google what we gotta do, and we'll be back on the road."

"And what if we can't fix it, huh?" said Jamboree, shaking her head. "We're not going to make the rehearsal now, which means Angie misses her chance."

"It's okay," Angie said.

"No, it's not," said Jamboree. "See, Angie won't tell you it's not okay, but I'm done pretending. Things are not okay, Zeke. You keep me and everyone pushed so far back with all this—"

"I didn't get to disappear out of my life, Jamboree," Zeke said. "Okay? I was here. In Dryfalls. No makeover. Just me. The shit-bag girl with shit-bag parents and a shit-bag life. And I just had to deal, okay?"

"Your way of 'dealing' just blew it for Angie," said Jamboree.

Jamboree walked away from them and ducked inside the RV.

Immediately, Angie was conflicted. In films, this was the point at which she should follow Jamboree. Her life was, however, not a film. Clearly, as she had not magically become cool and all-knowing in the span of less than twenty-four hours. Which happened frequently in teen films. What would Mr. John Hughes do? If he were alive, of course.

Follow or don't follow? Follow or don't . . . Angie followed Jamboree into the RV.

"Hey," Angie said.

Jamboree dug through cabinets.

"My mom usually keeps antifreeze in here," Jamboree said. "If that's what's wrong."

The RV swayed ever so slightly as an eighteen-wheeler rushed past them.

"Zeke has to push it," Jamboree said. "Everything. It's like she has to prove something."

"Maybe she just doesn't want to be the girl with shit pics on the Internet," said Angie. "I mean, that would be hard to get over. Right?"

Jamboree shook her head.

"Yeah, it would," said Jamboree. "And that's part of it. I get it, but it's not just that. It's this other thing she does more and more—like nothing's a big deal. Like stealing those messages off Darius's phone. She was like, 'receipts I got 'em,' and I kept thinking two wrongs don't make a right, right? I think she knows it, but she just can't . . . She just can't."

Angie nodded, leaning against the counter beside Jamboree, the RV swaying from another eighteen-wheeler whipping past them.

"When you showed up at The Backstory with that postcard," said Jamboree, "it just felt like . . . serendipity. After not talking and . . . there you were. You."

Me what? Angie thought, watching a softness swell across Jamboree.

"Anyway," Jamboree said, turning back toward the cabinets.

Jamboree swung open doors and dug around. Angie slid into the bench, staring at the WHY NOT? postcard. Trying to figure out some answer, some solution, but she had no automotive repair skills.

Zeke and Darius climbed into the back of the RV.

"Where's Jam?" Zeke asked.

Angie nodded toward the bathroom as Jamboree emerged with a container of antifreeze.

"So, if it is overheated," Jamboree said, "we can try this. Otherwise, I don't know."

Darius took the bottle from her.

"I'll try it," Darius said, "when it cools off."

"Thanks," Jamboree said to him.

"Look," said Zeke, "I sort of really messed up. I'm sorry. You're my best friend, and I might have been a bit of a selfish jerk."

Jamboree tipped her head to the side. Ear poised higher than usual.

"Was that an apology?" Jamboree said.

"Dude, don't make me sky-write it," Zeke said.

"An admission of error?" Jamboree said.

"You're a jerk," Zeke said.

Jamboree reached over, hooking her arm around Zeke's neck.

"I'd hug you, but I might bust your bag," Jamboree said.

Zeke leaned into a hug anyway. A full-on, this-is-intimate-and-shouldn't-happen-in-front-of-other-people hug because it's stupid awkward. But there it was, happening. And then . . .

"Okay," Zeke said, wiping a renegade tear from her eye. "Enough of this kumbaya stuff. I texted Lash. Told her Angie would be ready. We just need to be there by nine o'clock. So, all is not lost and shit. We just have to rehearse here."

"We don't have any instruments," Angie said.

Darius shrugged. "It's punk. It's an angry kind of music. I think we're good."

Zeke slid into the booth, rifling through her messenger bag.

"I've been working on these lyrics," Zeke said, pulling out her notebook.

She flipped through a few pages before stopping.

"Give it a look," Zeke said. "Tweak what feels . . . not you."

Which is likely everything, Angie thought.

Zeke slid the notebook over to Angie.

A few moments later, Angie began nodding. Tapping her fingers. Mouthing some of the lyrics. She held her hand out for Zeke's pen. Angie began marking up the song. Breaking what had been a continuous poem-like thing into sections.

They flipped the notebook back and forth, Jamboree picking up Zeke's camera and filming the process.

Zeke recopied it one last time. Angie proofed the song. It was . . . perfect. Well, it was definitely punk.

There was only one very specific challenge remaining: Angie could not sing.

"I can't sing," said Angie. "Not even a little. I mean . . . no."

"It's not singing," said Darius. "It's punk."

"Cállate," Zeke said to him. "Punk *is* singing. It's about a middle finger to the establishment. To all the bento-box, prefabricated, suburban-manifested subdivisions — to the machine that oppresses our rights and binds our breasts. It's chaos in musical annotation. It's revolution!"

Angie was startled and oddly excited by this effusive declaration.

"You are a revolution, Angie," said Zeke. "Right?"

"Um . . . I guess?" Angie said.

Darius grinned.

"Okay, let's start easy," said Zeke. "Sing something you like."

Angie thought "Walking on Sunshine" was not the approach to take. Nor was "Hello" by Lionel Richie, nor the flood of songs she knew that lacked the ultimate cool rebellion Zeke hungered for.

"'Ain't No Mountain High Enough'?" said Angie.

"Damn," said Darius. "Your work's cut out for you, prima."

"No, no," said Zeke. "It's okay. It's got soul. Let's hear it. Transform that sound into a breathing, raging middle finger to the fascist establishment."

Pause.

Big dramatic what-did-all-of-those-adjectives-mean-in-regard-to-a-harmony pause.

"Don't hold back," Zeke said. "You are in the Cone of Creative Expression."

Jamboree crawled to the back of the RV, digging through a plastic bag of food, camera still recording.

"Did you just quote Ms. Miller's creative writing class?" Jamboree asked.

"Don't hate the Miller," Zeke said.

Angie began to hum the tune. She kept humming and humming and —

"You gotta say the words," said Zeke.

"Yeah, I just, um . . . I think I hum it better."

Zeke perched on the top of the bench, sneakers on the

edge of the table — a very unsanitary action that was possibly in tune with the punk scene. Angie was not entirely certain.

"Just try," said Zeke.

Angie stood up. Deep breath in . . .

Just be angry, Angie thought.

Her head lowered.

Her chin doubled.

Her mind went dark with all the things she did not like.

What erupted from her sweet, semichapped lips was a demonic, possessed-by-the-soul-of-the-Devil rendition of "Ain't No Mountain High Enough." It was truly vinyl-played-backward-on-a-record-player frightening!

Darius's mouth was agape.

"What?" said Angie. "Wasn't that angry?"

Zeke laughed. "Uhhhhh . . . that was definitely like a failed exorcism."

"That's bad," Angie said.

"It was . . . scary," Zeke said.

Immediately, Angie felt self-conscious.

"I can't do this," she said. "I don't like this. It's all too hard. I can't sing. I can't even do laundry without forgetting to pull Kleenex out of my pockets."

"How about this?" said Darius, leaning forward. "Do you like the song 'Ain't No Mountain High Enough'?"

"Yeah," said Angie. "Of course."

"What do you like about it?" he asked.

Angie closed her eyes to consider his question. The harmony by Marvin Gaye and Tammi Terrell played in the private listening station in her mind. Her head began to nod to the beat, her smile wide. She was . . .

"It's alive," said Angie. "It feels like nothing is impossible."

"Try to sing it the way you like it," Darius said.

"I don't understand," Angie said.

"Sing it the way it makes you feel," said Darius.

Angie took another deep breath in and exhaled. With her eyes shut, she thought about the song again. How it made her feel. But then, she went beyond its textured and bright hopefulness. She felt something longing and lingering between the words. An aching she had never considered. She began to try to sing that feeling instead.

What started as a hesitation in her voice caked in shyness soon burst open wide. Angie channeled a voice no one knew lived beneath her sweaty and plump exterior. Beneath her insecurities and fears, beneath her host of *ums*, was a rich and soulful voice. A voice that was pained and smooth, with a guttural hunger along the edge of notes. It was "Ain't No Mountain High Enough" unplugged, raw, and Angiefied.

When her eyes opened, Darius's grin startled her. Zeke's mouth was now agape. Seriously, a fly could have flown in there. Twice.

"Damn, Ang," said Zeke.

Jamboree beamed at Angie.

"Um . . . I've never done that," Angie said. "I mean, in the shower, but everyone kind of sounds like bad Adele in the shower, right?"

"I don't," Darius said.

"Angie," said Zeke. "Forget what I said about exorcisms. You sing you. I mean, you sing like you, but just add some — wait."

Zeke reached for her phone, scrolled through playlists, stopping on *You Punk My Chi*.

"Listen to this," Zeke said to Angie.

So began the crash course of punk music on the shoulder of I-75 South. The RV walls vibrating with the beautiful-gritty rebel-girl playlist of Bikini Kill, Destruye Y Huye, Sleater-Kinney, Siouxsie and the Banshees, and of course, Ms. Joan Jett.

Darius and Jamboree watched Zeke and Angie rehearse the song they had written, all while hoping for the engine to cool off fast and for Angie to continue to heat up.

Some Nights

Cincinnati, Ohio, was not Dryfalls. Interstates intersecting with interstates intersecting with more interstates. Cars sometimes swerving in and out of lanes. Headlights and fast-flow traffic. It was more than a Starbucks town. It was an almost-everything town. Stores, stadiums, and . . . lights. It had a pulse and an energy.

As the RV tore through a tunnel, Jamboree's attention was solely on one thing: the time. It was 8:40 p.m., and the band went on at nine o'clock.

A wrong exit only added to the tension as Darius took lead as navigator. He was a native Cincinnatian, after all. He crawled into the copilot passenger seat. Soon, they were in the heart and the rhythm, among the skyscrapers of downtown Cincinnati.

"Princess Diana's crown," Darius said, pointing up. "That's what they modeled the top of the building after."

Angie leaned over the console, catching a glimpse of the arching glass. Shimmering and shining in the darkness, downtown passed for parts of New York City. At least, the version Angie had seen in movies. It was everything brick and graffiti and . . . big.

She liked it.

She liked it very much.

But when the RV cruised up traffic-packed Vine Street toward the infamous Fountain Square, Angie's jaw dropped. Seriously, it dropped wide open. The intimate gathering Zeke had described was anything but intimate as hundreds and hundreds of people crowded the square. It was a shoulder-to-shoulder event.

"You said there would be ten people, maybe," Angie said, turning to Zeke sitting in the bench, phone pressed to her ear.

"They'll all be drunk by your set," Zeke said. "Don't worry about it."

"You are relying on every single person, out of hundreds, to be intoxicated and somehow miss the fat girl singing on a very real stage."

"Look, you wanted to sing with a band," Zeke said. "This is the gig."

Jamboree cut the wheel down a one-way street and turned into a paid parking lot.

"Just do what we practiced," Zeke said, slinging her messenger bag over her shoulder. "I texted them the lyrics. They've got something they can put under them."

"Zeke," Angie said. "There are hundreds of people."

"Over a thousand," Zeke said, gathering her camera and extra batteries. "Look, they're about to go on. I gotta go check in with Lash."

Angie was prone to panic. This was not a headline in the world of news. But this—not only did she have to sing, but in front of so many people.

"I'm gonna step out," Darius said. "Pay for the parking."

"Oh, wait," Angie said, reaching for money.

"It's good," Darius said. "I got it."

"Thanks."

Jamboree climbed over the console and into the back of the RV.

"We'll be there in a second," Jamboree said to Darius.

"It's cool," he said. "Take your time."

Angie was clammy and sweaty and not ready for any part of this. Dancing with Jamboree plus two or even roller-skating—those were seemingly achievable, but standing in front of hundreds of people? Angie's mind spun in constant rotation: What would Ms. Joan Jett do?

Surely she would go out there, regardless, and be fearless. She was, after all, Ms. Joan Jett. One of the founding queens of rock 'n' roll and punk. And in her absolute bad-assery, Ms. Joan Jett had played for the United States Armed

Forces abroad on more than one occasion. Not even the threat of the tyranny of terrorism would keep Ms. Joan Jett from the stage.

Angie, however, was not Ms. Joan Jett. At that moment, everything in Angie said *go home.*

Her chin lowered.

Her chin doubled.

This was not an attractive moment for her. Even her truly awesome thrift-store shirt and maroon Doc Martens, trimmed with costume jewelry and an ode-to-Wonder-Woman leather cuff could not hide what was always underneath: Fat Angie.

"Hey," Jamboree said. "You thinking freak-out or paradoxical?"

Angie could not look at her, the panicked defeat all too real.

Jamboree sat beside her on the bench, the two swaddled in the muffled music pummeling the walls of the RV from outside.

"She could have done this without a second thought," said Angie. "Everything came so easy for her."

Jamboree picked the postcard up from the table.

"Look, I don't care if you do this," Jamboree said. "We can grab some food, sit by the river and whatever. But the thing is, this isn't about *her* anymore. It's about you, Angie. You know, you can live your life in the shadow of a dead girl, or you can run screaming out of it. And let them all know you're here. You. For you. Not me or Zeke or that postcard. Just for you."

"Can you do that?" Angie asked. "Be you?"

"Maybe," Jamboree said. "I think."

Jamboree slid her hand into Angie's.

Was this the moment? The moment that Angie's broken heart for KC would be mended by a gay-bi-gay-girl kiss between her and Jamboree? It seemed an urge worth exploring. A question worth answering.

Angie leaned closer. Jamboree's head tilted and —

Zeke swung the RV door open. The two girls leaned away from each other as Darius stepped in behind Zeke.

"Hey," Zeke said. "We doing this?"

Had the kiss-almost-kiss really just happened again? Had that feeling of butterflies been a moment shared by both? Is this what Angie wanted? To kiss the cute and faintly scarred lip of Jamboree Memphis Jordan?

"Ang?" Zeke asked.

"Yeah," Angie said.

Jamboree slid out of the booth. Angie followed her, grabbing the urn and her backpack on the way out. A wall of humidity and heat slammed into her outside the RV.

"It's just around the corner," Zeke said.

They waited to cross the street. Cars cruised by, music pouring out their windows.

"I talked to Lash," said Zeke. "She said you're going up last, so don't stress."

Angie gave her the but-I-am-clearly-stressed look after fishing a creased birthday hat out of her backpack and slipping it on her head.

The crosswalk light signaled WALK.

"I don't want to criticize another woman's entry into the revolution but . . ." Zeke said, walking beside Angie. "But maybe lose the hat."

"It contains me," Angie said.

Jamboree laughed.

"Okay," Zeke said.

They rounded the corner and climbed the steps to Fountain Square.

"Dude, check it out," Zeke said, pointing her camera at a megascreen on the Macy's building across the street.

The concert stage live-streamed on the screen. Which meant . . . Angie would be on that screen. She gulped.

Jamboree leaned into Angie, "It's just a big TV."

"It's a really, really big TV," Angie said.

They wove through the crowd, inching closer to the stage. The air smelled like skunks and lit tobacco. Surely, there were no skunks in thriving downtown Cincinnati. Though Angie recognized the smell from Wang. It was definitely not skunks.

Zeke flashed a badge to security when they arrived. A very Agent-Scully-from-*The X-Files* coolness. As they walked around the metal barriers, Angie saw one thing. A very real, badass female-fueled band up close. This was happening. This was —

"Tampon Nation!" shouted the singer.

Guitars raged with the drums blasting through the speakers. Angie jammed her fingers into her ears.

"Who is that?" Angie asked, pointing to the singer.

"She's the physical manifestation of clickbait," shouted Zeke. "Her name is Lola, but she hates it when people call her that. She calls herself V."

Angie made a V in the air with her fingers.

"Yeah, it's super fucking pretentious, but she's Prince on guitar and Nicks on lyrics, so the band puts up with her. But she'll be cool with you. Don't be intimidated."

Angie was, without question, intimidated. For one, the band was a real band on a real stage playing real music that they likely practiced together. Two, the drummer was in a giant cat head and a sleeveless tuxedo. Three, the bassist, Lash, had a faux hawk, a multitier in shades of red and blue and yellow. Four, and most notably, Lola-Not-Lola was the complete, undeniable rock-star/punk-rebel package. Lead singer for Beware the Cat Scratch, per the screaming cat stenciled in the center of their drum set, she was a young, Latina Ms. Joan Jett, seasoned with her own edge. She stomped the stage in her combat boots, the neon green laces seeming to slither through the eyeholes. Her skinny jeans and thread of a T-shirt only amplified her stripped-down presence. Angie watched in awe as Lola-Not-Lola owned the stage. Without question, she knew who and what she was: a woman with a very loud guitar and a stellar voice.

Period.

They all waited for thirty-three punk music minutes during a set list that included songs titles such as:

"Patriarchy Nightmare"

"Snapchat My Heart"

"PM My Rage"

"I-270 Escape"

"Bashful Kitten"

"I Menstruate"

"Casualty of Gender Wars"

"Please, Please Hashtag My Cat"

"I Ate Your Map and Liked It!"

"Tic Toc"

Unexpectedly, Lola-Not-Lola unplugged her guitar from the amp and fell backward into the crowd. She was literally surfing, screaming would-be lyrics — inaudible, as she had no microphone. The band continued to play until the crowd delivered her back to the stage.

Angie could not do such an action.

She feared the expectation.

Moments later, the band closed out their last song, Lola-Not-Lola flinging her sweaty hair toward the crowd. A very unhygienic move.

"We've got a special treat for you Cin-ci-nasty!"

Lola-Not-Lola said into the microphone, her eyes on Zeke offstage.

Zeke turned her attention back to Angie. Jamboree and Darius pushed in, forming a huddle around her.

"Remember, it's just like we practiced, Ang," Zeke said. "Down with the establishment. Up with the woman."

"You got this," Jamboree said.

Angie's glance ticked toward Darius.

"Oh," he said. "It's all you."

"Making her debut from . . ." Lola-Not-Lola continued.

Angie took a deep breath. A very, very, very, very, very, very deep breath. That was a six-very deep breath, which almost put her into hyperventilation.

"Just breathe," said Jamboree.

Angie handed the urn and her backpack to Darius.

"You got this, Ang," said Zeke, camcorder already recording.

Lola-Not-Lola announced to the crowd, "Angie!" and stepped back from the microphone.

The crowd cheered, perhaps expecting someone more grand than the awkward teenager adorned by a creased birthday hat. Angie ascended the three wobbly steps to the stage. The lights made her squint. She tripped and was caught by the bassist.

"You cool?" said Lash.

Angie nodded.

Angie most definitely was not cool.

Angie was simply good at nodding.

Lola-Not-Lola motioned for Angie to continue to the microphone, the crowd a mix of chatter and curiosity. The Hole definitely expanded inside of her.

"Um . . ." she said into the microphone.

Her voice echoed.

No ums, no ums, no ums, Angie thought.

"Go, Angie!" shouted Jamboree.

Darius cheered, "Go, Angie."

Zeke threw her fist in the air.

"Revolution!" Zeke shouted.

Angie's eyes glazed over at the crowd looking at her. Her hand shook the microphone when she gripped it.

For a moment, it all became a flash of thoughts. A run-on sentence in her mind.

Lights, people watching, police sirens squealing down the street, her sister . . .

Stay here, Angie thought. *Don't go . . . there.*

Pause.

Deep, shaky-breath pause.

"One, two, three!" Lola-Not-Lola shouted.

The drummer clicked their sticks three times. The song's intro rolled out. Angie was late to her entry. Confused, the band stopped.

"C'mon," she heard moaned from within the crowd.

There was talking; some people peeled away from the stage. Zeke had the camera still rolling.

Lola-Not-Lola pulled the microphone stand from Angie. Angie's grip reflexively tightened.

"Get off the stage, fat ass," some guy shouted from the back.

Lola-Not-Lola leaned into the microphone. "Hey, body shamer. Fuck you!"

"Get her off the stage," he answered back.

"Cut it out," Lash said to Lola-Not-Lola. "This is six hundred bucks."

Angie's breathing became labored.

The Hole was expanding.

There was nothing to eat.

Nothing to consume.

Nothing to . . .

She . . .

SCREAMED!!!!!!!!

into the microphone, and held that primal fat-girl pain-shame scream in full shaking piercing-the-eardrum throttle for approximately four seconds. When she stopped, the crowd was truly quiet. Until some girls close to the stage laughed.

Angie's eyes fell to Jamboree. To Zeke, of course, still filming. To Darius, who grinned at her.

"Wow. That felt good," Angie said, pulling the microphone toward her. "Um . . . one, two, three?"

Feedback. Distortion of instruments, three drumstick clicks, then—it got LOUD! Louder than before. Angie pushed her sweaty hair off the front of her face, bobbing her head to the drum beat.

Lola-Not-Lola flew up and down on the exercise trampoline, managing to play guitar while kicking her feet in midair. The stage floor shook beneath them, clearly not assembled to entertainment equipment guidelines, but nonetheless it managed to bear all of their weight. The lights pulsed onto the stage, skittering through the crowd.

Angie leaned into the microphone. Too close, in fact, as her first few lyrics were muffled. The bassist motioned for her to move back. And when she did, she opened up her mouth and channeled the feminine revolution that was all her knowing of *Wonder Woman*, of Willow and Tara from *Buffy the Vampire Slayer*, and every episode of any music-based reality television competition she might have stumbled upon.

She sang!

"You screw with my head.
You screw with my heart.
You say the world is round
when I'm falling off . . . yeah!"

In front of hundreds of faces, Angie was doing something unthinkable. She was singing!

"Hey!
Sweet sixteen neighborhood scream queen.
My horror movie's where you shame me.
But uh-oh.
Oh, no!
I'm not scared anymore.
I'm not scared . . . anymore!"

Angie screamed into the microphone. And from that second scream, something unexpected happened in Angie. She changed the bridge of the song she and Zeke had written. She sang:

"Fat Girl!
Fat World!
Rebel Girl Revolution!
Fat Girl!
Fat World!
I'm the Amazon evolution!"

Lola-Not-Lola jumped off the trampoline and broke into a brief guitar solo before cuing Angie to continue. Angie grinned at Jamboree before tightening her grip on the microphone.

"Road warrior.
Down under girl explorer.

I'm taking over your civilization.
So make plans for the Fat Girl invasion."

Jamboree screamed, jumping up and down. Even Darius was jumping in place.

"You say I'm sick
to think this way.
Wanna cure my enormous vibration
with your transcranial magnetic stimulation.
Back off now because this glory ride
is a celebrated plus size!

Fat Girl!
Fat World!
Rebel Girl Revolution!
Fat Girl!
Fat World!
I'm not your sweet sugar imitation!"

Angie whipped the microphone off the stand. The cable tangled, diminishing her rock-girl cool for a moment. She sauntered alongside the bassist, unapologetic for the gyrating of her hips. The movement that did not quit. Angie was on FIRE!

"Oh . . . oh . . . Oooooo . . ."

She turned and played to the crowd.

"Hey . . .
Bet you think you're in charge.
Hey . . .
Bet you think you've got me right where you want me.
Right . . . yeah, right.

Fat Girl!
Fat World!
Rebel Girl Revolution!
Fat Girl!
Fat World!
I'm the new institution!

Ohhhhhhh!"

What was that note? What was that sound that did not, as the phrasing would go, suck? What was this voice and body doing?

"Fat Girl!
Fat World!
Rebel Girl Revolution!
Fat Girl!
Fat World!
I'm the new institution!"

Big percussive ending.

Lola-Not-Lola threw her arm over Angie's shoulders and leaned into the microphone. "Angie, everyone!"

People clapped and cheered. Not like in that *Encore! Encore!* clap-cheer the way they did in movies, but still, clapping and cheering.

"You got something to say," said Lola-Not-Lola. "Keep saying it, girl."

"Thanks," Angie said. "Um, V."

"You can call me Lola," she said. "I just do that to mess with Zeke."

Camera still rolling, Zeke went into full interview mode as Angie came down the stage stairs, "You changed the lyrics. That was awesome. How does it feel?"

"F-ing AMAZING!" Angie said.

Zeke and Darius were there but . . . where was Jamboree?

Zeke tipped her head to her right. Jamboree was talking on her phone, looking through the crowd. A guy rushed up behind her and spun her around and pulled her into a kiss.

Angie's heart sank.

Logically, it should not have sunk. They were, as previously stated, not a thing, an item, a couple. They were just friends. Friends who had almost-kissed-not-kissed in the RV. If this were a well-written movie, this would have been the moment where, after Angie was hoisted into the air, she and Jamboree would kiss. Their image freeze-framed on the screen, suspending the viewer in an eternal, joyful bliss with the credits running.

But Fat Angie's life was not that kind of life. There were no credits. No girl to kiss, because someone else was already kissing her.

"Is that . . . ?" Angie said.

"The Troy," Zeke said, turning off her camcorder. "The tractor beam for social acceptance is too powerful for her."

The trio watched Jamboree and Troy as Angie's concert high increasingly deflated.

Rule #9: Troy Wilson is a dick.

As dictated by the rules of the road trip, Troy seemed nothing like Angie's idea of a "dick." Not that she was entirely sure what she had imagined. Troy was stupid handsome. Stupid fit. Stupid fashionable in that not-trying-but-trying way. He was a teen magazine pullout poster in full three-dimensional space. Complete with purposely torn knees in fitted dark jeans. Hiking books that were never taken hiking. He was polished, rustic perfection. Unlike The Ethan from the creepy-ish gas station, Troy would make a great candidate in Mr. Charles Darwin's theory of survival of the fittest.

Troy placed his hands on Jamboree's face and said, "I missed you."

At least, it looked like "I missed you." It could have been *I heart you* or *I love you* or *I swallow you* or *I infect you* — but it read as *I missed you*. At least to Angie. And all it took was three apologetic words for the Jamboree Jury to settle on a verdict of not guilty by reason of missing. Even though he had cheated on her. Twice! Whatever weird energy she and Angie had was overwritten by "I miss you" and everything handsome, boy-band, and brooding that was Troy.

Their second kiss was stupid long and stupid sexy and could win an award if it were judged by a proper committee. Without question.

"Who wants to throw up?" Zeke asked.

They all raised their hands simultaneously.

Clearly concerned for Angie's plump but fragile heart, Zeke put her arm around her shoulders. "You cool?"

"Yeah, why?" Angie said.

"Because you look like the Cucuy stole your puppy."

"This is a cultural reference, isn't it?" Angie said.

"Don't get pulled in," Zeke said. "She doesn't mean it, but she's professionally indecisive."

"I'm not pulled . . . in-ish," Angie said.

Zeke nodded. "So, you weren't about to kiss when I opened the RV door?"

Darius threw a look to Angie. Angie quickly shook her head.

Jamboree broke away from Troy long enough to wave them over.

Zeke dropped her head back. "Don't make me."

Darius pushed her forward.

"Hey, man, what's up?" Troy said to Darius, attempting

some version of a handshake with a series of steps that made him look ridiculous.

"Troy, what a surprise," Zeke said. "Why are you fucking here?"

Darius nudged her.

"What?" Zeke said.

"My family is here for the weekend," said Troy. "I came with my cousin and her boyfriend to see the show."

He slid his arm around Jamboree.

Cringe.

More cringing.

"I saw Jamboree on the megatron, so . . . yeah," Troy said, grinning. "Oh, and hey. Good song. It was kind of like . . . I don't know, but it was . . . yeah."

Jamboree now cringed.

Angie looked at Jamboree. Angie's heart breaking-not-breaking but definitely, quite possibly breaking. It was a confusing moment for her.

"Listen, my cousin's friend is having this massive rave outside of town," Troy said. "Big-ass barn. DJ. Kegs. You guys interested?"

"We have things —" Jamboree said.

"You should go," Angie said to Jamboree.

The look between Angie and Jamboree was exploited by three of the longest seconds ever.

"Troy, can you just give us a second?" Jamboree said, pulling Angie away from the group.

As soon as they were out of immediate earshot, Jamboree said, "What are you doing?"

Angie's heart truly hurt. In that what-am-I-doing-but-I'm-doing-it-anyway hurt.

"You want to be with him, so you should be with him," Angie said.

"I don't know what I want," said Jamboree. "Can I just not know what I want?"

"I don't know," Angie said. "I mean, I don't think so."

Jamboree seemed to rush through a mental landscape of confusion and overwhelm.

"Look, about the RV moment thing earlier," Angie said. "Whatever that was or wasn't. Clearly, you're into him, or the idea of him or something. I don't . . ."

Jamboree dipped her head over her shoulder. Troy grinned. It was boyish and handsome, and there was nothing stuck in his teeth, which would have at least made him moderately human.

"You did really good up there," Jamboree said to Angie.

"Yeah."

Jamboree reached for Angie's hand, then stopped herself. What was this start-stop interest?

"Look, I'm just going to talk to him," Jamboree said.

"Yeah . . ." Angie said.

Don't show you're wounded. Don't show you're confused about being wounded, Angie thought.

She, of course, did not have what many refer to as a "poker face."

"Hey," Jamboree said. "We still have one stop left. Right?"

Angie had almost forgotten. The empty blank on the postcard. Angie's choice. As far as she was concerned, it could be the nearest clean restroom where she could hide and pretend everything did not feel upside down inside of her.

"Yeah," said Angie.

Angie watched Jamboree meet up with the Troy, the two of them disappearing into the crowd of lingering concert-goers. And Angie waited. Waited for the world to swallow her whole. She just could not decide entirely why anymore.

Grenade

Troy and Jamboree sat at a table in Fountain Square. A table approximately seventy-five feet from Angie and Zeke. In Angie's estimation. Of course, Angie was not good at the art of numbers, according to her couldn't-understand mother.

Is that actually true, though? Angie wrote in her therapeutic journal. *Am I really deficient at the art of numbers? I think about them all the time.*

$$y = x$$
$$\text{or}$$
$$y = 2x$$

I like coefficients. A coefficient never changes. My mom is not a coefficient. Jamboree is not a coefficient. They are constantly changing. Maybe I don't like the art of numbers because they are incongruent with the reality of people. People are not math. Are they?

Many of the concertgoers had dissipated from Fountain Square into the bars or nearby restaurants. The stage stood quietly in its metal-frame glory. Angie had done it. She had reached an unexpected height. She had sung and danced, and people had clapped. Why did she feel so melancholy? Was she so easily swayed by the possible rejection-not-real-rejection of Jamboree?

"Ang," said Zeke, playing back footage on her camcorder. "You cool?"

Angie dipped her head toward Jamboree. Trying not to be obvious, which was, well, obvious.

"Sadness has no coefficient," Angie said.

"Hey," Darius said, carrying a stack of plastic to-go containers. "Hope you're hungry."

Angie moved the urn off the table to make room for the Cincinnati signature three-way, a rather taboo description for pasta with chili and cheese on top.

"Dude, you'll have to run that by D," said Zeke to Angie. "I flunked algebra. Twice. Yo no hablo matemáticas."

"Run what?" Darius asked, pulling a chair up from another table.

"Nothing," Angie said, closing her journal.

Darius popped the clear top off, steam swirling. The sweet smell swam wildly through the air.

"That brings me home," said Darius. "Me and my dad, sitting on the square. Eating Skyline, throwing pieces of bread to the pigeons and watching the world walk by."

Zeke twirled the pasta with her plastic fork, melted cheese trailing as she lifted it. A visual that normally would have made Angie salivate. Oddly enough, she was not hungry. This perplexed her, as she had not eaten in over four hours. By all accounts, she should have been quite hungry. Immensely.

"I'm not gonna lie," said Zeke. "Always loved it when we'd come visit, D. This shit is dope."

"Nobody says dope," Darius said, grabbing a napkin.

"Vato, don't be reconstructing my verbiage," Zeke said. "It's dope. Take something, Ang. We got plenty."

"I'm not really . . . hungry."

"You okay?" Darius said. "I mean, if you want . . . there's burgers just behind us."

"No, it's . . . it's just—" Angie said.

"The Troy," Zeke said.

Angie turned her head toward Jamboree's table again. "She looks into him."

"She looks trapped," said Zeke. "Too scared to be who she is. Like, her mom's cool. She'll roll with it. Not like my mom . . . my dad."

Angie watched the Troy's smile. The way he gestured with his hands. It was all music. Like a love poem.

"He's . . ." Angie said, still looking at him. "Perfect."

"Girl, don't be seduced," said Zeke. "You open up that book, and it's full of heartbreak and betrayal. I'd shelve that shit before I got to page two."

"Did you make a wish?" Darius asked Angie, nodding to the fountain behind them.

"No," she said.

He wiped his hands and scooted back from the table.

"C'mon," he said. "You can't come to Cincinnati and not make a wish on the square."

Angie heaved a heavy sigh and followed Darius.

"The Genius of Water," Darius said, as they walked toward the fountain. "Forty-three feet tall. She is the symbol of strength and gratitude. She ain't messing around."

Angie smiled. So did Darius.

"That's what my mom says," Darius said.

They stood there, sprays of water lightly dusted their cheeks, forearms.

"You really loved it here, didn't you?" Angie asked.

Darius nodded. "It's my home. It's where . . . I fit."

"That must be nice," Angie said.

Darius looked at her.

"To fit somewhere," she said.

"You fit up there tonight," he said. "On that stage."

"I don't know. I guess. I just . . ." Angie shrugged.

Darius looked back at the water fountain, reached into his pocket, and fished out a couple of coins.

"You want a penny wish, nickel, or quarter?" he asked.

"Does it matter?"

"Yeah," he said, matter-of-fact. "A penny means it's the most special, most important wish of the year. A nickel means you'll settle for five pretty good wishes. And a quarter — it's the wild card."

Angie smiled, a wisp of disbelief on her face.

"I'm serious," Darius said. "The quarter means you get your wish. It just might not be what you expect. Those are the rules."

Angie's hand hovered over Darius's palm. Penny, nickel, quarter.

"What's a dime?" said Angie.

"Irrelevant because I don't have one," Darius said, grinning.

Angie smiled. Smiled with Darius A. Clark. Who was not a clear and obvious turncoat anymore. Who was, in some strange way, a lot like her. Well, kind of.

Angie picked the quarter.

"A gambling woman," Darius said. "My mother would appreciate that. She always picks the quarter."

They both admired the fountain. Then, on the count of three, eyes closed, they tossed their coins. Wishes made.

"I'm glad there wasn't a bus for you to go back to Dryfalls," Angie said.

"Yeah," said Darius. "Me too."

They stood there watching as water from the Genius's palms flowed down while plumes of water spouted up from the bottom. A panel of rainbow lights behind the fountain reflected blues and reds and yellows onto Darius's face.

"Can I ask you a question?" Angie said.

He shrugged. "Yeah."

"Are you really going to join?" Angie asked. "The military?"

He bit his lower lip, shifting nervously with his foot along the cement.

"I think so," Darius said.

"Why?" Angie said. "You could probably go to any school."

"So could your sister," Darius said.

"She was running from something."

"I think I might be running to something," Darius said. "It's hard to explain. I guess. Choices, you know?"

Angie looked at all the coins in the fountain. All the wishes made with eyes open. With eyes closed. Wanting—

"The cheese is congealing," Zeke called out. "Come on."

"Thanks for the wish," Angie said to Darius.

Darius nodded.

As they headed back to the table, Angie noticed Jamboree with her phone pressed to her ear, straining to hear. Her back to Troy. Jamboree turned toward Angie.

Something was wrong.

Jamboree leaned into Troy, then jogged to Angie's table.

"It's your brother," Jamboree said to Angie.

"What's wrong?" Angie asked her.

"He said he needed to talk to you," Jamboree said, holding the phone out to Angie.

Zeke and Darius waited to see if Angie would take it.

Angie reluctantly took the phone, pausing before putting it against her ear. Fearing something had happened to Jake — to KC. Sensing that whatever he had to say, it was most likely not good.

"Hey," Angie said to Wang.

There was a silence. A distracted silence with the sound of yelling. Then Wang said three significant and terrifying words: "Mom's home early."

Angie's face went incredibly long. Uncertain if the color had left her, it most certainly felt as though it had. Everyone watched Angie as she froze hard in place. Three words had literally activated the Hole inside of her. The Hole that had all but nearly dissipated. Or so she had thought.

Her couldn't-understand mother had come home early. Angie's mind flooded with possible excuses — some way to prevent her mother from losing her absolute mind. But then Wang said, "She wants her fucking urn."

And all that panic — all that had been scared and shaking — shifted inside of Angie. She turned toward the urn sitting on top of the table. Angie passed the phone back to Jamboree.

"Angie . . ." Jamboree said, ear back on the phone.

Angie grabbed the urn off the table. Her heart full of . . .

Rage

Angie squeezed the sides of the urn and began to pummel it onto the concrete, dropping to her knees and pounding it, again and again and again. So many agains that everyone lost track. Even Angie, which was very unlike her.

Jamboree and even Zeke attempted to approach her, but it was Darius who put his arms up to hold them back. When Angie was finally done, the urn was dented and scuffed. It was most definitely crushed into what would be a very unacceptable shape for her couldn't-understand mother. This was something Angie could not fix. Her room? It could be cleaned. Her breaking the rule of not leaving the house? Even that might have been explained in some way. But malice against the urn? Violence against her mother's symbol? There was no turning back. She had destroyed it.

Angie turned to all of them.

"My mom didn't even ask where I was," Angie said, trying to steady her breathing. "She didn't even ask if I was okay. She just wanted her urn."

Zeke shook her head, looking away. Jamboree stood there, her heart seeming to break for Angie. And Darius nodded in disbelief of what he seemed to strangely understand.

"She just wanted this," Angie said, picking the urn up.

And that was when she heard it. There was something in . . .

"Angie?" Jamboree said.

Angie unscrewed the lid, flipped the urn upside down and out fell . . .

"Shyamalan twist," Zeke said, turning her camera on.

A blue velvet bag had fallen out of the urn. Angie loosened the yellow rope drawstring. Inside was a plastic bag with a twist tie. Her sister's name was printed in all caps on a small, white label.

Angie's sister had been taped to the inside of the urn the entire time.

Jamboree knelt beside her.

"I . . ." Angie said. "I didn't know. I swear. I didn't know."

Jamboree nodded, taking Angie's hand.

The few parts of her sister that had come back were not resting in a custom ivory casket underground. She was there. In Angie's hand.

Now what?

Let Her Go

They had parked the RV in a well-lit area near the Ohio River. Everyone was exhausted; Darius and Zeke had passed out in the loft, Angie and Jamboree on the bench-converted-to-a-bed below.

Angie had fallen asleep cradling the urn, her heart aching and breaking and the Hole throbbing in the way it had July Fourth weekend. She woke up sometime after dawn Saturday morning, not even thinking to check the time on her watch. She tipped her head toward the windshield. A spray of misty golden hue illuminated Fuchsia Jesus and Rosie the Riveter on the dashboard. Angie had made it through the night knowing her sister was in the urn and managed not to absolutely implode from the grief of it.

Angie had made it.

She looked to her right. The WHY NOT? postcard stared at her from the floor. Angie reached down and picked it up. She had one stop left. A blank in the postcard that she needed to fill. For her sister. For herself.

"Hey," Jamboree said. "You okay?"

Angie considered Jamboree's question. Was she okay?

"No," Angie said. "I'm not. But . . ."

Jamboree leaned up on her elbow.

"I think . . . um," Angie said. "I think I know my last stop."

"Okay," Jamboree said. "I'll get the map."

"We don't need the map," Angie said. "We're already here."

Without saying anything, Jamboree seemed to know, and nodded.

Angie rolled out of the bed, stepping back into her concert boots. Still in the same outfit as the night before. Jamboree woke up Darius and Zeke. Groggy but awake, they all followed Angie out of the RV.

Angie turned to Darius. "Where's the river?"

He motioned with a nod and led the way.

It was the longest walk Angie had ever made. Longer than the 3,239 steps from her home in the cul-de-sac of Oaklawn Ends to William Anders High School. Longer than all the steps she had run when she'd left her sister's funeral, moments before the dirt hit the casket. Longer than the walk into her house after finding out her sister was missing.

This was the longest and hardest walk Angie had ever made. The urn by her side. Her heart in her throat.

The sunrise was cinematic on the water. Angie was sure Mr. John Hughes would have approved. Even if he was not known for his cinematography.

A barge skimmed the river, along with a few fishing boats. A bridge connecting Ohio and Kentucky yawned quietly in the distance. It was everything Angie and her sister needed. To say good-bye.

Angie knelt along the concrete steps, unscrewing the lid to the urn, removing the velvet blue bag and then the plastic one inside. Zeke stood beside Darius, leaning into him. Camcorder turned off.

This was it. This was the moment. Now and forever.

Two equally timed tears rolled down Angie's cheeks, racing for the edge of her round face, plopping onto her T-shirt. Her lips were tucked inside of her mouth. Her heart breaking, quite possibly into quarter sections, and not evenly.

Angie reached into her jeans pocket and pulled out a half-eaten bag of M&M's. She crushed a green one and dropped it into the ashes.

"The green ones are the best," Angie said, wiping tears with the back of her hand. "They make you laugh more, right?"

Her throat choked up.

Her face constricted.

Every part of her felt tense and tight and . . .

Breathe, she thought.

But breathing was so hard.

"I always wanted to think it was really brave, you know," said Angie. "What you did. Running in there, saving those people. Saving your, um, people. But . . . I really thought it was stupid what you did. Not thinking . . . how hard it would be. Without you . . . here."

Zeke wiped a tear from her cheek.

"You were my best friend," Angie said. "And I miss you . . . every single day. And I'm so sorry that I . . ."

Angie couldn't stop the sobbing. It came in a big wave. Jamboree put her hand on Angie's shoulder. Angie's whole body shook. She tried to catch her breath. She could do this. She had already done so much she thought she couldn't.

Angie straightened her back, wiping the snot and tears off with the neck of her T-shirt. Holding up her hand to say that she had this. Though she truly questioned whether she did.

"Um," Angie said. "I'm so sorry that I . . . that I didn't hug you. That day at the airport. That I was mad. That I didn't say good-bye. Please, please, please know. I love you so much, Nat. But, um. I kind of have to just . . . let go a little."

Angie's throat was so tight.

Tears streamed in streaks that seemed like they'd never stop.

Her head hurt from crying.

Her whole body, exhausted.

But she was going to follow through, because it was what her sister always did. Follow through.

Angie held the bag over the water glistening back at her. Deep shaking breath and . . . the ashes poured out. Catching a hint of the breeze and spreading across a patch of the Ohio River.

Angie slid the plastic bag back into the velvet bag, placing them both back in the urn. She stood up and beside Jamboree, Darius, and Zeke, all of them wiping tears from their faces.

And in all of that pain, there was this wash of . . . something Angie couldn't say aloud—didn't know how to, but it was there. In her.

Maybe we won't be friends tomorrow, Angie thought. *Or even the day after that. But right now we are. And in this shorter version of forever, I'm not panicking at the known or unknown. I'm just standing here. With all of them beside me.*

Watching her wash away.

The ride back to Dryfalls was a somber one. No music. No dance party. Just the inaudible sound of all of them wondering *Now what?* as they cruised down the interstate and back to their real lives. Driving a direct route. No detours. No impromptu stops. Jamboree behind the wheel, Darius in the loft, and Zeke hunched over the table, writing in her notebook, occasionally looking out the window or at Angie. At Angie sitting in the plush chair, scribbling in her therapeutic journal for much of the ride.

The urn now empty, and Angie full of something she could not understand yet.

The RV eased up along the curb a few houses away from Angie's, the engine idling. Her couldn't-understand mother's SUV was not in the driveway. A calm before the storm, as the cliché went. Zeke and Darius watched Angie gather the urn and her backpack and make for the side door.

"Angie," Zeke said. "Let us know what's up, okay?"

Angie nodded, taking one last look at the inside of the RV. Not knowing if she would ever stand inside it again.

Angie stepped out of the RV, meeting Jamboree at the curb.

"I guess this is . . ." said Jamboree.

"Yeah," Angie said, slipping her backpack over both shoulders.

The two stood there saying a good-bye loaded with uncertainty. The irony was not lost on Angie. It was how their friendship had ended years earlier.

"In movies, they always know what to say," Angie said.

"Yeah," said Jamboree. "It's easier when someone is writing all the stuff, right?"

"Yeah . . . unless they're a really bad writer. Then it's just montages and cheap laughs."

"Yeah."

Pause.

Extremely long, uncomfortable is-this-really-happening pause.

"I, uh . . ." said Jamboree. "I just . . . this seems so hard. This — right now."

"I had fun," Angie said.

"Me too."

"Except for the sad parts," said Angie. "Those were hard."

"Well, yeah," said Jamboree.

"But . . ." Angie said.

What was it? The pang Angie felt. It was not the Hole. It was a confusing yearning for —

"Anyway," said Angie.

"Yeah," Jamboree said, sighing.

"See ya," Angie said. "I hope."

Angie shook her head and walked toward her driveway. Then she stopped. She stopped because she had to stop. She thought about Mr. John Hughes and Ms. Joan Jett. She thought of her life in a montage even though she truly hated montages.

"Jamboree," Angie called out.

Jamboree walked back to the curb. Angie had called out to her because she needed to know something. She walked directly in a straight line for Jamboree.

"What's wrong?" Jamboree said.

Angie raised her hand and slid it behind Jamboree's

neck and . . . kissed her. Angie had instigated a kiss! A first time for the historically not-so-suave kisser. A deep, passionate, fantasized-about-this-for-years kind of kiss. Angie tingled all over. She ached. Jamboree leaned into her.

When they stopped, they both looked surprised by what had just happened.

"I didn't ask you," Angie said. "Was that okay?"

Jamboree kissed her back. Though not officially timed, it surely must have been more than five seconds. Maybe more than even seven. And while it was not Angie's first kiss, it somehow felt like it all over her body.

"That just made me exponentially happy," Angie said, in a whisper.

"Yeah," said Jamboree, also in a whisper.

Then she wrapped her arms around Angie's neck and hugged her. Angie melted into Jamboree.

"Let me know," Jamboree said. "What happens."

"Definitely," Angie said.

Jamboree walked back to the RV. Angie watched her buckle in, dropping the gear into drive and looking at Angie one more time before turning around in the cul-de-sac and driving away. Zeke's face was pressed to the window, her hands in the "rock-on" gesture.

Angie had kissed-kissed Jamboree Memphis Jordan. Like, with exhale and yearning. Angie stared down at her boots, reimagining the moment again and again and wow . . .

She surveyed the neighborhood. No one had seen the moment transpire. Not Jake. Not Wang. None of the neighbors. A plus in a life often plagued with minuses for Angie.

She turned toward her home. An Oaklawn Ends cul-de-sac centerpiece, the glitter-dipped yellow ribbons flowing along the tree trunk in her front yard. She tilted her head up to the sky. Not a single cloud, yet the storm was coming all the same. Her couldn't-understand mother would have a lot to say about things she could not understand. The question was: What would Angie say?

Home

Angie stood with her backpack firmly fitted onto her shoulders in what should have been the rubble of her bedroom. The furniture was upright. The posters, though crinkled, were stuck back on the wall. No shards of glass on the carpet. No visible ones, anyway. It was as if she had made her entire meltdown up.

"Hey," Wang said, standing in her doorway. "The rebel girl returns."

"Did you do all of this?" she asked.

He leaned against the doorjamb, popping his earbuds out.

"If Mom saw your room like that, she'd commit you no doubt," said Wang.

Wang didn't even clean his own room. Perhaps his heart was bigger than Angie could have ever imagined.

"Thanks," Angie said. "Really."

He shrugged, strutting inside and plopping onto her bed.

"It's cool," Wang said. "It freaked me out a little, you know. Coming home. Seeing your room . . . I thought maybe . . . maybe you were going to do something stupid again."

Wang rolled the toe of his sneaker on the tufts in her carpet, then cleared his throat.

"Instead," he said, "you maced Gary Klein?"

Angie exhaled, slipping her backpack off. She plopped on the bed beside him. Gary Klein. Leaving the house. Pouring her sister's ashes in the Ohio River. The offenses continued to stack higher and higher.

"I'm so screwed," Angie said.

"You kidding me?" said Wang. "My phone's been blowing up. Didn't Jamboree tell you? Gary's busted."

Angie didn't understand what Wang was talking about, as evidenced by her confused expression.

"Hallmark Channel ending threw you a bone in real life," he said. "One of his friends ratted him out. Posted a video online. It already got picked up by the news."

"Video of what?" Angie asked.

Wang slid out his phone. A few swipes and clicks. There it was. The video of Gary kicking Angie—knocking her down. Of everything that happened. Of all of them. Even Darius, standing there. Letting it happen.

"Everybody has seen it, yo," said Wang. "It's viral. He's hung out, for real. Like, that punk ass is toast."

Angie sat there, dazed. "Who posted the video?"

"That guy," Wang said, pointing at the phone. "Darius."

Darius had not only ratted out Gary and the other guys, but incriminated himself. Why?

"I heard Stacy Ann and some other kids vouched for you with the principal," Wang said. "But Gary can't dispute what's on video."

It was some kind of made-for-television-Christmas-movie ending. Was that Angie's new story? New life . . . really? It all felt too easy.

"This is good news, Ang," said Wang. "They can't kick you out of school for defending yourself. And they definitely can't press charges. Trust me. I know about this shit. I'm a professional nonprofessional criminal."

Angie grinned. Wang grinned. And what should have been a V for victory, arms-in-the-air moment wasn't. There was still the part two, the sequel to Angie's problems. Angie still hated sequels — now more than ever.

"Where's Mom?" Angie asked.

"Like she talks to me?" Wang said. "She came so unglued about that urn. I was thinking, like, 'Damn, it's not like you can't buy another one.' You know?"

"That one's special to her, though," Angie said.

"She's probably at John/Rick/Prick's," Wang said, checking the time on his cell. "Which means she'll probably be back soon. She hates his place. Says it smells like feet and glue. That's what she said to Joan anyway."

Angie nodded.

"You brought the urn back, right?" he said.

Angie nodded again.

"Yeah . . . it's on the mantel," Angie said, knowing it was now empty. Just like Angie's future when her mom realized it.

"Jamboree told me about the postcard," Wang said. "Made me laugh. Sounded like something she'd want to do with you. Sounded like her."

Angie nodded. This was her third nod in a row.

"Did you do everything?" he asked. "On the postcard?"

"Yeah," Angie said.

He grinned, nudging his sister.

"You sang, huh?" said Wang. "Man . . . I wish I could've seen that."

"There may or may not be video evidence of the audible crime," Angie said.

He smile-laughed.

"Wanna come chill in my room?" said Wang. "Watch MST *Manos: The Hands of Fate*." Wang emphasized the movie title with a cheesy eeriness.

"I think I'm going to just . . . be here," Angie said.

Now Wang nodded.

"Cool," he said, heading back to his room. "Holla at me when she gets home."

"Wang," Angie said.

"Yeah, what?"

The moment was prime for tenderness. For everything loving. For the bridge of love to be built between them.

Then Angie belched. It was loud and long and . . . wow!

"Nice," Wang said. "Work on your depth. Hashtag bethebelch."

Wang disappeared into the hallway. Soon Angie heard the click of his bedroom door, leaving Angie alone. Something felt . . . different.

She looked around her room. It somehow seemed smaller to her. The posters that had been on her walls somehow didn't fit her anymore. Even the stars on her ceiling were a little more plastic than magic.

Angie stood up and wedged her hand between her headboard and wall, peeling away a taped, quart-sized ziplock stash of candy. She untaped candy bars from the bottom of desk drawers. She poured out a shoebox of Blow Pops, taffy, and Jolly Ranchers onto her bed.

A sugary mound of delicious, mouthwatering delights lay before her. She pulled a gas-station plastic bag out of her backpack and threw all the candy inside. She knotted the bag handles and carried it to the garbage can on the side of the house. Suspending the bag over the trash, she debated if she could let it go. Not forever. Just for now.

Breathe, she thought. *Just breathe.*

She dropped the bag inside and closed the lid, thinking

of the new list of rules she had started in her therapeutic journal on the way home.

Rules of Your Life Now
#1: Eat when you really want to. Not because you're scared, bored, lonely, and/or mad.

#2: Don't freak out when Rule #1 gets hard, because it probably will.

Angie looked across the street to Jake's well-manicured lawn, the sprinklers sprinkling. A deep compulsion to knock on his door tugged at her. Yes, he'd lied, and it was an egregious offense by her standards of friendship. Yes, he lied about dating Stacy Ann Sloan, which was not a wound she knew how to heal. But there was one thing Jake had been right about in all of his wrong. The one thing Angie had not done: listened. And Jake had always listened to her. Which, right then, made her realize she had truly, quite unknowingly, made a mistake. So Angie stepped off the curb and into the street, walking toward Jake's house.

She was halfway there when her couldn't-understand mother's SUV approached the cul-de-sac. Angie stood there as the car eased into the driveway. The brake lights ignited then exhaled off.

Angie's adrenaline elevated. It was clearly too late to run, to try to avoid what was unavoidable.

Angie's mother remained in her SUV for a longer-than-anticipated time, per Angie's Casio calculator watch. Finally, the door opened. Her heels clicked against the concrete driveway as she got out. She straightened her wrinkled suit skirt before shutting the car door, never looking directly at Angie.

Connie continued walking into the house, chin up. Momentum, as always, forward.

Angie instinctively followed her mother, shutting the front door behind her. Her mother stood in the entryway, purse still on her shoulder.

"Mom . . . I—" Angie said.

And that was all Angie said.

Because Connie slapped Angie across the face. So hard, in fact, that Angie fell back a step. The intensity of the action surprised Angie. The burn-sting undeniably painful.

"What did I say to you?" her mother asked, a shaking boil rolling in her voice.

Historically, Angie's mother did not believe in physical punishment as a means of discipline. Apparently, her views on the issue had changed, as evidenced by Angie's pulsating cheek.

"What did I say to you?" Connie repeated.

Connie put her purse down on the hall entry table, her keys in the designated key tray. Everything in its place. Everything but Angie and Wang and their couldn't-show-up father and their dead sister. And the family dog, Lester, who would not answer to his name.

"Not to leave the house," Angie said.

"What did I say to you?" Connie asked.

Angie was confused by her mother's persistence.

"I already answered your question," Angie said.

"Don't," Connie warned.

There was a chilled heat in her tone, something Angie had heard only once before, and Angie was truly scared.

"Where is my urn, Angie?" Connie said.

"Mom, I need to explain . . ." Angie said.

"Where is my fucking urn, Angie?" Connie shouted.

Frightened and surprisingly angry, Angie could not decide how to adequately navigate what to say. Certain that her mother was very likely to strike her again, she pointed toward the living room.

Connie proceeded toward the mantel, her stride stiff, but as always, precise. She lifted the urn, examining the damage done to it by Angie's own foray into rage the night before. Her couldn't-understand mother's fingers traced the dents and scratches — the scuffs that could not be undone. Soon becoming very aware of the lighter weight, Connie unscrewed the lid. She fished out the blue velvet bag, almost maniacally opening it and sliding out the plastic one. Only the faintest of dusty imprints remained inside of it.

"Mom . . ." Angie said.

"What did you do?" Connie said to Angie.

She marched back toward Angie. There was no stop to her go as she began to whale on her daughter.

"What did you do?" Connie demanded.

Connie struck Angie again and again and —

"Mom!" Wang said, halfway down the staircase. "What are you doing?"

"Go to your room," Connie told Wang.

Her tone stopped him on the fifth stair from the bottom.

"Go to your room," their couldn't-understand mother said to Wang again.

Connie's attention steered back to Angie. There was no escaping the betrayal they both felt right then. Angie's fear was replaced with anger.

"Where is *she*, Angie?" her mother said. "Where is my daughter?"

"You mean the good one, right?" said Angie. "That's what you said to Joan. On the phone. 'Why did it have to be my good one?' Yeah, I'm sorry it was your good one, too, Mom. I've been sorry every single day since she disappeared. That it wasn't me."

"I didn't say that," Connie said. "You're pulling things out of context."

Connie scrambled to formulate one of her courtroom counterarguments. Only this was not court, and she was ill prepared for anything as raw and honest as what lay between all of them.

"You should have told us," said Angie. "You should have told us *she* was in the urn."

"What?" Wang said.

Connie shook her head.

"Look at you, Angie," said Connie, palms opened at her daughter. "Look at you. I never know what's going to *set* you off."

"Mom," Wang said, his voice faint. "Is it true?"

There had been visitations to the cemetery. Easter and Memorial Day. On their sister's birthday. Visitations Angie had never gone to, but Wang had. Every one of them.

"She wasn't there?" Wang said. "Mom!"

"See something from my perspective," said Connie to them.

"I can't . . . breathe with all of your perspective, Mom," said Angie. "There is a hole inside of me. Just expanding with lies and camera etiquette and . . . shame. With modulation I don't even understand. Do you know what — what *I* feel? How much *I've* hurt?"

"Oh, I know, Angie," said Connie. "Trust me, we all know. Everyone knows that Angie is depressed. That Angie needs attention. That Angie —"

"You told us she was in that coffin," said Angie. "That you put her in the ground."

"It was a symbol," said Connie.

"Screw your symbols!" Angie said. "Some things are just what they are. She died. Period. She died scared. Period. She died because you wouldn't understand, and she had to run from your expectations. Period."

"It is not my fault—" said Connie.

"We're suffocating, Mom," said Angie. "In stupid yellow ribbons. In . . . statues and all the things you keep doing, for what? She's gone."

Connie wiped a tear from her face. Evidence that somewhere in there she felt something deeper than disgust and rage. Maybe.

"Are you done?" asked her mother.

Angie was done.

Angie was not done.

No, she was done.

Angie's delay, however, signaled she was done to Connie.

"Where is she?" Connie asked.

Angie considered her answer for 2.3 seconds. Knowing that the saying aloud would be the point of no return. It would be—

"The Ohio River," Angie said, looking away from her mother.

Connie's hand trembled as she pressed it over her mouth.

"Angie," Wang said, trying to piece everything together. "Where is . . . is she?"

The click of Connie's heels drummed on the wood floor. She gently set the urn on the entryway table. Carefully placed the bag inside and screwed the lid back on. Holding both hands along the sides of the urn, she rocked her head back and forth, ever so slightly.

"She was my daughter, Angie," Connie strained to say. "You had no right."

"She wouldn't want to be in that urn, Mom," Angie said. "She'd already been in a cold and dark place. She'd already—"

"You had no right," Connie said, throwing the urn against the door behind Angie.

Angie instinctively shielded her head with her arms.

"Mom," Wang said.

The urn rolled on the floor and behind Angie.

Connie struggled to recompose herself. To contain all of the loose and frayed parts that she couldn't let them — let anyone — see.

The three of them stood there in the same space. The same not-knowing-what-comes-next space. They stood there approximately eleven seconds. It felt like eleven months. Eleven months and seven days.

Wang's phone chimed, breaking the silence, snapping Connie out of her trance-like state of frazzled. She walked back to the entryway table, methodically picking up her keys and purse, wiping tears from her face. She walked toward Angie, who flinched ever so slightly. Wang stepped down a stair.

Connie paused, noticing Angie's shirt.

"Change your shirt," Connie said. "It has a stain on it."

And that was it.

Uneasy.

Queasy.

Connie walked past Angie and the urn and out the front door.

The oxygen was still poisoned by their mother's refusal to hear, to see, to . . . understand.

"This is so messed up," Wang said, wiping angry tears from his face.

He sat on the stairs and cried so hard — something Angie hadn't seen him do since their sister was found . . . and pronounced gone. Angie walked over to her brother and sat beside him. He leaned into her and sobbed. Her unemotional brother cried, and in that moment, she felt something she could not fully articulate. It was an idea. Growing inside of her. Expanding.

Something she would have to write about in her therapeutic journal.

"Everything is so messed up, Ang," Wang said.

"I know," Angie said.

She wrapped her arms around Wang as they both held on.

Where Do We Go From Here?

It was Monday. One p.m., to be specific.

While the details of Angie's suspension were still resolving, the question of Whispering Oak remained. Angie's fate would be determined by her therapy session. A session Wang had urged her to lie at before he left for school that morning.

Lying felt wrong, but so did Whispering Oak.

Connie eased her leased SUV up to the curb outside Angie's therapist's office. Connie kept the engine running.

"Aren't you coming?" Angie said.

Connie made the slightest of gestures that meant no.

Neither Angie nor her couldn't-understand mother had said a single word or exchanged direct eye contact since their near-the-stairway throw-down. They sat quietly for approximately twenty-nine seconds. Twenty-nine seconds of the gas-guzzling engine running. Of the air conditioner blowing in Angie's face. Of all the pain and anger and disappointment between them.

"I know you don't understand," said Angie. "Sometimes I think . . . you'll never understand. And, um . . . I don't want it to be that way. And, um . . . I can't tell you that you're doing your best because I don't believe—"

Connie shook her head. "Get out of the car."

"Mom, I just need you to—"

"You disobeyed me. You disposed of your sister's . . ." Connie couldn't say it.

"Why are you so afraid of—"

"Get out of the car, Angie!"

Angie waited, hoping some evidence of a heart would emerge. Wanting to believe that the motherly instinct she had read about in gorillas might have a fighting chance in her mother's much smaller chest. But Connie, sadly, could not go there, as the cliché went.

Angie had begun to dislike clichés in that moment and would add them to her List of Dislikes.

Angie pulled the door handle toward her and got out.

The distance between Angie and her mother should have been only a few feet. It honestly felt immeasurable. Haunting and hollow and filled to flooding capacity with all the disappointment and disillusionment between them.

Connie looked at her watch and then out the windshield. Never at her daughter.

"I'll walk home," Angie said, shutting the door.

The SUV tires crunched against the unpaved parking lot, dusting the other cars as it drove away.

Angie sat quietly for the first two and one-half minutes of her therapy session.

"I see it all sometimes," said Angie. "All of us, together. Like pictures in plastic, pressed in photo albums. Flat. Frozen. But if I look closely, I can see everything that was wrong — is wrong. She was always between us. The Elmer's Glue, but we needed like . . . um, Gorilla Glue. Something."

The new woo-woo therapist listened.

"My mom hates me," Angie said, her face twisting, trying to not cry.

"Why do you think that?"

"Well, I poured my sister's ashes in the, um, Ohio River," said Angie. "She can't even look at me. But . . . she never really can — could. Does. She just sees everything, um . . . that isn't her. That isn't my sister. I can't be my sister, and she wants to keep . . ."

Angie paused, tears bubbling.

"Shaping me," Angie said. "Trying to figure out how to make me into something I'm not. Something straight and narrow and . . . correctly sized. I can't do that."

"No," said the therapist. "You can't."

Quiet.

More quiet.

"Why did you dispose of your sister's ashes without telling your mom?" asked the therapist.

"Because she would never let her go," said Angie. "Because she would keep her contained in that cold and dark and . . . it's not what my sister would want. She was like, um, the sun. She was so bright that I think we all had to kind of squint. You can't really see things the way they are when you squint, you know? They just look a little different."

The new woo-woo therapist nodded.

"And I think maybe that's why my mom can't see her," said Angie. "I really wish she could."

Angie's eyes closed, tears rolling. It was all coming back. In waves, hard and genuine. It was the pain that went beyond the Hole.

"I wanted it to be . . . quiet Thursday night," said Angie. "I was in my room and I heard 'Free Fallin'' in my head again, and for a moment, it got so easy. To think about letting go? And that's when—I panicked. Because it felt so . . . I don't know."

"Stay with it," said the therapist. "What don't you know?"

Angie was reluctant to proceed.

She did not like the therapeutic process.

It required her to be—

Be what?

"Real," said Angie. "Like in how angry I was with my

sister. How I couldn't admit it. How, um, I couldn't . . . say it."

"Are you mad at her?"

"No," Angie said. "I'm not now. I don't think."

"And what did you do?" said the therapist. "How did you interrupt the panic?"

Angie considered the question. Remembering the destruction of her room. It was a temporary fix but not the solution. The letter had also been a temporary fix, but still not a solution. Her feelings for Jamboree, the trip? They were not the answer. The most real and absolute answer.

"Living," Angie said, somewhat surprised by her own answer. "Wanting to live, even if it was hard. It was what I wrote . . . in, um, my therapeutic journal. This sort of epiphany."

"What was your epiphany, Angie?"

Angie squeezed the edges of the journal before opening it, flipping the pages, many pages, and then stopping.

"Life is heart and ache," Angie said.

The new woo-woo therapist gently, quietly, unrolled the warmest smile.

"Yeah," said the therapist. "It is."

"You can't have one without the other," Angie continued.

There was no cheesy orchestrated music swelling triumphantly in the background. Just silence and the slightest ticking of the therapist's clock. The therapist shifted in her recently reupholstered chair. And then, the therapist, who rarely made notes, noted on a legal pad:

Recommending additional outpatient therapy and no inpatient, long-term treatment facility. Deeply grieving the loss of her family.

We Were Made
for This

The sounds of Prince spinning on vinyl wrapped around the sides of the RV and spilled out the screen door. Angie stood there in the dark watching Jamboree stretched out on the bench-converted-to-bed, flipping through the pages of a book. Nervous to actually be there, but there Angie was.

"Hey," Angie said.

"Hey," Jamboree said, planting her book facedown.

She slid out of the bed and opened the screen door.

The exchange of looks could have been forever if forever could be multiplied by a number equal to pi. In Angie's estimation, it felt that way, though it was mere seconds, at best.

"Come in," Jamboree said. "I was just waiting for Zeke."

"I can come back or —"

"No," said Jamboree. "Sit down. We're just going to watch a movie."

Angie sat on the edge of the converted bed, her head tilting and looking up. Jamboree had laminated and taped the Ohio map to the RV ceiling. The Christmas lights glistened like stars poking through small holes of the places they had been.

Jamboree sat beside Angie.

"What do you think?" Jamboree asked.

Angie couldn't stop smiling. "I think wow."

"It's my first real adventure," Jamboree said.

"You've been to Europe," Angie said.

"Yeah, but this was my first solo drive in the RV," said Jamboree.

There was a pulse-racing look between them. Jamboree's lips parted. The slightest of breaths escaped. Then Angie gulped and looked away. She was so nervous. She didn't want to be Nervous Angie. She just wanted to be —

"Wang told me your mom came unglued," Jamboree said. "You okay?"

Angie shrugged. "No, but yeah, you know?"

"No," Jamboree said.

"It's . . ."

Angie stopped herself. Yes, it was complicated, but she disliked that word. Immensely. Because it did not say anything specific. She didn't want to be nonspecific.

"It's going to be weird for a while," Angie said. "I mean, maybe forever. I don't know. But I went to therapy today, and it was . . . real. And I *think* that's okay?"

"Yeah," Jamboree said.

"Plus, I don't have to go to Whispering Oak. I just get to . . . figure things out. Which is kind of scary, but I don't know. Feels okay."

"I can't believe your mom let you out of the house, though," said Jamboree.

"She's at some support-group thing tonight," Angie said "For parents who, um, lost children. My therapist *overly* suggested it. Along with anger management. I didn't even know that was a thing. Management for anger. It sounds like . . . corporate."

They smiled, but it was layered in so many different fragile feelings.

"I was scared that she was going to send you away," Jamboree said. "I didn't want to lose you again."

"I didn't want to lose me again either," Angie said.

Both of them were wrapped in the music of Prince, the smell of microwave popcorn, and the brushing of tree limbs along the roof of the RV.

"Got another list?" Jamboree asked.

Angie half smiled.

Jamboree lightly nudged Angie.

"What are you thinking about?" she asked. "Freak-out or paradoxical?"

Angie grinned.

"I'm not good at this," Angie said.

"You were good at it with KC."

"Everything was just different with KC," said Angie. "She . . . I just kind of followed along. I didn't have to know anything, um . . . because she just knew."

The wind rustled through the trees, the leaves in full commotion.

"I don't think that's how it's supposed to be," said Angie. "Just following. Because if that person goes away, then what? What do you follow?"

"Yeah," Jamboree said.

They sat there kind of awkward and quiet.

"About that kissing thing," said Jamboree. "Um . . . I wanted to kiss you since seventh grade. And it totally freaked me out to want something like that. We live in Dryfalls, you know?"

"Yeah," said Angie.

"You know how people are. How they treat Zeke. I mean, my mom's Catholic-cool, but I thought . . . I just thought I was going to go to hell or she'd go to hell. I mean someone was definitely going to hell. Everything was just . . . I was just so . . . scared to feel that way."

"Yeah," said Angie. "I get the scared."

"Then we ended up on this road trip and . . ." Jamboree said. "Then you kissed me and . . . Yeah."

"Yeah . . ." Angie said.

And it seemed their conversation had plateaued, because nothing but Prince and a lot of awkward silence was happening. Now, after the act of full-on, unbridled kissing, they knew the most intimate things about each other. Want and breath and quiet moan and exhale. The kiss had been, without question, that intense, and in some degree of replay in Angie's mind. Intense and now real.

"So, Troy?" Angie asked.

"Yeah, that's over," said Jamboree.

Angie nodded. In fact, she seemed to have perfected the nod over the last few days.

"KC?" Jamboree said. "Wang said . . . he said she's coming back."

"Yeah," Angie said.

She was not thrilled that Wang had spilled the KC-returning beans to Jamboree. Angie was still trying to process KC's message for Angie via Wang, because Angie still did not have her phone or computer or iPod or life back. All of it on a bizarre behavior layaway. KC had written:

> Hate Dallas. Hate living at my dad's.
> Miss you so much. Let's talk about talking.

Angie would have done anything for that message a week earlier. Anything! Yet she'd decided not to respond.

Silence in that Prince-is-shredding-the-guitar-but-we-aren't-saying-anything kind of silence.

"It's good, right?" Jamboree said. "That she's coming back."

"Yeah," Angie said.

More of the above-mentioned kind of silence.

The confused longing held its prolonged proximity. The questions. The answers. The needle of the record player not automatically picking up when it reached the end of the album generated a scratching noise. It was a sound that Angie did not like. She stretched and put the needle near the beginning of the record. Surely, all could come to knowing with Prince in the background.

May His Royal Badness live forever, Angie thought.

When Angie leaned back up, her forearm pressed against Jamboree's forearm. Now it was thighs and forearms touching. A dangerous, heart-racing array of hormonal desire.

"Can I ask you something?" Jamboree said.

"Yeah," Angie said, unusually fast.

"Are you still in love with KC?"

Angie heaved a sigh. When would she not be in some form of love with KC Romance? KC was her first love ever. Even if KC joined a cult, wore flip-flops with fake rhinestones, preached religion on street corners, and claimed to speak to extraterrestrial life, Angie would still love her. Though it would be challenging, her heart would still contain some amount of love for the girl with a purple heart tattoo on her neck. She was KC Romance. There seemed no way not to love a girl by that name.

"I probably shouldn't have asked," Jamboree said. "That's weird, right?"

"I don't know how I could ever not love her," Angie said.

"Sure," said Jamboree. "That makes . . . a lot of sense. She's pretty amazing—seems amazing. You know, not that I know her, but . . ."

Jamboree tripped over her words, seeming to try to shield herself from rejection. Angie understood that feeling. It plagued much of her life.

"But I'm not with her," said Angie. "I mean, I'm here. With you. And I was thinking maybe we could figure this friendship thing out. And see maybe about the other part of . . . you know, um. Where there's, uh . . . you know . . ."

Angie was truly dying a thousand emotional deaths in her rambling.

Dramatic pause.

Continued dramatic pause.

"Yeah," said Jamboree. "I know."

Rule #3 of your List of Rules of Your Life Now: *Don't be afraid to ask people for what you need.*

With Prince's "Take Me with U" filling the air around them, they talked the way friends would. About music and movies and places they wanted to see. About all the things big and small. Why Not?

Move in
the Right
Direction

With a newly cleared record, per Darius releasing the video of her fight with Gary Klein, Angie walked 3,239 steps from her house to Williams Anders High School. She walked past the glitter-dipped yellow ribbons still tied to many of the trees, though a few had been taken down. She walked past the statue of her sister guarding Main Street. Past The Backstory, whose marquee was now empty. She walked past many of the places that had seemed to overwhelm her with memories before.

Wang loitered in the student parking lot with his usual group of malcontents and troublemakers (as her mother referred to them). When they all started to head inside, Wang stopped.

"Angie," he called out. "You want to walk in with us?"

A couple of the guys snickered. He turned and shoved one of them. The guys tried to gauge whether he was serious or not. Wang turned back to his sister.

"Thanks," she said to him, realizing the miracle that had just transpired. "I'm good."

Her brother had acknowledged her as a human being worth walking into the socially charged hallways with. It was a moment of unbelievable proportions. One that she would surely have to document.

Wang threw her a nod and strutted inside.

Angie was looking toward the parking lot for Jake when she saw Darius being dropped off in the front of the school. Both of them seeing each other. Angie unsure if she should wave or half wave or not wave. Thankfully, Darius eliminated the confusion by throwing a head nod and walking toward her.

"Hey," Angie said.

"You're still here," he said.

"Yeah," Angie said. "Thanks to you. For telling the truth."

He nodded, looking off at everyone heading into the building.

"I knew I'd be off the team," Darius said to Angie.

Angie didn't understand.

"If I said I lied, if I told the truth," Darius said. "I knew I'd be off."

"But you didn't do anything," Angie said.

"Exactly," said Darius. "I almost let it all happen."

Darius went off in his own thoughts for a moment.

"It was the right thing," said Darius. "To finally stand up. You know?"

Angie nodded.

"It's hard, though," he said, grinning. "Coach said he was sorry, but he had to set an example. Everybody involved was dropped. And Gary he's . . . yeah."

Angie lowered her head.

Darius leaned down into her sightline. "Hey."

She looked up at him.

"Don't ever stop living your story," he said. "For anyone."

Angie nodded.

Darius walked toward the school. "Keep making those wishes, Angie. I'll see you around."

He jogged up the school steps and disappeared behind the glass double doors.

Jake's car cut up into the parking lot. The glint of the chrome popped in the sun. Angie tugged on the straps of her backpack. There were so many things to say. The sequence of topics bled into one another as Jake approached her. She was hurt and mad and somehow beyond elated to see him. The emotional trifecta was unexpected.

"Hey," Jake said.

"Hey."

Jake heaved a heavy-hearted Jake sigh: moderately

awkward, but somehow intensely layered. It was a behavior that Angie knew. She found it oddly comfortable.

"Do you think about breasts a lot?" Angie asked.

"I'm sorry?" he said.

"I think about them sometimes," she continued.

"Um . . . I don't know," Jake said. "Maybe. Sometimes."

"I always wanted to ask you that."

He nodded. "Okay."

He waited.

And waited.

"Anything else?" Jake asked. "Other pieces of human anatomy?"

"Not right now," she said. "Wait. No. That's it for now."

"Are you okay?" asked Jake.

Angie considered the question for approximately . . . well, she did not know how long. She had left her watch at home. A first.

"Yeah," said Angie, noticing the scars on her wrist. "I'm good."

Jake nodded. He was also very good at the art of nodding. In fact, they were in a kind of nodfest that seemed like it might not end. At least, not until the bell rang.

"I kissed Jamboree Memphis Jordan," she said.

"Hmm," Jake said.

"You're the only person I've told," said Angie.

"Well, that's cool," Jake said. "I mean, she's had a crush on you forever."

"What?" Angie said.

"Yeah," he stated, matter-of-fact. "It was pretty obvious when we were in junior high."

"Not to me," Angie said. "Why didn't you say something?"

"You weren't gay-girl gay, like, until, what?" Jake said. "Last year? And you were all about KC. Didn't really seem like mine to put out there."

Angie shook her head.

"Look, I'm sorry I didn't tell you —" Jake said.

"That's not what I'm mad about."

"All you are is mad at me."

"All you do is lie, Jake," said Angie. "First about some promise with my sister to look out for me — then about Stacy Ann."

"It's so hard to just be honest with you sometimes," Jake said. "Because *I* know how much you've been hurt. The people who have hurt you. Because you really are my best friend, and I just . . . I don't want to be the reason Angie fell apart again or Angie was disappointed or Angie was heartbroken."

Angie did not know this version of Jake. She had made him out to be all things perfect. All things specifically specific, but he wasn't.

"You can't lie to me and say we are best friends," Angie said. "That's not best friends, Jake. I'm not sure exactly what it is, though."

Jake nodded.

"Okay, so truth," said Jake. "My parents are kind of . . . they might be over. And it's just . . . been . . . hard."

"Jake . . ."

"I'm sorry that I lied," said Jake. "About Stacy Ann. About everything."

"I'm sorry I didn't listen," said Angie. "To anything."

Jake paused, leaning his ear toward her.

"What was that?" Jake said. "Was that an apology?"

"Don't push it," said Angie. "You still lied. And I'm not going to be best friends with Stacy Ann."

The bell rang.

"No one's asking you to," Jake said. "Just so long as you're best friends with me. Because it's pretty lonely without you."

A loose strand of hair swung out across Jake's eyebrow. It was a cute look.

Jake began walking inside, and Angie instinctively walked with him toward the entrance. Then she stopped, kids jogging past her.

"What?" he said.

"I'll see you at lunch," said Angie.

"You sure?" he asked.

"Yeah," Angie said. "Very."

In that moment, Angie had come to the realization that she could, in fact, walk into William Anders High School alone. She did not need a human/emotional shield. Not that there might not be looks and giggles to duck from. Her life was, in fact, never going to be a made-for-television Christmas movie.

But it was hers.

Jake disappeared inside the glass double doors. Angie rolled the volume dial up on her Walkman playing her mixtape *Ain't No Mountain High Enough on Repeat Thirteen Times*. She left her foam headphones around her neck. Not needing to block out all the noise but craving a soundtrack for the morning nonetheless. A soundtrack of her choosing.

Every step she made toward the towering stairs, a renewed sense of self emerged.

Her sister had died. That fact would never change. Angie, however, was still there, and maybe that could be okay.

As she walked through the courtyard and past the gym, the sound of dribbling echoed. It was a sound that became, in that moment, inviting to Angie, in a way she would never have anticipated it could again.

The idea of her roundness shifted in that moment. It was no longer the bane of her existence. It was her. Size, and all that had happened.

Angie maneuvered through the crowded hallway of kids lingering at lockers, shuffling to class, her thumbs pressed to the straps of her backpack. Her chin was raised, not doubled. Her smile widened as she turned the corner toward the senior lockers. Zeke and Jamboree stood in the middle of the morning chaos, Zeke filming Jamboree at her locker.

Angie continued to walk toward them, the faint vibration of music pouring out of her headphones. She thought about Zeke's Fact or Fiction game, and in her mind, it went something like this: *Fact or Fiction. Fat Angie. If I were a superhero, that would be my name. Enter: Fat Angie. My name is Fat Angie. This is my story.*

And what happened next? Well, it was not what anyone would have expected.

There was a girl. Her name was Angie.
She had fallen in love . . .

with herself.

ACKNOWLEDGMENTS

Fat Angie: Rebel Girl Revolution has always been about and for the young people. For the kids who held the first book in front of their faces and said "Everyone is Fat Angie." Kids like Ruby and Emelie from Texas, Elizabeth from Pennsylvania, Michelle from New Jersey, Kamari and Destiny from Illinois, and Ms. Scott's English class in California. You and thousands of other young people have taught me that this book could be for any kind of reader. Always know that your voices matter and will continue to be the creative revolution this world needs!

Creating this book was definitely not a lone effort, so immense thanks to Joan Powers for her insightful editing of this strange, funny, dark, rebellious, and sometimes heartbreaking story. Thank you to Andie Krawczyk, Tracy Miracle, Anna Gjesteby Abell, and Sawako Shirota for empowering me to reach readers everywhere. Matt Roeser, your book covers are truly iconic works of art, and I am honored to have another one. And while I can't believe I'm saying this, I LOVED the process of copyediting for the first time because of Maya Myers and Maggie Deslaurier and proofreaders Amy Snyder and Jackie Houton. You were meticulously masterful and wrote the best margin notes ever!

Erin Murphy, thank you for your wisdom, tenacity, compassion, and humor. I am a better artist working with you as my agent. Among many things, you remind me of the value of storytelling and growing with it.

Andrea Cascardi, thank you for seeing the potential in a very different kind of story when I originally wrote *Fat Angie*. Larry P., you helped me realize what was important in life and on the page.

Kurt, thanks for always believing in my writing and filmmaking, and in my desire to make the world a more accepting place. I love you mad for it. Extra big love to my Belgian family of Anouck, Ayden, and Esperanza and to my chosen family: Sally and Karl Miller; Frances Gordon; Dave, Tanya, and Mel Bartlett; Maddie Murray; and Rachel Watson.

And to mi hermana from another mama, thanks for being the artist and the human being who empowers young people, writes nonstop, grows food, shovels snow, raises two fantastic kids, and still manages to show up for your friends. For that, I am unbelievably grateful.

My gratitude runs deep for my artist friends G. Neri, Galen McGriff, Elly Swartz, Margaret Coble, Cynthia Levinson, Kirstin Cronn-Mills, Hannah Moushabeck, and Jim Bailey. Each of you reminds me what really matters in this world and keeps me tethered to it. And thank you to Pat Zietlow Miller for knowing I could be brave.

The list of amazing teachers, librarians, booksellers, bloggers, and festival organizers who continue to support *Fat Angie* and the documentary *At-Risk Summer* is beautifully long. Among them, I'd like to acknowledge Katrina

Gonzales, Jenny Paulsen, Eva Goins, Erica Scott, Helen Read, Kim Summers, Jennifer Salas, Dr. Carstensen, Brenda Kahn, Dr. Bercaw, and David Weaver.

Life comes with losses. It's one of the sad and painful realities we face. One of them was my dear friend Amanda Cunningham. She never had the opportunity to read any of my books, but I celebrate her magnificent life by inspiring others the way she inspired me. And Linda Sanders-Wells, who was my best friend and who said before *Fat Angie* ever sold, "This book will change lives."

As unusual as it might sound, I have to thank the brilliant Lenny Kravitz (whom, in full disclosure, I've never met), whose song "Are You Gonna Go My Way" inspired the first book and makes a cameo here. His art lit the fire to mine, and that can't go unrecognized. Art inspires art.

Last but not least: Gordo, you are my best friend, and I get the joy of being in a relationship with you. Thank you for your unwavering support, late-night story chats, and adventures, and for loving me back.